The Courting Campaign

REGINA SCOTT

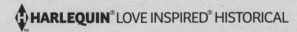

HARLEQUIN® LOVE INSPIRED® HISTORICAL

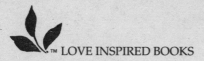 ™ LOVE INSPIRED BOOKS

ISBN-13: 978-0-373-82976-7

THE COURTING CAMPAIGN

"You seem uncommonly outspoken, for a nanny," Nick said. "Why would that be?"

Miss Pyrmont straightened. "I suppose because other nannies fear for their positions too much to tell the master when he's behaving like a fool."

Nick stiffened. "I beg your pardon?"

"You have the sweetest, brightest, most wonderful daughter, yet in the three months I've worked here, you have never visited the nursery. You didn't even know who had charge of her. You spend all your time out here—" she gestured to his still-smoking laboratory "—risking your life, risking leaving her an orphan. That, sir, I find foolish in the extreme."

Nick raised his brows. "So you have no regard for your position to speak this way."

Her smile broadened. "I have tremendous regard for my position. I would defend your daughter with my life. But I don't think you'll discharge me over strong opinions, Sir Nicholas. You need me. No one else would agree to serve in this house. Good day."

Nick watched, bemused, as she marched back to the Grange.

He could not remember any member of his household speaking to him in such a bold manner. He needed to learn more about this woman who was taking care of his daughter.

Books by Regina Scott

Love Inspired Historical

The Irresistible Earl
An Honorable Gentleman
*The Rogue's Reform
*The Captain's Courtship
*The Rake's Redemption
*The Heiress's Homecoming
†The Courting Campaign

*The Everard Legacy
†The Master Matchmakers

REGINA SCOTT

started writing novels in the third grade. Thankfully for literature as we know it, she didn't actually sell her first novel until she had learned a bit more about writing. Since her first book was published in 1998, her stories have traveled the globe, with translations in many languages including Dutch, German, Italian and Portuguese.

She and her husband of more than twenty years reside in southeast Washington State with their overactive Irish terrier. Regina is a decent fencer, owns a historical costume collection that takes up over a third of her large closet and is an active member of the Church of the Nazarene. You can find her online blogging at www.nineteenteen.blogspot.com. Learn more about her at www.reginascott.com.

All that the Father gives me will come to me,
and whoever comes to me I will never drive away.
—*John* 6:37

To Meryl, Sarah and Linda, who understand the true meaning of family, and to our heavenly Father, who welcomes us all to His table

Chapter One

The Grange, near the Peak District, Derbyshire, England

June 1815

"He'll blow us all up this time, he will."

At the maid's prediction, Emma Pyrmont glanced up from where she'd set her charge's afternoon tea to steep. The scullery maid, laundress and chambermaids had their noses pressed to the glass of the Grange's wide kitchen window. Even Mrs. Jennings, their cook, was peering over their shoulders, her ample bulk blocking some of the summer sunlight.

"It's more like steam than smoke," the white-haired cook said with certainty born from experience.

"Looks more dangerous to me," argued Dorcus Turner. Even though Emma had only been working at the Grange for a few months, she'd noticed that the buxom chambermaid had an opinion on every subject. "I'll bet the master is coughing." She elbowed the laundress. "And there'll be more smelly clothes to wash, too."

Emma returned her gaze to the elegant teapot sitting in front of her on the worktable in the center of the kitchen. The curve of the silver gave back a reflection of her face, from her light blond hair to her pursed lips. It seemed she had an opinion on the matter, too, but she wasn't about to voice it. She had no business caring what her employer, Sir Nicholas Rotherford, did in his makeshift laboratory to the south of the Grange. It was not her place to rescue the master from his folly. In this house, her place was in the nursery.

And thank You, Lord, for that! You've kept Your promise to never forsake me, even when others haven't.

"You may be right," Mrs. Jennings said, and Emma could see her shifting this way and that as if trying for a better view. Her blue wool skirts and white apron brushed the worn wood floor. "Perhaps it is smoke. Come have a look, Miss Pyrmont, and tell us what you think."

Emma lifted the lid on the teapot and peered inside. Not quite there—the tea looked far too pale. And that meant she couldn't avoid the cook's request by claiming her duty. Biting back a sigh, Emma slid the lid into place and went to join the group by the window.

The Grange sat at the end of Dovecote Dale, with its back to the Derbyshire peaks and its front looking down the dale and the swirling waters of the River Bell. The house had been built of creamy stone in the last century and was a solid block with a portico at the front and a veranda at the back. She knew the master had turned one of the nearest stone outbuildings into some sort of laboratory where he conducted experiments, but she'd made it a point not to learn what sort and why.

Now she could see that gray smoke was seeping from under the wooden door. But a light gleamed through the paned windows, and a shadow of someone tall crossed in front of it. Whatever he was doing, Sir Nicholas did not appear to have taken any harm.

"It isn't dangerous," she promised the concerned onlookers. "You only need to worry if the smoke turns black."

The maids gaped at her as she returned to her tea.

"As if she'd know," Dorcus grumbled.

"An expert on smoke, are we now?" Mrs. Jennings challenged the maid. "Get about your duties, all of you, or you can be sure I'll bring the matter up with Mrs. Dunworthy."

The threat of Sir Nicholas's widowed sister-in-law, who had come to manage the household for him four years ago, sent them all scurrying from the kitchen. Emma breathed a sigh of relief. She had only caught a glimpse of her reclusive employer as she sat in the back pew for Sunday services and he sat near the front of the church. She rather liked keeping her distance. She was fairly certain he'd been a caller at the house where she'd lived in London, and she didn't want him to wonder how she'd found her place working at the Grange. The fewer people who knew about her background, the better. She couldn't risk her foster father learning where she'd gone.

But Mrs. Jennings did not seem disposed to let the matter go. She walked over and laid a hand on Emma's shoulder, the touch surprisingly light for an arm so large and capable.

"Very clever of you, miss," she murmured. "How did you learn about smoke?"

Emma smiled at her. Though she couldn't remember her grandmothers, she thought Mrs. Jennings a perfect example. The thick strands of her white hair were tucked neatly into her lace-edged cap. Her brown eyes often twinkled with merriment. From her round face to her wide feet, she exuded warmth and affection. Mrs. Dunworthy might run the household now, having displaced Mrs. Jennings's once-larger role, but everyone knew the cook was the heart of the Grange.

Still, Emma couldn't tell Mrs. Jennings the truth about her past. Mrs. Dunworthy had insisted the matter remain between her and Emma. The lady thought Sir Nicholas might take offense if he knew his daughter was being cared for by a woman who had had an unconventional upbringing.

"I had foster brothers who experimented," Emma told the cook, knowing that for the truth. Of course, they hadn't experimented because it amused them, as it probably amused a gentleman like Sir Nicholas. They had had no choice in the matter.

"Ah, so you understand this business of natural philosophy!" The cook leaned closer with a satisfied nod. "I thought as much. I've had my eye on you, Miss Pyrmont, ever since you joined this household. You see, we have a problem, and I think you're just the one to solve it."

Emma busied herself adding a bowl of lumped sugar to the tray she would carry to the nursery. Sugar and tea had been kept under lock and key where she'd been raised, but Mrs. Jennings was more generous about who was allowed access to the costly goods.

"I'm always happy to help, Mrs. Jennings," she told the cook as she worked.

"I know you are. You've been a real blessing to this family. Wait a moment." She hurried to the larder and back and set a plate on the tray with a flourish. "Here.

I baked you and Miss Alice the biscuits you both like so much."

Emma grinned at the cinnamon-sugar treats. "Thank you! Alice will be delighted. Now, how can I help you?"

She glanced up to find Mrs. Jennings back at the window again, this time with a frown.

"It's Sir Nicholas," she murmured, more to the view than to Emma. "He's lonely, you know. That's why he spends so much time out there."

Emma thought more than loneliness motivated her employer. She'd seen the type before—men whose work drove them until family, friends and even faith had little meaning. That was not the sort of man she wanted near her. She lifted the lid on the teapot again and was relieved to see that the tea was a rich brown. Time to take it to Alice.

"You could save him."

The lid fell with a chime of sterling on sterling. Emma hastily righted it. She could not have heard the cook correctly. "I should get this to Alice," she said, anchoring her hands on the tray.

Mrs. Jennings moved to intercept her. Concern was etched in her heavy cheeks, the downturn of her rosy lips. "He needs a wife. He doesn't move in Society anymore. He doesn't associate with the lords from the neighboring houses when they're in residence. How else is he to meet a marriageable miss?"

"Marriage?" The word squeaked out of her, and she cleared her throat. She had once dreamed of the sort of fellow she would marry, but she was beginning to think he didn't exist. That didn't mean she was willing to compromise her ideals.

"I am not a marriageable miss, Mrs. Jennings," she

said, using her sternest tone. "I am Alice Rotherford's nanny. I like my post."

"But wouldn't you like to be mistress of this fine house instead?" Mrs. Jennings asked, head cocked as if she offered Emma another treat as delicious as her famous cinnamon-sugar biscuits. "To travel to London like a lady when he presents his work to those other philosophers in the Royal Society?"

Emma shook her head. "Mrs. Dunworthy is mistress of this house. And I have no need to see London again, I promise you."

"And sweet little Alice?" Mrs. Jennings pressed, face sagging. "Wouldn't you like to be her mama rather than her nanny?"

A longing rose up, so strong Emma nearly swayed on her feet. How sweet to see Alice beyond childhood, to guide her into her place in the world. Emma knew how some might try to minimize the girl, to stifle her gifts claiming she was merely a woman. She'd had to fight that battle for herself. She could protect Alice, help her achieve her dreams, whatever those might be.

But she'd known the restrictions of her job when she'd accepted the post. Nannies might be beloved by their charges, but they were often only useful until the governess or tutor arrived.

"I'm afraid I cannot help you in this instance, Mrs. Jennings," she said, lifting her tray and keeping it between them like a shield. "If you'll excuse me, I must see to my duties." She turned for the door, blocking her sight of the cook, the window and Sir Nicholas's pursuits.

A gasp behind her made her glance back, thinking the cook meant to plead. But Mrs. Jennings wasn't looking at her. The cook's gaze was once more out the window, and her plump hand was pressed to her mouth.

Dropping her hand, she turned anguished eyes to Emma. "You have to help him, miss. You're the only one who understands."

"I understand that I have a responsibility to Alice," Emma started hotly, but the cook shook her head so hard a few white curls fell from her cap.

"No, miss, your responsibility right now is to the master. You see, the smoke's turned black."

Out in his laboratory, Sir Nicholas Rotherford placed another damp cloth over the glowing wool and stepped back to cover his nose with the sleeve of his brown wool coat. Carbon always turned acrid. He knew that. He'd figured it out when he was eight and had burned his first piece of toast over the fire. He should have considered that fact before treating the wool and attempting to set it ablaze.

Now the smoke filled the space, and he could no longer even see the locks of black hair that tended to fall into his face when he bent over his work. His nose was stinging with the smell, and he shuddered to think what was happening inside his paisley waistcoat, where his lungs must be laboring.

But he had work to do, and nattering on about his health wasn't going to get it done.

Behind him, he heard footsteps on the marble floor he'd had installed in the old laundry outbuilding when he'd made it into his laboratory. No doubt his sister-in-law Charlotte had come to berate him again for missing some function at the Grange. She couldn't seem to understand that his work was more important than observing the social niceties.

Of course, it was possible she'd noticed the smoke pouring from the building and had come to investigate.

"It's all right," he called. "I have it under control."

"I'm certain the good Lord will be glad to hear that when you report to Him an hour from now in heaven," a bright female voice replied. "But if you prefer to continue carrying on this work here on earth, I suggest you breathe some fresh air. Now."

Nick turned. The smoke still billowed around him, made more visible by the light from the open doorway. He could just make out a slender female form and…a halo?

He blinked, and the figure put out a hand. "Come along. You've frightened the staff quite enough."

It was a kind tone, a gentle gesture, but he could tell she would brook no argument, and he was moving before he thought better of it.

Once outside, he felt supple fingers latching on to his arm and drawing him farther from the door. The air cleared, and he sucked in a breath as he stopped on the grass closer to the Grange.

It was sunny. He could see the house, the planted oak forests on either side, the sweep of fields that led down the dale toward the other houses that speckled the space. Odd. He was certain it had been pouring rain when he'd set out for the laboratory that morning, the mists obscuring the peaks behind the buildings. How long had he been working?

"Take a deep breath," his rescuer said.

The advice seemed sound, so he did as she bid. The clean air sharpened his mind, cleared his senses. Somewhere nearby he thought he smelled lavender.

"Better?" she asked.

"Better," he agreed. His gaze traveled over her, from

her sturdy black boots to her muddy brown eyes. She appeared to be shorter than he was, perhaps a little less than five and a half feet. What he'd taken as a halo was her pale blond hair, wound in a coronet braid around a face symmetrical enough to be pleasing. Her brown wool dress with its long sleeves and high neck hardly looked like heavenly apparel.

But then how could he be certain? He'd been avoiding thoughts of heaven and its Master for several months now.

"Who are you?" he asked.

She dipped a curtsey, but her pink lips compressed as if she found the question vexing. "Emma Pyrmont." When he continued to wait for clarification, she added, "Alice's nanny."

He eyed her and batted away a stray puff of smoke. "You're the new nanny?"

She raised her chin. "I have that honor, yes. Is there a problem?"

"No," he admitted, although he wondered at her tone. Was that a hint of belligerence? "I merely expected someone older."

"Mrs. Dunworthy was satisfied with my credentials," she said, chin a notch higher. Interesting—how high could a woman raise her chin without sustaining a neck injury? Not a topic he'd choose to pursue, but he might pass it on to one of his colleagues who specialized in anatomical studies.

"And I'm hardly new," she informed him. "I've been here three months."

Three months? He had lost touch. It felt more like three days since his sister-in-law had informed him that the previous nanny had quit. Nanny Wesling was one of many who had fled his employ after his reputation as a natural philosopher had been questioned, even though she'd initially moved to Derby with the family. He had never heard what she had found about the Grange to be so unsatisfactory.

Still, the young woman in front of him did not conform to his notion of a nanny. He would have thought the wisdom that came from age and the experience of raising children to be requirements. She looked too young, at least five years his junior. He also hypothesized that family connections or beauty would be lacking, as either could qualify a woman for an easier life as the wife of a well-situated man. While he could not know her family situation, that bright hair and smile would certainly allow her to make some claim to beauty. If she'd been dressed more like the young ladies of the ton, she would likely have found any number of young men eager to pursue her.

But she did not appear interested in pursuit. In fact, the way her foot was tapping at the grass, this lady already regretted looking in on him, as if she had far more important things to do than possibly save his life.

If she was Alice's nanny, he had to agree.

Alice! He glanced about, seeking the dark-haired head of his daughter. "Tell me you didn't bring Alice with you," he ordered.

She frowned at him. "Certainly not. I thought a four-year-old should be spared the inhalation of carbonic fumes." She shrugged. "Old-fashioned of me, I'm sure. Clearly you prefer it."

He should take umbrage, but she said it all with such a pleasant tone he could not argue. That trait alone probably made her an exceptional nanny.

He should find out.

He immediately banished the thought. This was not

an experiment requiring acute observation and documentation. This was a female in his employ. Besides, Charlotte had been clear in her requirements for managing his household. She had the responsibility for Alice and the staff. He had the responsibility of staying out of her way.

Still, questions poked at him, as they always did when he was confronted with something he didn't immediately understand. A few moments' investigation would not hinder his other work. The smoke would need a little time to dissipate in any event.

He tapped the fingers of his right hand against his wool trousers, gazed at her down his nose. "If you are not here with Alice, how did you know I required assistance? The nursery is on the opposite side of the Grange, if memory serves."

She clapped her hands as if he'd said something particularly clever. "Excellent! At least the smoke hasn't addled your wits." Lowering her hands, she added, "I was in the kitchen preparing tea. And as you appear to have taken no immediate injury, I should return to my duties." She curtsied again as if ready to escape.

But he wasn't ready for her to go. He had too many questions, and he needed answers before forming a hypothesis. "You seem uncommonly outspoken for a nanny," he said. "Why would that be?"

She straightened. "I suppose because other nannies fear for their positions too much to tell the master when he's behaving like a fool."

Nick stiffened. "I beg your pardon?"

Her smile was commiserating. "I don't believe the smoke has affected your hearing, sir. Let me see if I can put this in terms you would appreciate. You have miscalculated."

He frowned. "In what way?"

"You have the sweetest, brightest, most wonderful daughter, yet in the three months I've worked here, you have never visited the nursery. You didn't even know who had charge of her. You spend all your time out here—" she gestured to his still-smoking laboratory "—risking your life, risking leaving her an orphan. That, sir, I find foolish in the extreme."

Nick raised his brows. "So you have no regard for your position to speak this way."

Her smile broadened. "I have tremendous regard for my position. I would defend your daughter with my life. But I don't think you'll discharge me over strong opinions, Sir Nicholas. You need me. No one else would agree to serve in this house. Good day."

Nick watched, bemused, as she gathered her dusky brown skirts and marched back to the Grange, her pale hair like a moonbeam cutting through the vanishing smoke.

Singular woman. He could not remember any member of his household speaking to him in such a bold manner. Of course, most members of his household avoided speaking with him entirely. Something about his work unnerved them as if he meant to test his concoctions on them rather than to use the chemicals to help develop a new lamp for mining.

Still, he could not argue with her assessment. He had been neglecting Alice. His skills were either insufficient in that area or unnecessary. His daughter had people who loved her, cared for her, made sure she was safe. The coal miners he was working to support had no such protection. They risked their lives daily in the mine on his property to the east of the Grange. Why shouldn't he risk his health for them?

He'd already risked his reputation.

And, he feared, he was about to risk it again. Other noted philosophers were laboring like he was to find the secret to producing light under the extreme conditions underground. They enjoyed the challenge. He knew personally the deaths that would be prevented. What was needed was a lamp that would burn without exploding in the pockets of flammable air that appeared without warning.

Yet, as he returned to the laboratory and began to clean away the remains of his failed experiment, he found himself unable to focus. It seemed another study beckoned, one in which he had every right to investigate and every expectation of immediate success.

He needed to know this woman who was taking care of his daughter, how she came to be in his household and how she knew exactly what kind of smoke was streaming from his laboratory.

Chapter Two

Emma fended off Mrs. Jennings's tearful thanks for rescuing her beloved master, hefted the tray of tea and biscuits and headed for the nursery. All the while she seethed at the incident at the laboratory. The insufferable, insensitive lout of a man! How could he be so cavalier about his life?

When she'd entered that wretched laboratory of his, she'd expected to find him lying on the floor, gasping like a fish plucked from the River Bell by the anglers who loved it so. Instead, he'd stood tall and proud like a blacksmith at his bellows, the curling smoke wrapping him in power and mystery.

She snorted as she took the last turning of the servants' stair to the chamber story. Power and mystery? Nonsense! He might have raven hair and walnut-brown eyes that peered out from under the slash of his brows, but he was just a man. A man with very mistaken priorities!

And the person who should have been his first priority was waiting for Emma just inside the door of the nursery.

"Nanny!" Alice Rotherford clutched her favorite doll

close and ran to Emma's side, pink skirts rustling. Her snowy skin, big violet-colored eyes and thick black hair set in curls made the four-year-old resemble a porcelain-headed doll herself.

Emma gave her a hug and glanced up to see the maid who helped in the nursery rising from the rocking chair by the fire. "Everything all right, Ivy?"

"She was good as gold, Miss Pyrmont," the maid assured her with a fond smile to Alice. She came to the door and took the tray from Emma to carry it to the table at the back of the cheery room.

At least Sir Nicholas didn't scrimp when it came to material things, Emma thought as she followed. The main room of the nursery boasted its own rose-patterned china and crystal glasses, low shelves crowded with picture books and bright building blocks, one trunk full of clothes and accoutrements for Alice's dolls, another full of outside toys like balls and skipping ropes and a dollhouse large enough to suit even the most extravagant tastes. Why then was he such a miser when it came to spending time with his daughter?

As Emma reached the table where Alice took her meals and her lessons, Ivy leaned closer to whisper, "Bless you, miss, for saving us all. Dorcus told me how you're going to marry the master. Without a wife, we'd be stuck with Mrs. Dunworthy forever."

Emma recoiled to glare at her. "That is entirely enough of that sort of talk."

Ivy quailed, hanging her blond head while bobbing a curtsey. "Of course, miss. Sorry, miss. I'll just go help Mrs. Jennings with supper." She scurried out of the nursery.

Emma took a deep breath to calm herself. Dorcus must have overheard the conversation with Mrs. Jennings. So even now the maids knew the cook expected Emma to turn the master up sweet. Well, they were all doomed to disappointment. He had no time for courting; he had no time for his daughter! And she refused to marry a man with the ink of science running through his veins.

Alice was regarding her solemnly, and Emma could only hope that nothing of what she was feeling showed on her face or in her actions as she smiled down at her charge.

Alice held up her doll. "Lady Chamomile missed you."

Emma curtsied. "My deepest apologies, your ladyship. You know I would never keep you waiting unless it was very important."

Alice giggled and pulled the doll close once more. "She says you are forgiven, but you must ask her permission before leaving the room again."

So now she was even taking orders from a doll! Emma shook her head and held out her hand. The soft touch of Alice's little fingers reaching into her grip reminded her of her purpose here, and it certainly wasn't to charm the master.

"Let's have tea," she said to the girl as she led her to her chair. "I'm sure Lady Chamomile would enjoy that. Mrs. Jennings sent up biscuits."

"Oh, biscuits! Do you hear that, Lady Chamomile?" Alice climbed up to her seat and set her doll in a chair nearby. Emma sat and began to lay out the tea things.

But even going about such a routine task, her feelings betrayed her, for her hand trembled on the pot. She set it down carefully. Perhaps she should be honored that Mrs. Jennings thought her capable of winning the master's love. She was sure some nannies would jump at the chance to rise in position. She wasn't one of them. And did they think she merely had to dress in fine muslin and bat her eyes, and he would fall on his knees to propose?

She supposed she could wear colors that made her hazel eyes look green or gold instead of a drab brown. She could cover her work-reddened hands with silk or fine leather gloves, just as she wore long sleeves to cover the small scar of a burn on her arm. Unfortunately, she thought she stood a better chance of gaining his attention by dipping herself in whale oil and lighting herself on fire. At least then he might take the time to observe how long it required for her to expire!

"Lady Chamomile is very hungry," Alice announced. She swung her feet against the rungs of her chair, hands clasped in her lap. From the chair next to her, her doll cast Emma a baleful glance.

"A lady knows how to wait," Emma replied. And when waiting will never solve anything, she silently amended. A shame Mrs. Jennings didn't understand that.

Emma poured the tea through strainers into the cups. Between leaving it to rescue the master and carrying it up the stairs, it was no longer hot enough to steam. But Alice didn't mind. After Emma added sugar, Alice puffed on her cup as if to make sure the brew was cool enough to taste, then did the same with her doll's cup.

Sitting across from Lady Chamomile and next to Alice so she could help if needed, Emma could only smile. Alice was a darling child. How could Sir Nicholas be so determined to stay away? Many of the orphans who had been raised with her for a time in the asylum had gone on to loving homes, their new parents caring for them. Then, too, she'd heard of families in which the children were raised entirely by servants. She wouldn't have a position if the Rotherfords didn't need someone to oversee the child. But if Alice had been her daughter, she would never have left her solely to the care of others.

"And the biscuits?" piped up a hopeful voice.

"Oh, yes. Sorry!" Emma passed the plate to Alice, who selected a treat for herself and one for her doll. Emma took the plate back and set it down. She needed to stop thinking about Sir Nicholas—his deep brown eyes; the way he moved, purposeful, intent. She had found a good position at the Grange. She was safe here, from memories and from an uncertain future. She was not about to jeopardize that because the cook feared the master needed something besides his work to console him.

"And what have we here?" Mrs. Dunworthy said, coming into the nursery.

"Auntie!" Alice cried.

Emma stood out of respect for her mistress. Alice started to do likewise, but Mrs. Dunworthy held up her hand to keep the girl from climbing from her chair.

"Don't let me upset your tea, my sweet," she said to Alice, long face breaking into a smile. "I know how you love your biscuits."

Alice held one up. "We'll share."

Her aunt glided to the table and leaned down to hug her niece. "That's very generous, but perhaps another time." She straightened to eye Emma, and some of the warmth evaporated from her look. "May I have a word with you, Miss Pyrmont?"

She knew about the incident in the laboratory. She was here to tell Emma she had overstepped her role. Emma was certain of it. Funny. She would never have taken Sir Nicholas for a babble-mouth. She should have kept her own mouth shut, remembered she was merely a member of the staff, but she just couldn't stand his reckless disregard for his own life. Did he care nothing for Alice? Didn't he understand what could happen if he died? Emma remembered all too well the helplessness and fear when she had been orphaned, the pain of thinking no one cared about her. *Please, Lord, spare Alice that fate!*

Aloud she said, "Certainly, Mrs. Dunworthy," and followed her employer to the door of the nursery.

Mrs. Dunworthy stopped on the corridor side, far enough away that Alice couldn't overhear their conversation but close enough that Emma could see and attend to her if needed. Mrs. Dunworthy knew her business. She ruled over the household, yet somehow she never looked like a housekeeper. An elegant woman, tall, slender, with long fingers and etched features, she dressed in fine silk gowns and often put ribboned caps over her auburn hair. Now her gray eyes were narrowed, her mouth tight.

"Sir Nicholas," she said, "just informed me of a change in plans."

Emma nodded. She was going to be discharged. There went all her dreams of self-sufficiency. How could she find another post so far from London? She hadn't even earned enough yet to take the mail coach back to the city!

"He would like Alice to join him for dinner tonight," the lady continued.

Emma blinked. "Alice? Dinner?"

Mrs. Dunworthy nodded as if she could not believe it either. "I know. Highly unusual. But we must do what we can to humor him. We serve at six. Have her in the withdrawing room at quarter to the hour. I suggest the crimson velvet."

"Yes, Mrs. Dunworthy," Emma said, mind whirling. He wasn't going to sack her. In fact, it appeared he'd actually listened to her, for this very much sounded like an attempt to reconcile with his daughter.

"And as for what you should wear," the lady said, "have you anything presentable?"

Emma stared at her. "Me? Am I to eat at the family table, as well?"

Mrs. Dunworthy's lip curled as she answered. "That was Sir Nicholas's order. I suspect he is trying to make Alice feel at ease."

Perhaps. But she knew from experience the mind of these natural philosophers. Once a problem presented itself, they would not rest until they had poked, prodded and pestered the thing into submission. Was she the problem he meant to solve tonight? That would only lead to trouble.

"Surely there's no need for me to attend," Emma said. "I'm certain Alice would be equally at ease in your company."

"I'd like to think you're right," Mrs. Dunworthy replied. "I am perfectly capable of taking care of my niece."

Relief washed over Emma. "Then I'll just come back for her when dinner's over."

Mrs. Dunworthy quirked a smile. "I'm sorry, my dear, but it won't do. I couldn't talk him out of it. He's rather like a dog with a bone when he sets his mind to something. I suppose that's commendable in some circumstances."

So he was determined she attend. Emma felt as if her

stomach had dropped into her boots. "Yes, commend-able," she murmured.

"So, I fear you'll simply have to put up with us," Mrs. Dunworthy said. "Do you own a dinner dress?"

Not a one. Her foster family had never thought it necessary. The two brown wool gowns she alternated wearing now had been given to her in her former posi-tion. And Mrs. Dunworthy had not offered a blue gown, which seemed to be what most of the other staff wore.

"Nothing suitable for dinner with the family," Emma said.

Mrs. Dunworthy tsked. "And no time to cut down one of mine, even if we could take it in sufficiently for you. You'll have to come in your day dress, then. We'll see you downstairs at a quarter to six."

Emma curtsied in agreement as Mrs. Dunworthy turned for the corridor that led toward the adult bed-chambers.

Dinner with the family. It was a great honor usually reserved for governesses or land stewards, and then only rarely in many households, she'd heard. Certainly her foster father had never invited any of his staff or assistants to dinner. He wouldn't have spared the cost.

She winced as she returned to the nursery and her cold cup of tea. *Father, forgive me. I don't want to be so angry with my foster father, to hold a grudge. I would prefer to be grateful that he took us all in, gave us a place to live, a chance to learn a trade. I just wish he'd seen us as the family we all hungered for.*

A family that still didn't count her as a member. And dinner with Sir Nicholas was not about to change that.

Downstairs in his private suite next to his study, Nick grimaced as he mangled the second cravat. His valet was one of the servants who had refused to accompany him to the wilds of Derby, claiming he at least had done nothing to warrant exile. As Nick had had no plans to dress like the gentleman he had once been, he hadn't bothered to hire a replacement. He needed no help to don the simple country clothes he generally wore in his work.

But the cravat was another matter. Once he'd prided himself on a precise fold; now he barely managed a satisfactory knot. It didn't help that his hands were scalded from the fire today, and he was developing a blister on his thumb. The price for success in his work was high, but the cost of failure was unthinkable.

He managed to tie the third cravat into something passable and assessed himself in the standing mirror that had been his late wife, Ann's, joy. His hair was pomaded back from his face for once, but the change affected the perspective of his features, making them look longer and leaner. The black evening coat had a similar effect on his physique. The faintest hint of stubble peppered his chin, made more noticeable by the white of the cravat against his throat. Alas, at this hour he had no time to shave. And he couldn't risk damaging his hard-won fold.

Charlotte met him at the main stair. Tall and ascetic as always in her gray lustring gown, she looked so little like his fragile Ann that he sometimes wondered whether they had truly been sisters. Still, he'd read a fascinating essay in *Philosophical Transactions,* the journal of the Royal Society, about the inheritance of physical characteristics. Charlotte's dark straight hair and thin lips could certainly be attributed to some ancestor, probably one who had frightened the Vikings out of England.

"Are you determined to run off my staff?" she greeted him.

So she was still smarting over his request to have Alice and her nanny join them for dinner. He didn't think her temper would calm if he explained that he merely wished to observe his new employee more closely.

"I would never attempt to interfere in your kingdom, my dear," Nick said with a smile. Ann had assured him he could be quite charming, but either he had lost his touch along with his scientific reputation or Charlotte was immune.

She didn't bother to accept his arm as they descended the stair, her chin set as firmly as those of the men and women in the gilt-framed portraits they passed. "Yet you are determined to embarrass our new nanny by insisting she dine with us. The poor thing doesn't even own a dinner dress. How could you be so cruel?"

Nick's smile faded as they took the turning of the polished wood stair and started down for the main floor, where alabaster columns lined the corridor that ran through the center of the house. Scientific pursuit was hardly cruel. He needed to observe a phenomenon to build a hypothesis about its usefulness. Relying on secondhand observations, such as Charlotte's, could result in a flawed analysis.

"She needn't feel compelled to dress for dinner," he pointed out. "This isn't the Carleton House set."

"It certainly isn't," Charlotte quipped as they reached the bottom of the stair. "And you are not the Prince Regent. But by failing to dress as we do, Miss Pyrmont makes it all the more evident she doesn't belong at the table. She's a sweet girl from a good family, Nicholas.

You cannot expect her to like the fact that she must work for her supper."

Now there was a bit of data, if lamentably second-hand. He had found little sweet about Miss Pyrmont this afternoon, with the exception of her smile. He would have placed her closer to the acidic end of the scale. And it was not uncommon for women of good family to take positions as an upper servant. Charlotte would know. His sister-in-law had married poorly and been left a destitute widow. If he hadn't asked her to come preside over his household, she would be serving in some other house, likely as a governess or companion.

"If you are determined she needs a gown," he said, "give her one of Ann's. Someone ought to take pleasure from them."

Charlotte stared at him, her skin stretched tight over her long nose. "Have you no respect for her memory?"

Guilt wrapped itself around his tongue and stilled it. A day didn't go by that he didn't think of Ann, her quiet insights, her dry laugh. He still didn't understand how he'd so failed to misread the evidence of her illness until it was too late to save her. But he'd realized he couldn't linger over his grief or he'd go mad.

As if his guilt had shouted into the silence, Charlotte patted his arm, face softening. "Forgive me. I just miss her so."

Nick touched her hand. "We all do. But you know she frequently donated her time and her gifts. I suspect she wouldn't mind someone else using her things."

Charlotte nodded, but she moved ahead of him to enter the withdrawing door near the foot of the stairs first.

Nick came more slowly. He knew Charlotte grieved the loss of her sister. But life was for the living, and holing himself up with his regrets would not solve the problems facing him.

Nor would it help him understand his daughter's nanny. She was waiting for him in the withdrawing room, and despite Charlotte's concerns, he thought Miss Pyrmont looked as if she belonged there, even in her plain brown wool dress. Perhaps it was the way she held her head high or the smile on her pink lips. Perhaps it was the way she clutched Alice's hand as if to protect her. She met his gaze with an assessing look that made it seem as if he had strayed into her withdrawing room rather than the other way around.

For some reason, he wondered what she thought of the space. The withdrawing room wasn't nearly as fussy as some he'd seen when he'd spent time in Society. Everything was neatly done in geometric shapes, from the gilded medallions on the walls and ceiling to the pink and green concentric circles of the carpet that covered the hardwood floor nearly from wall to wall. The white marble fireplace provided sufficient heat, the wall of windows and brass wall sconces sufficient light. The furniture was arranged in groupings, but a chaise in the corner provided rest for a retiring lady, or so Ann had always said.

He thought Miss Pyrmont would never be so retiring. But that hypothesis remained to be tested.

"Ladies," he said with a bow. "Thank you for joining me this evening."

Miss Pyrmont curtsied, and Alice copied her, a tiny figure in her red velvet gown. Charlotte smiled at her niece with obvious fondness.

"I believe Mrs. Jennings has dinner ready to be served," she said. "Shall we?" She didn't wait for his answer. She accepted Alice's hand from her nanny and strolled toward the main door, which led into a salon and then the corridor.

Nick held out his arm. "Miss Pyrmont?"

For the first time, she looked uncertain. She glanced at his outstretched arm, then up at his face as if trying to understand the gesture. If she was from a good family as Charlotte had said, she should have been escorted in to dinner more than once. And even if she hadn't, surely the master of a house could be expected to act with chivalry on occasion.

He could see her swallow against the high neck of her gown. Then her gaze darted past him, and she straightened her back as if making a decision. She marched to his side and put her hand on his arm. Despite the determination in her stiff spine, the touch was light, insubstantial, directly disproportionate to her temperate. It was almost as if a butterfly accompanied him to dinner.

Shaking his head at the fanciful thought, he led her from the room.

Chapter Three

Here she was, being escorted to dinner by the master as if she were a guest in this house. How silly! She should have refused his arm. But Emma had seen Mrs. Jennings peering into the room a moment before the cook had scurried back to her work overseeing the serving. The smile on Mrs. Jennings's broad face said she was delighted beyond measure to see Emma with Sir Nicholas. Emma simply couldn't bring herself to discourage the kind woman.

So she walked beside him through the salon with its tall alabaster columns holding up the soaring ceiling, and down the black-and-white marble tiles of the central corridor. Sir Nicholas looked almost presentable in his evening black, a silver-shot waistcoat peeking out from his tailored coat. So he knew how to dress for Society. He simply chose to avoid Society as he avoided his daughter.

"Mrs. Dunworthy tells me I have inconvenienced you," he said as they headed for the dining room at the front of the house.

And why should he care if he had? That was his

right as her employer. "Nonsense," she said. "I'm very glad you wanted Alice with you tonight. Thank you."

A crease formed between his midnight brows, as if he wasn't sure why she was thanking him for paying attention to his child. "And how is Alice getting on here?" he asked.

"Fine," she assured him as they reached the door of the dining room. "Though it is a little quiet, when you aren't catching things on fire."

He chuckled, and the warm sound sent gooseflesh skittering across her arms.

Oh, no! She was not about to be charmed by this man. She would put her reaction down to the wonder of dining in such style. And wonder was entirely warranted.

The Grange dining room was as large as the withdrawing room, with an elegant white marble fireplace on one pale green wall and three windows looking down the valley on the opposite wall. A cloth-draped table that could likely seat thirty ran down the center, with four places set at one end in fine china, sparkling crystal and gleaming silver. Candles in silver sconces glowed along the walls; lilies in a jade urn adorned the table. She'd never seen anything like it.

Mrs. Dunworthy was already seated to the left of the head, with Alice on the right. Sir Nicholas escorted Emma to the seat next to her charge and then went to take his place at the top. As he sat, his sister-in-law gazed at him expectantly, and he frowned a moment before bowing his head and asking the blessing. It seemed he was so rusty at being in Society he'd forgotten how to say grace!

A portion of the wall in one corner swung open from the warming room, and Dorcus and Ivy in caps and aprons carried in porcelain platters of dressed lamb and trout with mushrooms, followed by macaroni in a creamy cheese sauce and asparagus. Emma tried to ignore her host and focus on Alice, selecting small portions and plainer foods from the abundance offered. Alice alternated between squirming in her chair over every new experience and staring about her with wide eyes.

"And how are you this evening, Alice?" her father asked after all had been served and the maids had withdrawn.

Emma relaxed a little. If he spent the meal talking with his daughter, everything would be fine. She glanced at Alice, who was examining her trout as if she expected it to start swimming about the table.

"Lady Chamomile is very unhappy," she told the fish.

Emma frowned. She'd figured out her first day at the Grange that the doll's feelings generally mirrored Alice's. What was causing her charge concern?

Sir Nicholas frowned, as well. "I hadn't realized you'd visited our neighbors. Which estate is Lady Chamomile's?"

Emma bit back a laugh. So, he didn't know about the doll. She was fairly certain Alice wouldn't explain. In fact, the girl was returning his frown as if giving the matter great thought. Emma couldn't help herself.

"I believe Lady Chamomile owns a castle," she offered, hiding her smile with a dab of her napkin.

Alice nodded solemnly. "A big castle."

"Does she indeed?" Mrs. Dunworthy said, but Emma could see she was trying not to smile, too.

"Interesting." He fiddled with his silver fork as if the

movement helped spur his thinking. "I don't recall anything approaching a castle in Dovecote Dale."

"Unless you count the Duke of Bellington's country estate Bellweather Hall," Mrs. Dunworthy pointed out. "Of course, Bell is still in London I imagine, wrestling with some weighty matter in Parliament while his mother and sister lead the social whirl."

Bell. They could speak of a duke with such familiarity. Even though dukes had been known to sponsor her foster father, she felt the gulf between her and this family widening.

"Then you visit Lady Chamomile often?" Sir Nicholas asked, obviously intent on discovering the truth about the matter.

"Most every day," Emma assured him. "Isn't that right, Alice?" She glanced at her charge.

Alice nodded again. "And she sleeps with me at night."

His black brows shot up.

Mrs. Dunworthy laughed, a silvery sound that surprised Emma. "Oh, Miss Pyrmont, have pity on my overly logical brother-in-law and explain about Lady Chamomile before we perplex him any further."

He turned his gaze to Emma's, dark, directing. Oh, but this was too good an opportunity to forego. Emma offered him her sweetest smile. "Lady Chamomile," she said obligingly, "is a very grand lady and Alice's favorite doll. We shall have to introduce you to her, Sir Nicholas. Perhaps you could join us for tea, tomorrow."

She had only meant him to spend more time with Alice, but Emma knew she'd overstepped her position again by the way Mrs. Dunworthy's smile faded.

"I hardly think that's necessary," the lady said.

Emma swallowed and dropped her gaze to her plate. "Forgive me. I meant no disrespect."

"No offense taken," she heard Sir Nicholas say, and she wasn't sure if he was speaking to her or his sister-in-law. "I only regret my work keeps me so busy that I must decline your invitation to join Alice and Lady Chamomile."

Alice sighed.

Emma's hand clenched on her fork, and she could not bring herself to pick up a mouthful of the meal. Too busy! He was too busy to spare his daughter a moment for tea. What was so important?

It wasn't material need that motivated him—the amount of silver, from the cutlery to the candelabra, said the Rotherfords had more than enough income. He didn't seem to be studying anything that would immediately save lives, like Dr. Beddoes and Mr. Davy used to do at the Pneumatic Institute in Bristol, where they used gases to help people fight off consumption. He didn't even seem to have a sponsor or patron who expected results from an investment; at least she'd heard no word of it in the servants' hall. Why couldn't he find time for Alice?

"As I cannot join you tomorrow," he continued, obviously unaware of her frustration, "perhaps you could be so good as to answer a few questions now."

Her anger melted as quickly as it had come. This was what she had feared. Emma swallowed though she'd eaten nothing. "Questions?" She glanced up at him.

His warm smile would have assured her in other circumstances. Now she thought it stemmed from having something else to observe and study. "Yes. A very wise woman recently suggested that I should know more about the person who cares for my daughter."

He meant to learn all about her. That was the way of natural philosophers. Still, she could hardly blame him. After all, she'd been the one to exclaim over the fact that he didn't know his daughter's nanny.

"I like Nanny," Alice announced. She took a big bite of asparagus and made a face.

Mrs. Dunworthy seemed equally prepared to defend Emma. "I assure you, Nicholas," she said, "I reviewed Miss Pyrmont's credentials thoroughly before I employed her."

"I'm certain you did," he replied with a nod of approval, slicing through his lamb with brisk efficiency. "I'd merely like to hear about them myself." Before his sister-in-law could argue further, he turned to Emma. "For instance, Miss Pyrmont, where were you born? Where were you raised?"

He could not know the position in which he had placed her. When Mrs. Dunworthy had made her nanny, the lady had ordered Emma not to speak of her background.

"There are some in this household," Mrs. Dunworthy had said then, looking down her long nose, "who will never appreciate the plight of an orphan. I would prefer not to burden you with their disdain."

Was Sir Nicholas one who would judge her? She glanced at her mistress for guidance, but Mrs. Dunworthy's gaze was fixed on her brother-in-law, and her mouth was set in a tight line. It was up to Emma. She took a breath and told him the truth.

"I'm an orphan, Sir Nicholas," she admitted. "I don't remember much about my parents. I was a fosterling at the asylum in London."

She thought she might see curiosity or dismissal in his gaze, but his look softened. "I'm sorry. It couldn't have been easy to find a proper place in the world with that start. I commend you for rising above it."

Tears threatened, and she dropped her gaze to her plate once more. *I'm only here because of Your grace and strength, Lord. I know that. Thank You!*

"Do try some of the trout, Miss Pyrmont," Mrs. Dunworthy said kindly. "It's quite good."

Emma knew. An angler brought fresh fish to the Grange almost daily. Mrs. Jennings made sure they all ate well. Did Mrs. Dunworthy think otherwise, or was she giving Emily time to compose herself?

"London is a long way from Derby," Sir Nicholas said to Emma as if his sister-in-law had never spoken. "How did you come to find yourself here?"

"Because she answered my advertisement in the newspaper, of course," Mrs. Dunworthy said. It was the truth. Emma had asked to read her previous master's discarded newspapers before they were used for cleaning. The request for a nanny all the way up in Derby had been a Godsend, for it took her far from all those who might seek to bring her back under control.

"So you were looking for a better position," he surmised.

Emma nodded and was thankful that the maids entered just then to clear the first course and bring in apple pie, trifle and ice cream. Alice started squirming again.

Emma didn't think Sir Nicholas would let the matter drop, so she wasn't surprised when he took up his questioning again the moment the maids left.

"Why Derby?" he pressed, spooning up a bite of trifle and holding it before him.

"Oh, Nicholas," Mrs. Dunworthy said with a sigh, "stop quizzing the girl!"

"I merely wish to know her better," Sir Nicholas protested. "Alice's recommendation carries great weight with me," he smiled at his daughter, "but a gentleman needs to deal with facts."

Of course. Facts, never feelings, were what a natural philosopher relied on. He had to observe, chronicle. The well-being of his subject was never a consideration.

Well, if it was facts he wanted, she could certainly provide them.

"Allow me to elaborate, then," she said, setting down her own spoon. "I had three younger foster brothers of whom I was given charge when I was nine, so I've more experience than you might expect caring for children. All of us were adopted by a gentleman in London, and I was given care of his two daughters, as well. I attended all the same lessons they did, so I know how to read and write in English and some Latin, and I'm good with numbers. Immediately before coming here, I worked for an apothecary and his family, where I learned a bit about diseases and how to prevent and cure them."

"Exceptional," he said, and she sat a little taller. Alice sat up, as well. Emma thought even Mrs. Dunworthy looked a little more confident about the outcome of this conversation.

Until he said, "Who taught you Latin?"

He had to pick that one. She should have left it out, but some part of her had wanted to impress him.

"Nicholas," Mrs. Dunworthy said, "you are starting to browbeat the girl. Miss Pyrmont has volunteered her accomplishments. Be happy with that and enjoy the rest of your meal."

His smile of apology was more like a grimace. "Very well, Charlotte. Forgive my inquisitive nature, Miss Pyrmont. It is part and parcel with the way I work, I fear."

She thought her smile was just as strained, for she very much feared the same thing.

Mrs. Dunworthy began asking Alice questions, then, and as they chatted, Emma found herself watching Sir Nicholas. Much of his food remained untouched on the plate, his long-fingered hands resting on the tablecloth beside it. His right hand was twitching, one finger beating time on the damask to sounds only he could hear. Though he answered any question put to him readily, his gaze no longer focused on the people around him. His body was present in the room, but his mind had already wandered.

Anger pricked her. Alice deserved a father who would love her. Emma was certain they existed; she'd read about them. In fact, as soon as she'd learned to read, she'd devoured stories about families. In the books she loved, fathers were kind and wise, and mothers firm but loving. Men and women married because they were deeply in love, enough to overlook all fault of upbringing or misfortune. As an orphan, Emma had been denied such a family. Why should Alice face the same fate, when her father was very much alive?

Alice said something clever, and Sir Nicholas smiled in obvious appreciation. For a moment, his gaze lit on his daughter, and those analytical eyes warmed, his angular features relaxed. In fact, he had rather expressive lips, the bottom more full than the top. Now they smiled in such a way as to cause a hitch in her breath.

Emma blinked. Why, it seemed he had potential! Perhaps he'd invited Alice to dinner for more than a chance to question Emma. Perhaps he truly cared about his daughter.

What if she could encourage him? What if she could bring him and Alice closer? Mrs. Jennings seemed to think he needed a mother for his child. Perhaps what he really needed was to learn how to be a father.

She smiled as she attacked her apple pie with enthusiasm. She knew exactly how to solve Mrs. Jennings' problem, and her own. She would indeed start a campaign to court Sir Nicholas, for his daughter.

Nick was surprised to hear the clock on the mantle chime eight even as they finished the last of the second course. It appeared dinner had passed more quickly than it usually did.

Alice yawned.

Miss Pyrmont smiled at her. "I think perhaps we should make our curtseys, Miss Alice."

Alice giggled. "You don't have to miss me. I'm right here!"

Her nanny's smile grew, and Nick knew his must match it. "Miss Pyrmont is right, Alice," he said. "It's time for bed." He rose and pulled out her chair so she could climb down. Those violet-colored eyes, so like her mother's, met his, and he felt as if someone had taken out his heart and squeezed.

Singular sensation. Singular thought.

"Good night, Papa," she said.

Throat surprisingly tight, Nick bowed to her. "Good night, Alice."

As he straightened, she took Miss Pyrmont's hand and turned to Charlotte. "Good night, Auntie! Sleep tight. Mind the bugs and fleas don't bite."

He had never thought pink a violent color until it erupted in Miss Pyrmont's fair complexion.

Charlotte threw down her napkin and pushed back her chair to stand. "Bugs and fleas? In my household?"

Nick barked a laugh and instantly regretted it for Charlotte's head came up and Miss Pyrmont's head hung.

"It's something I learned as a child, madam," she murmured. "It must have slipped out."

Alice glanced between the two of them. "I like it. I don't want the bugs to bite me."

"Of course not," Nick assured her. "But I'm certain if any bug even considered entering this house, one look from your auntie would drop him dead in his tracks."

Charlotte glared at him, but he thought he heard a smothered laugh from Miss Pyrmont.

He bowed to his daughter again and to her redoubtable nanny. "Good night, ladies. Thank you for joining me for dinner. It has been most engaging."

"Good night, sir," Miss Pyrmont said and hurried Alice from the room as if her very life was in danger.

Seeing the look on Charlotte's face, he thought she might be right.

"I apologize, Nicholas," Charlotte said, picking up her napkin as she returned to her seat. "Of course I knew about Miss Pyrmont's unfortunate early years, but I had no idea she would share anything so common with Alice. I will discharge her tomorrow."

Nick stopped himself from sitting. "Discharge her? For a child's rhyme? Nonsense."

Charlotte cocked her head. "Then it doesn't trouble you that we know nothing of her parentage?"

"Hardly. It doesn't matter what she was when she was born. It matters who she is now. She seems to genuinely care for Alice. Surely that is what Alice needs."

Charlotte nodded as if satisfied. "Very well, then. She stays. But I will keep a closer eye on her."

He pitied Miss Pyrmont. "Is that necessary? I seem to recall you saying she came from a good family, though how that's possible given she's an orphan, I'm unsure."

"I meant her foster family, of course," Charlotte said with asperity. "I knew her foster mother years ago."

By her tone, he gathered he was supposed to have known this fact. He wasn't sure why. But then, while Ann had always encouraged his scientific pursuits, Charlotte lacked all appreciation of reasoning, as it seemed she could question nothing, not even herself.

"As Miss Pyrmont mentioned," Charlotte continued, "her foster family took in her and three boys from the orphan asylum to raise. It was a fine act of Christian charity."

"So it would seem," Nick mused, finger tapping his thigh. "Though considering such a background, our nanny seems rather outspoken."

"She exhibits a certain independence," Charlotte agreed, and he thought he detected a trace of envy in her crisp voice. "But I don't think her attitude will infect Alice. She's too young to understand such things."

He relaxed his hand. "I rather hope a spark of independence rubs off on Alice. I'd hate for my daughter to grow up an average sort of girl."

She quirked a smile. "I doubt you'll have any problem there."

No, Nick thought as he bowed and left her to her thoughts. His problems at the moment were far bigger, and neither his daughter nor the intriguing Miss Pyrmont could help him solve them.

Chapter Four

Emma took her time settling Alice to sleep that night. The little girl was still wound up after dinner, telling Lady Chamomile all about the food, table settings and conversation. She seemed genuinely delighted with the whole affair. Why, then, had she claimed that Lady Chamomile was so unhappy?

Emma put the question to the girl as she tucked her into the child-sized poster bed in her bedchamber off the main room of the nursery suite.

Alice snuggled deeper under the goose-down comforter. "She is unhappy because she is an orphan."

The answer cut into Emma. "Not all orphans are unhappy. Some know the Lord has better plans for them."

Alice sighed, closing her eyes. "That's good. But I think Lady Chamomile would be happier if we could find her a papa."

Emma stroked Alice's silky hair back from her face. "I'll do all I can, Alice. I promise."

She started the very next day at Sunday services. Dovecote Dale was served by a fine stone church in the center of the valley. Though the Duke of Bellington had responsibility for it, all four of the wealthy families—the Rotherfords at the Grange, Lord Hascot at Hollyoak Farm, the Earl of Danning at Fern Lodge, and the Duke of Bellington—had endowed gifts so that the little country chapel lacked for nothing. The building and bell tower had a fresh coat of white paint below a gilded steeple. The stained-glass windows glittered in the summer sun.

Inside, carved oak seats marched along the center aisle, and banners in rich silk draped the walls leading up to the alabaster cross. With his flyaway hair and silver-rimmed spectacles, the Reverend Mr. Battersea always seemed in awe of the place, honored to be given charge of their souls.

With the servants from the four estates, Emma listened with her usual interest to the readings and the sermon. But she was careful to be the first one on her feet and the last one to sit when the service called for the congregation to change positions. She wanted to take advantage of every opportunity to observe Sir Nicholas near the front.

From his absorption in his work to the way the staff seemed to revere him, she'd assumed he was a man like her foster father, though certainly not with Samuel Fredericks's ability to denigrate those he saw as lesser beings. She was fairly sure her foster father was in a class by himself in that area. Mr. Fredericks attended church in his finest clothes, arriving in his best carriage. He worshipped with head high and shoulders broad, as if he wanted everyone around him to notice or he saw himself as a peer of the Lord instead of a humble penitent.

Sir Nicholas was different. Oh, his clothes were of fine wool and soft linen, but they were a bit on the rumpled side, and his cravat was more simply tied than that of Mr. Hennessy, the butler from the Earl of Danning's lodge. Though she never saw Sir Nicholas pick up the *Book of Common Prayer* to follow the service, his lips seemed to be moving in the appropriate responses. Yet she detected little change in him, as if he were merely doing what he'd done a dozen times before.

Lord, what am I to make of this man? Last night I thought I saw a glimmer of a good father. But if he cannot give his heart to You, how can he give it to his daughter?

She received the beginning of an answer that afternoon, at the weekly Conclave.

Once a month, each member of the household received a Sunday afternoon off. She and Mrs. Jennings had the same day, and the cook had quickly introduced Emma to the place the servants gathered at the Dovecote Inn, not far from the church. The inn was a rough-stone building with flower boxes under the windows. More boxes under the overhanging eaves made homes for the doves for which the area was famous. On the upper floor lay a large private dining room, and it was there every Sunday afternoon that some collection of the local servants met to celebrate or commiserate their lots.

Some of the other houses, Emma knew, were more generous, so a few of the Conclave attendees like Mr. Hennessy were there nearly every Sunday. Others, like her, came once a month. Someone usually brought the largess of a master's table—today it was fresh apricots from Lord Hascot's orchard. And there was always tea and talk around the polished wood table.

The last time Emma had attended she'd brought her knitting and sat quietly on one of the tall upholstered chairs by the window, listening to the talk around her and the coos of the doves outside. She'd noticed that the unmarried servants tended to flirt with each other. She paid them no mind, as they didn't seem to be serious.

Today, she had another purpose anyway, so she chose a seat near the stone hearth and confessed her goal to Mrs. Jennings.

"God bless you, Miss Pyrmont," the cook said, face brightening. "You can count on my help—anything you want."

"I'm trying to think of an activity Sir Nicholas could do with Alice," Emma explained, edging forward on her seat as the other servants milled around them. "Something that might encourage him to forget his work for a time. You've known him for years, haven't you? What did he like to do as a child?"

"Read," Mrs. Jennings answered promptly, brushing back her skirts from the glowing fire. "Everything and anything. He knew the Latin names for things by the time he was Miss Alice's age, and he knew most of the Gospels by heart by the time he was eight. He liked Luke the best. Said it had more facts."

Of course. She'd suspected he set a great store by facts. And perhaps that was why he'd felt no need to use the *Book of Common Prayer*. He might well have memorized that, too! She studied the apricot she'd plucked from the bowl. "Did he have any favorite toys? Good friends?"

"Any so-called friends he found at Eton and lost in London," the cook replied tartly. "But I'll not gossip."

"I will," Dorcus said, ambling closer. The maid also had the afternoon off, but Emma had noticed she'd spent her time batting her eyes at a strapping footman from the duke's household. "You should know what's what, Miss Pyrmont," she said now, pulling up a chair to sit beside Emma and the cook, "especially if you mean to become mistress of the Grange."

"I have no such intentions," Emma informed her, biting into her apricot to forestall additional comment. As if she'd ever consider marrying a man like Sir Nicholas! Her ideal husband would value his family, put their needs first.

"The more fool you, then," Dorcus replied. "Being called a cheat never colored a fellow's money."

"That's quite enough from you," Mrs. Jennings declared. "Sir Nicholas is no cheat. If he says he made the right calculations, then he did."

Dorcus rolled her eyes, but she rose and returned to her pursuit of the footman.

The cook leaned closer to Emma and lowered her voice. The warm scent of vanilla washed over Emma. "Never you mind her. All you need to know is that some of those philosophers questioned Sir Nicholas's work. He left London because of it and gave himself completely over to his studies. All the more reason for you to carry on with your plan. And as for toys, he was quite partial to kites. Seems he'd read about some experiment by an American gentleman and was keen to repeat it."

Kites, eh? Oh, for a windy day! But lacking that, surely there was something she could use from Mrs. Jennings's stories.

Emma's mind began to conjure up any number of activities designed to woo Sir Nicholas away from his work. She would have loved to speak further with the cook, but she could see Dorcus casting them looks. Best not to fan that flame. Emma thanked Mrs. Jennings and made polite conversation with the other servants until it was time to return to the Grange.

So, Sir Nicholas had studied from an early age, she

thought as she walked up the lane from the village, the sun warm on her dark wool gown. Again, she wasn't surprised. Indeed, the only surprising thing about her discussion with Mrs. Jennings was the reason Sir Nicholas found himself rusticating in Dovecote Dale.

His scientific calculations had obviously incensed his fellow natural philosophers to the point that he no longer felt comfortable among them. He must have made a tremendous mistake indeed. In her experience, it took a great deal to convince learned men to castigate their colleagues. Certainly she'd wished someone in authority to berate her foster father for his inhumane practices. But it seemed experimenting on children did not rise to the level of offense among the Royal Society.

There, she was starting to sound bitter again. She could feel her emotions like acid on the back of her tongue. One of the reasons she'd wanted to escape London was to leave her past behind, before those emotions poisoned her outlook, her hopes and her future. She was not about to give in to them now.

Help me, Lord. I know You must have sent me here for a reason. Show me the good I can do. Help me be a blessing.

Her own blessing was waiting for her on her return. In fact, Emma heard laughter before she reached the nursery.

As she paused in the doorway, she saw that Ivy was chasing the little girl around the table, her blue skirts flapping. Alice giggled each time she managed to evade capture. Ivy stopped immediately on seeing Emma, tugging down her apron and adjusting her lace-edged cap.

"Begging your pardon, miss," she said, with a quick curtsey to Emma, "but someone *would* refuse a tickle."

She glanced pointedly at Alice, who covered her mouth with both hands. The giggle still slipped out.

Emma ventured in. "Tickles before dinner? What am I to do with the pair of you?" She clucked her tongue with a smile.

Alice dropped her hands and hurried to the table, slippers skimming the rosy carpet. "Do you wish a tickle, too, Nanny?"

Now Ivy giggled before a look from Emma sent her hurrying out to help Mrs. Jennings finish the Sunday dinner.

"Not at the moment," Emma assured her charge. "And I'm guessing the rest of the household is not up to laughter either on a quiet Sunday evening."

Alice climbed up into her chair and waited for Emma to push her up to the table. "I didn't mean to make so much noise," she said, face scrunching. "I know I shouldn't bother Auntie or Papa."

All at once the ideas that had been germinating in Emma's mind sprouted into bloom. Her smile grew.

"Not at all, Alice," she said, pushing the girl up to the table and going to her own seat to wait for the dinner tray to arrive. "I believe your father needs something to wake him up. And I know just how we can go about it."

The next morning, Nick scowled at the scrap of wool sitting on his worktable. Two days ago the stuff had burst into flame immediately; his laboratory still gave off the grit of charcoal from the smoke even though he'd spent Sunday afternoon airing the place and setting up his next experiment. Today, under a different chemical treatment, the material would not so much as smolder. That didn't bode well for success.

It had sounded like a relatively simple problem to

solve. Coal miners required light to do their jobs deep underground. Coal mines gave off firedamp, a noxious gas that appeared to be a form of the swamp gases Volta had studied. Combine a flame with a patch of the gas, and the resulting explosion could kill dozens. The Fatfield Mine in Durham had lost thirty-two men and boys just two years ago after their candles ignited firedamp.

Still, the solution eluded many. Dr. William Clanny had developed a method of using water to force the air into a lamp, protecting the flame from the gas. While ingenious, the device was impractical to carry into the mines. Sir Humphry Davy, the chemist, was approaching the matter from a heating perspective. An enginewright named George Stephenson thought burnt air was the key to separating the flame from the firedamp.

Nick had been working with a team of natural philosophers led by Samuel Fredericks to consider the properties of the materials that could compose a lamp. They had thought they'd come across a likely combination of candidates, but their first attempt to test the lamp had resulted in the deaths of three men and a boy a little older than Alice.

The muscles in his hand were tightening; he shook them out. Obviously this composition would not meet his needs. He required something that would burn in the presence of oxygen but not firedamp, not the other way around. He'd have to start over.

He rocked back on his stool, took a deep breath. He was certain the secret lay in the composition of the lamp's wick. He'd already had a glassblower create the appropriate chimney to partially isolate the wick from the gas and the blacksmith create the brass housing for the fuel. He'd tried wool, cotton and linen and various combinations of fuel, to no avail. One attempt was too flammable. Another, like this, wasn't flammable enough. There was no easy in between.

Which somehow reminded him of his life of late.

Outside, he heard a noise. More like a bump and shuffle, really. Very likely the gardener was attempting to replace the shrub Nick had withered when he'd dumped a batch of chemicals after he'd first moved to the Grange. He'd learned to be more cautious in his disposal habits. He didn't want Alice to accidentally come in contact with the stuff.

Perhaps he ought to try silk next. Kressley had recently proposed its use in commercial lamps. But he wasn't sure it was practical by itself. Perhaps coated with some chemical to moderate the flammability.

The noise outside was rising in volume now, and he thought he made out words. Was that someone singing? He could place neither the tune nor the key.

Nick shook his head to clear his mind. It didn't matter what was happening outside. He had work to do. His family's income came in large part from the leasings of the mine to the east of the Grange. He felt as if he owed it to those men personally to find a safer way for them to work.

He still remembered the first time his father had taken him to the mine, on a gloomy day when Nick was eight. Nick had been about to leave for Eton, and his father seemed to see Nick's imminent departure as reason to spend time together. Certainly Nick could find no other logical hypothesis for why his father had suddenly remembered his existence.

They'd driven to the mine in the gig, his father at the reins, but obviously determined to show his knowledge of the place. He'd pointed out the shadowed entrances, the stiff metal outbuildings, the men and boys laboring under the weight and darkness. His father's face had glowed with pride as he described the prosperity, the accomplishment.

Nick had been more interested in how the mine worked. He'd prevailed upon his father to allow him to be lowered in one of the baskets into the pit. He hadn't been afraid, even as daylight disappeared and blackness swallowed him.

Open-flame lamps produced more light at the bottom, where scarred walls told of past discoveries. Sitting on the floor had been a boy of six, face grimy, clothes grimier. One small fist enclosed the handle of a wooden door built into the wall.

"What are you doing?" Nick asked as he stepped from the basket onto the uneven floor.

"Manning the wind-door," the boy replied with pride. "We open and close the doors to keep the air flowing." As if to prove it, he heaved on the handle, and air rushed past Nick, setting the basket beside him to swaying.

That grimy face was the one he saw when he thought about the need for his safety lamp.

Something hit the door of his laboratory, hard. The memory faded. Enough of that nonsense. Each day down in those mines, hundreds of men and boys risked their lives. While it was not entirely his fault a replacement had not been found, he could not forget that a mistake of his had cost lives as well as his status as a natural philosopher. He would not rest until...

"What on earth is all that noise?" he demanded, jumping off his stool. He strode to the door and jerked it open.

Alice gazed up at him, little fingers barely grasping a battledore. The wooden racket was nearly as long as she was. Her eyes seemed disproportionately large for her face, but one look at him and they brightened. "Papa!"

"Alice," he returned, bemused

"Good day, Sir Nicholas," Miss Pyrmont called from a short distance away. She swung her battledore up onto the shoulder of her brown wool gown. He seemed to remember the game that required the rackets also involved a shuttlecock that was cork at one end and feathers at the other. Hardly sufficient to make noise. He struggled to develop a hypothesis about the source of the thuds against his door.

"Miss Pyrmont," he greeted her. "Why are you here?"

She cocked her head as she strolled closer. She wore no bonnet. Perhaps they were not required for a nanny as they seemed to be for other ladies. Certainly Charlotte and Ann had never left the house without one. Either way, the sunlight blazed against her pale hair.

"We're playing a game," she explained with a smile as she approached him. "I would think that would be obvious to a gentleman given to observation."

Alice was still gazing up at him as if equally surprised he hadn't figured it out.

"I can see you are playing a game," Nick replied. "What I don't understand is why you must play it here."

"Don't you like games?" Alice asked.

That was not the issue, but he didn't think her nanny cared. Indeed, the look in Miss Pyrmont's muddy eyes as she stopped in front of him was nothing short of challenge.

"Games can be enjoyable," he started, when Alice dropped her battledore and seized his nearest hand with both of hers.

"Oh, good!" she cried. "Come play!"

He took a stutter-step forward to keep from bowling her over. "No, Alice. Not now."

He had meant the tone to be firm, but not sharp. His daughter obviously had a different interpretation. She stopped and dropped his hand, and her lower lip trembled. "I'm sorry. I thought you wanted to play with me."

How was he to answer that? Alice could not understand what drove him. She was too little to remember her mother's death much less the recent tragedies associated with his work. She couldn't know the depth for which he needed to atone. Only God knew how much Nick had failed, another reason he found it hard to take his concerns to the Almighty.

Miss Pyrmont had reached their sides. She knelt, brown skirts puddling, and took Alice's hands in hers. "I'm sure your papa would love to play with us, Alice. We simply caught him at a bad time." She glanced up at him. "Isn't that right, sir?"

Nick blew out a breath. "Yes, just so. Thank you, Miss Pyrmont."

She gave him a quick smile before returning her gaze to Alice, whose face was still pinched.

"Your father has important work to do," she explained. "We wouldn't want to keep him from it."

"Noooooo," Alice said, the length of the vowel proclaiming her uncertainty.

"Thank you for understanding, Alice," Nick said. "I'll be done soon, and then I'll have more time for games."

Alice brightened again. How quickly she believed him and with no evidence. A shame his colleagues didn't have such faith in him. A shame he'd lost such faith.

Miss Pyrmont rose, all smiles, as well. In fact, he

noted a distinct change in her appearance when she smiled, as if she somehow grew lighter, taller. The change seemed to lighten his mood, as well. Curious.

"I'm so glad to hear you're making such progress, Sir Nicholas," she proclaimed. "Do you think you will be done today, then?"

He could not be so encouraging. In fact, her brightness suddenly felt demanding, asking things of him he knew he could not achieve. Nick took a step back. "Not today, no."

"Tomorrow then?" she persisted, following him.

"I cannot be certain," Nick hedged, glancing over his shoulder for the safety of his laboratory.

"The next day, then," she said with an assurance he was far from feeling. "We should celebrate over tea."

"You'll like tea, Papa," Alice said as if he would be experiencing the brew for the first time. "The bubbles make kisses."

Kisses? Though he knew for a fact that tea and kisses did not equate, he found his gaze drawn to the pleasing pink of Miss Pyrmont's lips. As if she'd noticed his look, she took a step back, too.

"What time should Alice and I be ready for you to join us?" she asked.

She seemed to assume his agreement this time. Assumptions were dangerous things, to be used only when no source of direct observation or calculation was available. He did not think it warranted in this instance. Surely Miss Pyrmont had observed that he was too busy for a social convention like tea.

"I fear I cannot give you a precise day when I will be finished," he told her. "Now, if you'll excuse me, I should get back to my work. I suggest you find somewhere else to play."

Alice seemed to crumple in on herself, and he felt as if a weight had been placed on his shoulders. He wished once more he knew how to make her understand. Perhaps she would appreciate his work one day, when she was older. He could imagine having her sit beside him as he explained his process, his hypotheses. She could help him think through his logic, question things he'd perhaps taken for granted. It seemed he needed someone like that in his life, or he would never have overlooked the mistakes in his calculations, much less his wife's illness.

But as he turned to go, he caught sight of Miss Pyrmont's face. Her chin was thrust out, her eyes narrowed, as if she could not understand him. She was certainly mature enough to realize the importance of his work, might even have been of some use to him in furthering it. But if possible she looked even more disappointed than Alice.

With him.

Chapter Five

"He wouldn't even take tea with her," Emma lamented to Mrs. Jennings a short while later. "You've seen Alice's face when she wants something. How can anyone refuse?"

Mrs. Jennings tsked in sympathy. She and Emma had snatched a few moments' reprieve in the servants' hall behind the kitchen. Under Ivy's watchful eye, Alice was taking her afternoon nap upstairs, though the little girl generally protested.

Now Mrs. Jennings sat on a high-backed chair at the table that ran down the center of the hall, flanked by benches. Ivy had confided it was the only place Mrs. Dunworthy hadn't supplanted the cook when Sir Nicholas's sister-in-law had come to manage things. Seeing Mrs. Jennings sitting in the chair, one competent hand thumbing through her recipe book by the light from the fire and the floor-to-ceiling windows overlooking the peaks, Emma thought the cook still looked like the queen of this castle.

"You say no to Miss Alice when it's not in her best interests," Mrs. Jennings pointed out, eyeing a recipe with a frown as if doubting it was good enough for her master.

Emma began casting the next row of stitches on the sock she was knitting for Alice. "How could spending time with her father not be in Alice's best interests?"

Mrs. Jennings flipped the page in her recipe book. "Poor man. Sometimes I think she reminds him too much of Lady Rotherford, God rest her soul."

Sir Nicholas being a knight, there could be only one person the cook referred to: his late wife. Emma sobered. "I never thought of that. I was told she died when Alice was a baby."

"Three years ago now, it was," Mrs. Jennings confirmed, gaze going out the window as if she saw that day again. "She was such a pretty little thing, like Alice, though more fragile, mind you."

Sometimes she thought Alice was fragile enough! The sock Emma was knitting for her would almost have fit Lady Chamomile's porcelain feet.

"How did Lady Rotherford die?" Emma asked.

"Consumption." The cook shivered as if the memory chilled her and refocused on her recipe book. "Started with an occasional cough. None of us paid it any mind. But then Millie noticed blood on her ladyship's handkerchief when doing the laundry, and it seemed her ladyship just got weaker and weaker until there was nothing left of her."

Now Emma felt the chill and wished the wool she was using had already been fashioned into a shawl. "Thank the Lord, Alice was spared."

Mrs. Jennings nodded, tagging down a corner of one page in her book. "We were all thankful. But Sir Nicholas, oh, it broke his heart. They had been promised since they were children, you see. Everyone said it was a love match."

A love match. Emma nearly sighed aloud at the thought of it. The books she'd borrowed from her foster sisters were full of stories about love denied and ultimately triumphant. She wanted to believe men and women could come together out of love, that someday she'd meet a man willing to overlook her lack of family and fortune and appreciate her for herself. That sort of love seemed entirely too rare.

But if Alice Rotherford had been conceived in love, how could Sir Nicholas thrust her away now? If Emma had had a smidgeon of such love, she would have treasured it.

"And Alice?" she asked. "Did he have the same degree of affection for her?"

Mrs. Jennings shut her recipe book before answering. "You have to understand," she murmured, gaze on Emma's. "Lady Rotherford was never strong. Birthing Alice took a great deal out of her. I think that's why the consumption carried her off so quickly. I don't believe Sir Nicholas blamed Alice, mind you. He simply had his hands too full with her ladyship to pay the child much mind."

Emma hooked her needles into the sock to keep it from unraveling and gathered up her things. "You said her ladyship has been dead for three years. From what I can see, it's his work that's keeping him busy, not family concerns."

"You mustn't be so hard on him, miss," Mrs. Jennings protested. "I know he cares for Alice. He's always made sure she had someone to look out for her, proper food and sustenance."

"Food and sustenance aren't the same as love," Emma replied, rising.

Mrs. Jennings chuckled as she too rose to return to her work. "Oh, I wouldn't be so sure. More than one of the Rotherfords have found their way to my kitchen over the years when they wanted something to comfort them."

Emma smiled at her. "I suspect it was your presence rather than the food that brought them comfort, Mrs. Jennings."

The cook returned her smile as they headed for the kitchen together. "Thank you for that, my dear. I try to make my kitchen a place of welcome, as the good Lord intended. But I know that food can bring comfort as well, something warm, perhaps, to take the chill from life, something a little sweet to cover up the bitter."

On her way to the servants' stair, Emma paused to eye the cook. "Was Sir Nicholas ever one of the Rotherfords who came seeking comfort?"

Mrs. Jennings face saddened. "All too often, the poor mite. It wasn't easy growing up alone in this house."

"Then I think we have an opportunity before us," Emma said, mind clicking through options.

Mrs. Jennings cocked her head. "What are you thinking?"

Emma grinned. "I propose we conduct an experiment, Mrs. Jennings. I've heard it said that the shortest way to a man's heart is down his throat. Let's test that theory."

Nick noticed that something had changed the moment he bit into dinner that night. The difference did not appear to be in the eating arrangements. The table had always seemed too long to him, a waste of space.

He and Charlotte took up less than one tenth of the length, by his rough estimation. He should probably have simply requested a tray in his study each night, but he somehow thought Charlotte deserved not to eat alone. And after a fruitless day like today, even Charlotte's judgmental company was to be preferred to the silence of failure.

So if it was not the arrangements or the company that differed, it must be the food. Another bite of the new potatoes confirmed it.

"Is Mrs. Jennings well?" he asked Charlotte, trying not to grimace. Charlotte never responded well to anything she considered criticism of her household.

"I've heard no complaints from below stairs," Charlotte said, lifting a small portion of the trout. "Why do you ask?"

He sniffed the next forkful before tasting it. Yes, something was definitely missing—parsley perhaps? Either way, the food was not to his liking. He pushed back his plate. "It all seems rather bland tonight."

"I taste nothing unusual," Charlotte countered, with the supreme confidence of one who knows about such things.

"Perhaps it's the company then," Nick said, and immediately regretted it as she stiffened. "Forgive me, Charlotte. I meant no disrespect. I was simply thinking that dinner was more interesting when Alice was here."

Charlotte's body settled into her seat. "She is a dear. Perhaps I can advise Miss Pyrmont to have her ready on Mondays, Wednesdays and Fridays."

Odd logic. "Why only those days?" Nick queried.

Charlotte smiled at him. "I think she is a bit young to join us for dinner every night."

Was she? He hadn't been invited to the adult table

until he'd returned from Eton at fourteen, but he thought that was his mother and father's decision, not a general rule of Society. He'd visited the homes of friends where the children of the family were allowed at table as young as six.

"We had no difficulty with Alice last night," he reasoned. "If she causes trouble in future, we can reconsider the matter. Until such time, I see no reason why she can't eat with us."

"How very kind of you." Charlotte's praise held an edge, as if she gave it begrudgingly. He felt as if his chair was growing harder. He purposely reached for his glass and took a deep draught.

He could not understand Charlotte. Why was she so annoyed by his request to include Alice? He had never been opposed to the idea. Alice had simply been too young until recently to make the matter practical.

Knowing he needed sustenance for the next few hours, he pulled his plate closer and decided to attempt the trout.

"I suppose you'll need to do something about Miss Pyrmont's wardrobe," he said, remembering the conversation from the previous day. "I've never paid much attention to the staff's attire, but if that brown dress is the best we can do I obviously need to increase your household budget."

He had taken another sip from his glass and set it back down before he noticed that something else was missing. This time it was the sound of Charlotte's voice. Indeed, he wasn't even sure she was breathing. Glancing her way, he saw that she had drawn herself up and was regarding him fixedly. Odd. He hadn't been aware of a change in his anatomy or clothing.

"Why, precisely," she said, "do you wish to improve Miss Pyrmont's wardrobe?"

He hadn't realized that the hearth was deficient either, yet he was certain the temperature in the dining room had plummeted by at least twenty degrees. "You said she was mortified to take dinner with us last night because of her attire. If we intend to have her to dinner every night with Alice, her mortification must multiply by seven, by my estimation. Surely that is unacceptable."

"I see." She lay down her fork with such care Nick could only wonder whether she'd considered another use for it, and one that would result in his injury. "So what you really want is to have dinner with your daughter's nanny."

Nick kept his own fork in his hand with a distinct feeling of self-protection. "I am not opposed to dining with Miss Pyrmont. She makes intelligent, some might even say witty, conversation. She is pleasant to look upon. However, my thought was that Alice would need someone to attend her."

Charlotte's chin seemed to have shortened. Tightening of the muscles, perhaps? "Then you find me incompetent to assist your daughter in social settings," she said.

He never had understood why his words were so easily misconstrued. He thought he had a rather good grasp of the English language. Certainly his tutors had never complained. But when it came to Charlotte and even Ann, what he meant never seemed to be what they heard.

"My opinion of your competence should be evident by the fact that I leave all matters in this household to your attention," he told Charlotte. "As I already trespass on your generous nature by having you manage the staff, I thought perhaps you'd prefer to eat your dinner in peace and allow someone who is paid to see to Alice's needs assist her through dinner until she is experienced enough to do so herself."

He must have succeeded in communicating at last, for she dropped her gaze. "I see. Forgive me, Nicholas. I know I am not here because of my generous nature but yours. If you wish Miss Pyrmont to join us for dinner in the future, I will make the arrangements. It may take a day or two to work out the menus with Mrs. Jennings."

Nick wasn't sure why menus would be so complicated, but he thanked his sister-in-law for the effort. A glance at the trout and the new potatoes beside it confirmed he had no interest in either. Conversation held as little appeal. He rose, and Charlotte glanced up, eyes widening.

As she appeared to require him to state the obvious, he did. "I'm finished with dinner this evening. If you will excuse me, I have work to do."

Charlotte nodded, but he hadn't really expected otherwise. Theirs had never been a congenial relationship, and Ann's death had only made matters worse. At least in his work he had some hope of untangling difficulties, unlike Charlotte's unpredictable responses.

Yet his work continued to thwart him that night. He sat in his study, reviewing his calculations, considering alternative theories that had been proposed by his peers the last few months. Why couldn't he find the solution? Certainly there had to be at least one, and he had considered the possibility that there was more. Was he truly as deficient as his colleagues in the Royal Society had intimated when they'd cast him from their number?

He pushed such thoughts aside. He had evidence that

he had some pretentions toward knowledge—scores at Eton and Oxford, his work on the properties of common materials for industrial use that had earned him his knighthood. Until Ann's death, there had been no hint that his faculties could fail him. He wanted to think of that as the aberration rather than the rule.

He worked for much of the night, as was his wont, then woke early and took a turn about the darkened grounds to clear his head. He had noticed that movement seemed to stimulate thought, but in this instance no revelation presented itself.

By the time he returned for breakfast, he was in no mood for further arguments. Perhaps that was why he took one look at the breakfast tray the footman brought him—the lumpy gray porridge; the cold charred toast— threw down his napkin and marched to the kitchen.

"Mrs. Jennings," he began as soon as he stepped over the threshold. He had the momentary satisfaction of watching all movement in the room jerk to a stop. Miss Pyrmont, who had been preparing a tray on the worktable in the center of the room, stared at him, mouth pursed as if she offered a kiss.

Why did he persist in thinking about kisses? He shook his head to cast out the image and glanced around at the others. Mrs. Jennings stood by the fire, ladle raised above a pot and dripping so that the liquid sizzled on the hearth. The young maid by the sink dropped the cup she'd been holding with the unmistakable crack of breaking china.

That woke his cook. She thrust the ladle back into the pot, hurried forward and bobbed a curtsey. "Sir Nicholas, what's happened to bring you to my kitchen again?"

So she remembered the days he'd sought solace at her worktable. The kitchen had always been the warmest room in this house, not only in temperature but in the welcome he'd felt. That seemed to have changed. The maid was trembling as she picked up the chards from the basin. Miss Pyrmont seemed to be trembling as well, but the light in her eyes and the way she had compressed her lips suggested she was holding back laughter.

"Sir Nicholas?" Mrs. Jennings asked, head cocked.

Nick straightened. "I thought I should ask after your health."

His cook's snowy brows shot up. "My health? Whatever for?"

They were all staring at him as if the very idea was preposterous. Only Miss Pyrmont looked remotely sympathetic. She offered him a smile as she gripped the tray she'd prepared. He considered offering his help to lift it from the table. Indeed something positively urged him to rush forward and take it from her. What nonsense was that? She seemed confident and capable of carrying the thing, and it was clearly her duty.

So he turned his attention to Mrs. Jennings and his reason for visiting the kitchen again after all these years.

"Dinner last night and breakfast this morning did not seem up to your usual standards," he told the cook. "I was wondering what might have changed. If you are well, have you perhaps taken on an assistant?"

He glanced at the maid, who promptly dropped all the pieces of the cup into the sink again. Perhaps Charlotte had had reason to stare so fixedly at him last night. It seemed somewhere along the way he'd become ferocious.

"No assistant," Mrs. Jennings assured him. "A shame your dinner and breakfast were not to your liking."

She didn't look the least bit abashed. People who

were embarrassed by lapses in good judgment or behavior generally hung their heads, shuffled their feet,
made excuses. Mrs. Jennings was regarding him with
a smile he had always considered kind.

"Then can you assure me that future meals will return to their usual quality?" he asked.

Miss Pyrmont was definitely biting her lower lip
now. He could tell even though she'd bowed her head
and clamped her arms to her sides.

"Oh, I cannot say, sir," Mrs. Jennings replied. "I best
speak to Mrs. Dunworthy about the matter. I've been so
busy lately I don't have time for the little extra things."

He felt the same way. "Quite understandable," he
assured her. "For now, might I trouble you for some
of those cinnamon biscuits you generally put on my
breakfast tray?"

Mrs. Jennings set her finger against her lips. "Goodness me! I remember how you used to dote on those.
But I'm afraid I sent the entire batch upstairs for Miss
Alice. If you'd like some this morning, you'll have to
have breakfast with her."

Chapter Six

Oh, the clever woman! Emma hid her smile at Mrs. Jennings's decree and Sir Nicholas's obvious surprise. The cook had given Emma an opportunity. Emma intended to take it.

"Yes, Sir Nicholas," she said, hefting the tray. "I was just about to bring Alice her breakfast. Won't you join us?"

His look crossed from her to Mrs. Jennings and back again as if he simply could not believe them. Emma let her smile shine and hoped it looked more welcoming than triumphant.

"It won't take long," Mrs. Jennings encouraged him. "Miss Pyrmont is generally back downstairs in about a quarter hour. Your tray often takes longer than that to return."

Still he hesitated. A quarter hour? He was wrestling over sparing so little time for his daughter? She had her work cut out for her, it seemed. But at least breakfast was a start.

Please, Lord, help him agree!

"Very well," he said, and Emma sent up a prayer of

thanks. "I had something I wished to say to Alice in any regard."

He strode to Emma's side and held out his hands. "Allow me, Miss Pyrmont."

She felt his fingers brush hers and nearly dropped the tray at the unexpected warmth. She barely managed to transfer the platter to his control. Then it was his turn to look surprised.

"Something wrong, Sir Nicholas?" she asked.

He eyed her up and down, and she felt her color rising. "The weight to height ratio is off," he said.

Emma drew herself up. "I beg your pardon?"

He frowned. "The tray is heavier than I expected for a woman of your slender frame." He glanced at the cook. "I seem to remember we had a footman in the nursery when I was young."

Mrs. Jennings's round face did not show the annoyance Emma was certain she was feeling that she could no longer address the problem herself. "We've had trouble keeping our fellows on the staff for some time, sir."

Though she didn't say it, Emma suspected the issue lay in Mrs. Dunworthy. They had men who worked outdoors—grooms, gardeners, the head coachman Mr. Dobbins—but only a single footman indoors, and Charles often looked a bit harried to be at Mrs. Dunworthy's beck and call. A household this size generally boasted a butler, kitchen help and more maids. Even Dorcus, who served as Mrs. Dunworthy's maid, had to do double duty, helping with cleaning and serving. But perhaps Mrs. Dunworthy had decided that having fewer staff was wiser so far from London.

Sir Nicholas obviously thought otherwise. "When you see my sister-in-law," he said to the cook, "ask her to assign a footman to the nursery. Tell her it was my suggestion."

Mrs. Jennings nodded, but Emma considered protesting. She'd been carrying Alice's tray for months. And she'd carried much heavier things in her foster father's home. But truth be told, she wouldn't have minded a little extra help.

"Thank you, Sir Nicholas," she said with a curtsey. "This way."

That he had never taken the servants' stair was evident by the way he glanced around at the narrow steps, the dim light from the single window high on the wall. Perhaps she should have gone up the main staircase with him beside her, but that route to the nursery was much longer, and Alice had already been waiting for her breakfast. Besides, servants did not take the main stairs. Ever. That point had been pressed upon her by her foster mother.

"Are there other needs in the nursery?" he asked.

She could tell by his frown that the matter concerned him. The fact that Mrs. Jennings had removed the seasoning and sweets from his food had opened his eyes to things he had taken for granted, just as Emma had hoped. Now she needed to turn his thoughts toward Alice.

"Alice has all she needs materially," she assured him as they took the first turning. She nodded toward the top of the stairs ahead of them. "She has her own room, just off the nursery, with me on the other side. She has books, toys and clothes to spare. What she needs is company."

He glanced at Emma. The frown caused a line to appear in his forehead, pointing down his nose to his lips.

Among all those angles, their softness was in direct contrast and all the more apparent. She had to look away.

"I never had company in the nursery," he mused.

"You had your father and mother," Emma reminded him.

"Your assumption is ill-founded," he replied as they passed the ground floor. "My mother preferred to spend her time in London. I don't remember her at this house. And my father did not visit the nursery."

Something inside her twisted. Was that how he had been raised? Small wonder he didn't see the need to visit Alice! But, oh, what he was missing! She may not have been raised in a family where all children were loved and valued, but she knew such families existed from the many stories she'd read. People didn't make up stories no one would believe. If those authors wrote about happy people, she reasoned, then at least some examples of the breed must be found. Surely that's what Alice deserved. Surely that was what the Lord expected for all His children.

"Well, the people in the home where I was raised had long left the nursery," Emma told him as they took the final turn. "But the schoolroom was never lonely."

"I cannot imagine this nursery is lonely either," he said. "Not with you in it."

Emma blinked. Was that a compliment? No, surely not from a natural philosopher. He meant because she was a competent nanny or that two people were sufficient to ward off loneliness or some more logical construction.

"I cannot be with her every minute," Emma protested as they reached the top of the stairs. "Ivy spells me from time to time so I can prepare lessons or fetch a tray. I receive a quarter hour off every afternoon and a Sunday afternoon once a month."

"A whole afternoon once a month," he said. "However do you fill it?"

Because his sarcasm was evident, she didn't answer directly. "It's more than I had in my previous position. Mrs. Dunworthy runs an orderly house. Your concern should be for Alice, not your staff."

"Indeed," he said, but she didn't think he believed her. She led him into the nursery.

Ivy glanced up and then hopped to her feet from her place at the table as Emma and Sir Nicholas came through the door.

"Papa!" Alice cried, rushing forward.

For a moment Emma thought the tray would come crashing down, but he managed to balance it while his daughter hugged his legs.

"Good morning to you, too, Alice," he said. "If you'd return to your seat, I'll join you for breakfast."

She disengaged and scampered back. Ivy had evidently set the table, for the nursery china lay waiting at three places, as usual. With a terrified glance at the master, Ivy hurried to her duties in cleaning and airing Alice's room after the night.

Emma went to the cupboard to fetch a fourth set of dishes. Out of the corners of her eyes, she saw him set down the tray on the table and move to take the seat closest to Alice, where the third set of china lay.

"Lady Chamomile sits there," Alice informed him.

Emma turned with the place setting in her hands, expecting him to laugh off Alice's concern, remove the doll from the seat. Instead, halfway down, he twisted to avoid sitting on the doll and straightened. "My mistake. Is the seat on the other side taken?"

"No," Alice replied with a gracious wave. "You may have it."

Emma bit her lip to keep from commenting. As she brought him a place setting, he was glancing about the room as if seeing it afresh, as well.

Please don't let him fix on things, Lord. You know Alice needs more than material possessions.

"Thank you, Miss Pyrmont," he said as she set his place. Now she felt the warm walnut gaze on her. For some reason, that made it hard to take her seat and focus on laying out Alice's breakfast.

Her charge sighed at the toast and chocolate. Sir Nicholas accepted the cup of chocolate but frowned as well at the thoroughly cold toast.

"It's never warm by the time I climb the stairs," Emma apologized. "We've tried covering it, but it just gets mushy."

"The heat from the toast allows water to condense on the underside of the metal covering," he replied. He glanced around the room once more. "You have a fire, I see. No toasting forks?"

"Mrs. Dunworthy believes that allowing Alice too close to the coals could be dangerous," Emma explained.

"Possibly," he agreed. "But perhaps the new footman can do the toasting. I'll see that Mrs. Jennings sends up a fork."

"Lady Chamomile likes biscuits better than toast," Alice said, shifting her gaze from Emma to her father and back.

"Oh, biscuits!" Emma rose and went to the cupboard to retrieve them. "Mrs. Jennings says your father likes these every bit as much as you do, Alice." She set the plate down between them and had to hide her smile as they both reached for one of the sweets at the same time.

Alice eyed her father. "You must save some for Lady Chamomile."

He inclined his head. "I would never steal a lady's biscuits."

He said it with equal gravity, a solemn promise, and Emma felt her frustration with him thawing further. How odd. Sir Nicholas might not steal biscuits, but it seemed that he had the capacity to steal a few hearts, her own included.

It was Nick's theory, tested by observation of his colleagues, that a man must be cautious with things he allowed to control his actions. Ministers and tutors had warned of the folly of gluttony, the danger of drink. Until today, Nick would not have ranked cinnamon-sugar biscuits on the same scale. Yet here he sat, attempting to make conversation with a four-year-old and a porcelain-headed doll, just so he could partake of Mrs. Jennings's masterpieces.

Yet something suggested it wasn't only the biscuits that kept him in his seat at the little table in the nursery. Each time he spoke with Alice, Miss Pyrmont's face took on the strangest look, as if her skin and eyes had developed translucent properties. It was enough to make the humblest of men feel decidedly worthy.

"And what are your plans for the day?" he asked Alice. It was a gambit that had never failed to win him at least a quarter hour of discussion with Ann.

Alice frowned as if giving the matter considerable thought. He had met few children her age, but it seemed to him that she was more serious than most. Certainly he and Ann had been serious children, preferring books to battles with tin soldiers, drama to comedy at the theatre, a minuet to the more sprightly country dances.

"I believe we are going to study our letters," Alice said, "then take a turn out of doors." Her rendition was such a perfect imitation of Charlotte's superior tone that he had to smile.

"Perhaps your father would like to join us on the lawn," Miss Pyrmont put in.

He started to demur—after all, he had work waiting, but then she added, "We intend to conduct an experiment, you see."

Nick swallowed the last of the biscuits. "An experiment, you say?"

Her eyes sparkled. He'd considered them a muddy color, perhaps brown or dark gray, but now with her sitting so near him at the table, he could see they were a clear color somewhere between blue and green. Interesting. Perhaps the shade changed with the color of her clothing. If Charlotte followed through on arranging for newer gowns, he could test that hypothesis.

"What's a spare mint?" Alice asked.

"Perhaps your father should answer that," Miss Pyrmont replied. "He's conducting one in his laboratory beside the Grange."

Alice regarded him with wide eyes, as if he'd done something quite heroic. Nick wiped his hands on the napkin beside his plate. "An experiment," he explained, being careful to enunciate the word properly for her, "is a way to address a question when no one knows the answer."

"Like what?" Alice asked.

"Like which kind of biscuit you prefer," Nick temporized, "or what color gown would look best on Miss Pyrmont."

Miss Pyrmont blushed, a shade the color of the roses Ann had liked to tend in their small garden in London. Perhaps that was the color he should suggest to Charlotte. It would certainly look better on her than that dreary brown.

Alice giggled. "That's easy. Cinnamon biscuits and purple."

"Purple?" Miss Pyrmont was clearly trying not to laugh. "Why purple?"

"Lady Chamomile likes purple," Alice said.

"And I'm certain a lady of her station would look charming in it," Nick said. "I'll tell you what, Alice. Let us conduct an experiment right now. Can you find me something blue, say the shade of the sky on a clear summer's day?"

Alice slid down from her seat and hurried to a chest that lay against the far wall.

"What are you doing?" Miss Pyrmont asked, though the smile on her face said she wasn't opposed to the game.

"Humor me," he said.

Alice came scurrying back with a china plate the size of a guinea. Part of Lady Chamomile's tea set, perhaps? "Very good," Nick said, as he accepted it from her. "Now perhaps something yellow, the color of the daffodils that used to bloom in your window box in London."

Alice frowned, then hurried off toward her bedchamber.

"And do you dash off looking for things in your experiment, Sir Nicholas?" Miss Pyrmont asked.

"I only wish it were that easy," he replied. "Ah, excellent, Alice. That slipper will do nicely. Now something pink, the very color of Miss Pyrmont's cheeks."

As Alice regarded her steadily, Miss Pyrmont's color rose.

"Now, now," Nick said with a smile. "That is most unsporting, Miss Pyrmont. How can we determine the proper shade if you keep changing it?"

A chuckle escaped her. "How very inconvenient of me."

"I know!" Alice cried, and she went dashing to her dollhouse.

"There must be some point to all this," Miss Pyrmont said.

"There is a point to everything I do," Nick replied. He eyed the doll dress Alice had brought back. The bodice was a light shade of pink, the skirt darker. "Well done, Alice. Now that we have the right materials, let us conduct our experiment." Remembering his mistake earlier, he inclined his head toward the doll. "Lady Chamomile, might I prevail upon you to allow Alice to sit next to her nanny?"

"She says she is delighted to assist," Alice reported, picking up her doll and dumping her unceremoniously in another chair. She wiggled into the empty seat and looked up at him. "What now, Papa?"

"Pick up the saucer and hold it up to Miss Pyrmont's face," Nick instructed.

"Oh, I say," Miss Pyrmont started, but she blinked as Alice held the piece of blue china next to her nose.

"There, you see?" Nick proclaimed, leaning closer. "Her eyes look blue, and her skin becomes the color of your mother's pearls. Try the slipper."

Alice nodded eagerly, set down the china plate and reached for the slipper. But when she held up the yellow, she frowned. "She's turning color again. It's not so nice."

"Well, I'm very sorry," Miss Pyrmont said, with a bit more asperity this time, "but it's a little difficult to control the shade of one's skin."

Nick nodded. "Quite true. But even if she wasn't turning color, Alice, I think you can see that the yellow doesn't have nearly so pleasing an effect." He reached for the doll dress and held the satin up to Miss Pyrmont's face. As he had conjectured, the pink very nearly matched the color of her cheeks, and he thought perhaps the feel of her skin might approximate the softness of the material.

Where had that thought come from? Indeed, where had any of this come from? He'd merely been attempting to teach Alice the rudiments of experimentation. He had no business building an hypothesis of the feel of Miss Pyrmont's skin.

He dropped the gown to the table and stood, focusing his gaze on his daughter. "Well, Alice, what do you conclude from our experiment on color?"

"Blue," Alice said. "Nanny looks best in blue."

"I concur," Nick said. "You might mention that to your aunt. I believe she's planning on purchasing new gowns for Miss Pyrmont."

"New gowns," he heard Miss Pyrmont say, and he thought the words held confusion. "Why?"

"Because you and Alice will be joining us for dinner again very soon," he said.

He had hoped for a good reaction, and certainly Alice's applause was gratifying. But he couldn't help glancing at Miss Pyrmont to see how she would take his decision. Her grin seemed to make the room brighter, his efforts more laudable. Meeting his gaze, her smile only grew.

As if she saw that his smile answered hers, she

quickly bent to gather up the empty plates and stack them on the tray to return to the kitchen.

"And can I help you with your experiments?" Alice asked.

How well she pronounced the word this time. "I'm afraid not, Alice. Mine are not nearly so pleasant as this one. You see, I am attempting to develop a special lamp that boys can carry into the ground so they can see their way."

Miss Pyrmont gasped. He hadn't thought anyone outside the sphere of the mining community would be so fascinated by his work to warrant that sort of reaction, but when he glanced her way again, he saw that she had paled.

"Is something wrong, Miss Pyrmont?" he asked.

"No, nothing," she said, much more quickly than she had said anything else to him. "I simply find it commendable that you would develop a safety lamp. The coal miners certainly need it by all accounts."

She knew the name of the device without an explanation. Interesting. Though the explosions at the mines were well reported across England—the public having an insatiable desire to read of disasters, it seemed—he did not think the work to solve the problem nearly so well presented. How had a nanny learned of it?

Before he could ask, she rose. "I should return the tray to the kitchen. I'll leave you and Alice to chat and be right back."

He didn't even have a chance to protest before she'd fled the room.

"Odd," he said aloud in the wake.

"She will return," Alice promised him as if she thought he doubted. She came around the table to lean against his arm. "Let's do another experiment."

He smiled at her eagerness. "Like experiments, do you?"

"Oh, yes, Papa. Don't you?"

"Very much," he assured her. "But sometimes we must ask a number of questions before we can start the experiment. Let me ask you some. Do you like your nursery?"

She nodded. "Oh, yes."

"And your lessons?"

Another nod.

"And your nanny?"

Alice squeezed his arm. "Oh, yes, Papa. Nanny is the best nanny ever."

She was so certain, her violet eyes wide. She had only one other nanny for comparison. He had had two—Alice's previous lady and his own. Though he seemed to remember a fondness for his nanny, he did not think he would have been as certain of her place in his affections. Of course, that could have been his failing, not hers. He had ample proof that he was not skilled in matters of the heart.

"I'm very glad to hear that," he told his daughter. "Such a remarkable nanny deserves our thanks."

Alice nodded, releasing her hold. "You should get her a present."

Nick regarded her. "What an excellent suggestion, Alice. I will see to it. Now, let's see what your maid is up to in your bedchamber. I have a question for her, as well."

Chapter Seven

Emma flew down the stairs, heavy tray and all, and pulled herself to a stop at the bottom to catch her breath. That's why Sir Nicholas kept starting fires! He was trying to develop a material that wouldn't react with firedamp.

She knew all the theories—the segregation of oxygen from the more flammable air, the lower-heat possibilities of various materials, the properties of tallow and whale oil. This was the same research her foster father had been conducting. She'd thought he and Sir Nicholas might know each other from the Royal Society, but she'd never thought they might be collaborators!

The china was rattling on the tray. She forced her hands to still. Firedamp might react to heat, but at the moment she was reacting from fear. She refused to give in to it. Much as she hated the unwavering logic of these natural philosophers, she had to agree with them that emotions had their place, and not when she was trying to make a sound decision.

Still, her first thought was to run away again, leave before her foster father showed up at the door. But she wasn't entirely certain he cared that she'd gone or would seek her return. One thing she did know: she mustn't allow fear to ruin what had been a wonderful position for her.

Even if her foster father still wanted to control her, she had no real reason to suspect that he knew where she was. Despite the fact that he and Sir Nicholas were studying the same problem, she also had no evidence they were collaborating. The colliers around the country had reached out to several noted philosophers, she knew—her foster father, Samuel Fredericks, and the chemist Sir Humphry Davy among them. The owners of the coal mines could easily have sought Sir Nicholas's help as well, particularly as he had a coal mine on his property, she'd been told.

Of course, her foster father frequently partnered with other philosophers to solve some problem. Sometimes they even competed with each other to be the first to discover the answer. This business of firedamp had intrigued him in particular. She remembered him expounding on it over dinner one night.

"England runs on coal," he'd told his wife and two daughters by birth as they sat around the cloth-covered dining table. Neither Emma nor her three foster brothers were allowed to eat at that table. They'd been fed in the kitchen when they were small, while the family was dining. As they grew older, they had eaten afterward so they could help with the serving. That day she and Jerym, the eldest of the boys, had been standing along the papered wall, waiting to remove the plates.

Samuel Fredericks had picked up his crystal goblet and gestured with it, like a choirmaster ordering his singers. He was a large man, with heavy jowls and a ponderous nose. When his bushy brows drew down in a scowl, she and her foster brothers knew it was time to disappear for a bit.

"We must have more coal, so they must dig deeper," he'd told his wife. "And the deeper they go, the more of this noxious gas they encounter."

"And when you have found a way to protect them from it, you can require that they dig deeper indeed," his wife had agreed, her graying blond ringlets bouncing in her enthusiasm, "in their pockets, that is." She tittered at her own wit.

"Now, now," Mr. Fredericks had cautioned as his daughters snickered, their coarse manners clashing with the finery of their lace-edged silk dinner dresses. "Science can provide a service to the nation, and I am honored to play a part." He drained his glass and held it up. "Fill it again, boy, and be quick about it."

Be quick about it. Her foster father had expected instant obedience, to every command. He hadn't expected her to refuse to marry the man he'd chosen for her or to run away from his suffocating household to work as a servant in another. But if she was to be a servant the rest of her life, it would be on her terms. She had to make sure that no one at the Grange ever told her foster family where she'd gone, just to be on the safe side.

You know I am trying to forgive him for the way he treated me and the boys, Father. But forgiving him doesn't mean I should give him the ability to hurt me again.

She felt the truth of that statement echoing through her. Taking a deep breath, she raised her head and moved into the kitchen to return the tray.

"How did it go?" Mrs. Jennings asked as soon as she sighted Emma.

Emma set the tray on the worktable. "Very well, thank you. In fact, he's still with her."

Mrs. Jennings clapped her hands. "Oh, well done, Miss Pyrmont!"

"I didn't leave him much choice," Emma admitted, going for a towel to wipe her hands where some of the chocolate had spilled. "And I don't dare leave him alone with her for too long, or Mrs. Dunworthy will think I'm being lazy."

"Of course," Mrs. Jennings agreed, dropping her hands. "But don't give up on him. He deserves to know his daughter as much as she deserves to know him."

Emma quite agreed. After the way he'd behaved in the nursery, her confidence was growing that she could convince Sir Nicholas to spend additional time with his daughter. She was more concerned what he'd do if he ever learned she'd come from the house of another natural philosopher, and a leader in the group that no longer welcomed him.

She made sure she'd regained her composure by the time she reached the top of the stairs once more, but it turned out she needn't have worried. Ivy was helping Alice wipe her face and fingers after breakfast, and Sir Nicholas was nowhere in sight.

"Sorry, miss," the maid said as if sensing Emma's disappointment. "I finished with my duties in the night nursery, and the master asked me to watch Alice so he could return to his laboratory."

"He must work on his experiment," Alice said with grave concern. "Those little boys need a light."

Emma was certain he'd called them boys to help Alice understand. Surely children didn't work anywhere so dangerous as a coal mine. "So it would seem," she replied. "And we have our own experiment to conduct."

Alice brightened. "More colors?"

"No, something better," Emma promised, thinking of her plans. "Though it may take us a day to prepare."

With any luck, she reasoned, the time between breakfast and their next encounter with Sir Nicholas would give him a few moments for his work. He needed to feel as if he'd made progress before she interrupted him again.

Unfortunately, Emma was the one to be interrupted.

She and Alice had just settled at the table the next afternoon, the big book of letters spread before them. Alice was regarding the letter *B* with such a deep frown that Emma felt compelled to question her.

"I don't know if I like it," Alice said, as if she was in charge of determining the shapes and functions of letters.

Emma smiled. "I think you will find *B* a fine letter. But you must mind his tail else he might sting you." She swooped down on Alice and ticked her on the ribs. Alice squirmed with a giggle.

Just then Dorcus hurried into the nursery. The maid's head and color were both high, telling Emma the woman had either run half the way or been ordered to do an unpleasant task, or both.

"Yes, Dorcus?" Emma asked, straightening.

"Mrs. Dunworthy would like to see you," the maid said. "Now. I'm to stay with Miss Alice if Ivy isn't here."

"Ivy has gone down to help in the kitchen with the baking," Emma said, rising and feeling her own color rising, as well. "You can help Alice review her letters."

Dorcus nodded and moved to the table, but as she passed Emma she whispered, "I never learned how to read, but I'll do my best, miss. Just watch yourself, now. She's in a taking."

The advice only made Emma less eager to obey the summons.

As she left the wing that housed the nursery suite, the quiet assailed her. The Grange had been built to house a large family, with six bedchambers on this story, and two more comprising the master suite on the ground floor. Now Alice was the only child in residence, and she'd been sequestered in the nursery.

The plastered walls of the corridor that ran down the center of the chamber story were decorated with massive paintings of landscapes and sailing ships. No people were in evidence in them either. In fact, Emma didn't sight another person until she rapped on the door to Mrs. Dunworthy's sitting room and Charles, the footman, opened the door for her to enter.

Like the rest of the Grange, the room was bright, with pale silk on the walls and multipaned windows opening to a balcony overlooking the peaks. Mrs. Dunworthy sat near the fire at a white enameled desk with long gilded legs, quill posed over parchment. Her day dress was of fine lustring that caught the light as she moved, the neck, sleeves and hem dripping with ecru lace. Circumstances might have brought her to serve as a housekeeper in her brother-in-law's home, but she remained every inch the lady.

Just as the man with her kept proving to Emma that he was capable of acting every inch the gentleman.

Sir Nicholas rose from the settee on the other side of the fire and came forward. "Miss Pyrmont, thank you for joining us."

Mrs. Dunworthy's mouth worked, but she kept her head down and her pen scratching across the parchment.

Why would they both need to speak to her? Had she offended Sir Nicholas by leaving him alone with Alice this morning? She curtseyed, careful to make sure the movement included them both. "Sir Nicholas, Mrs. Dunworthy. I understand you wished to speak to me."

Still the lady did not look up from her paper. "Sir Nicholas," she said, "would like to see you gowned properly."

So he had pursued the matter. She'd thought his experiment with colors was just a game for Alice. Very likely he thought the suggestion no more than a conclusion to his efforts. What good to learn something new if not to share it?

"That is very kind of you, sir," she said, mindful of the footman standing with his back to the wall behind her, "but I'm sure my dresses will do for my work."

"There, you see, Nicholas?" Mrs. Dunworthy set her quill into its crystal holder with a gentle wave of the white feather. "Miss Pyrmont is entirely satisfied with her wardrobe."

That frown had appeared again, drawing her gaze to his lips once more. At the moment, they were compressed in a tight line as if he were considering his response. "That was not the impression you gave me earlier," he said to his sister-in-law.

Had they been discussing her? Somehow she had thought Sir Nicholas was happily unaware of the household's workings.

"I cannot be held responsible for how you take my attempts at conversation, Nicholas," Mrs. Dunworthy said.

His frown grew. "If that is true, then I cannot be held responsible for your inability to understand me. Still I do not remember having such difficulty when Mrs. Jennings ran the household."

Mrs. Dunworthy rose, slowly, majestically, as if every muscle was held in tight control. Emma would have been tempted to quail before such a look, but Sir Nicholas merely continued to regard her as if he had discovered a change in a well-known element.

"You have made it my duty to see to the staff," she told him. "I suggest you leave me to it."

If any other member of the household had dared to speak so severely to the master, Emma was certain that person would no longer be employed at the Grange. But instead of taking umbrage, Sir Nicholas straightened, and his brow cleared.

"You seem to be laboring under a false assumption," he said as if he had just determined the source of her enmity. "I am grateful for your assistance with the household and Alice. You are welcome to stay as long as you like. But this is my home. I make few requests, as you know. I expect them to be honored unless you have evidence that they are misplaced. I understand your reasoning that Alice cannot dine with us until you have determined an appropriate menu with Mrs. Jennings, but I will expect her and Miss Pyrmont tomorrow evening at the latest."

Mrs. Dunworthy's jaw was working again, but he turned his gaze on Emma.

"Miss Pyrmont, I have nothing but respect for your position and the way my daughter holds you in her affections. Surely providing you with a new gown or two and inviting you to join us for dinner as a token of my appreciation is not overstepping my role as your employer."

Her employer. She must remember that. It shouldn't

matter that she couldn't remember ever being given a present, much less a gown someone else hadn't worn nearly through. It shouldn't matter that his look was kind, that she could see her face mirrored in his warm, dark eyes.

But it did matter, and she felt tears building. Emma bowed her head to hide them and dropped a curtsey again. "Thank you, Sir Nicholas. I'm glad to find my service acceptable."

She thought that would be all, but as she straightened, he laid a hand on her arm, right over the spot of her burn. He could not know that puckered flesh lay below her sleeve, and the spot had stopped hurting long ago, but she had to keep herself from flinching. Then she realized that the touch was as warm as his gaze.

"Your work is more than acceptable," he said. "It is exceptional. You've given Alice someone to care about." He released her with a smile. "Besides Lady Chamomile, of course."

"Of course," Emma said with an answering smile, hand going to cover the spot, still warm from his touch.

"That's settled then," Mrs. Dunworthy said brightly. "I trust we have kept you from your work long enough, Nicholas. I will take care of matters from here."

He inclined his head. "Thank you, Charlotte." With a nod to Emma, he left the room, the footman holding the door open for him.

"Leave us a moment, Charles," Mrs. Dunworthy said, and Emma felt as if a storm was gathering. She heard the snick of the door closing.

"It seems that blue suits you better than brown," Mrs. Dunworthy said in the silence that followed.

Emma wasn't sure what to expect from the mercurial lady, but she thought at least she should explain.

"That business of blue was part of a game he played with Alice this morning. I'm sure whatever color you choose will be suitable, madam. And I am very grateful for your kindness."

She hoped she sounded suitably humble, but her words had little effect. Mrs. Dunworthy swept out from behind her desk, auburn head high.

"And apparently I'm also to hire a footman to spare your back. Are your duties too much for you, Miss Pyrmont?"

Feeling as if she'd been attacked, Emma raised her head, as well. "Not at all. I have never complained."

"Not to me. But it seems you have a great many things to confide in Sir Nicholas."

She made it sound as if Emma had been angling for prettier clothes, easier working conditions. Nothing could have been further from the truth. But Emma knew she had to go carefully. Whether Sir Nicholas realized it, whether the rest of the staff appreciated it, Mrs. Dunworthy held the power over the household. If she took Emma in dislike, she could most likely prevail even against Sir Nicholas to have Emma discharged.

Emma kept her gaze on the wall, her body still, her face neutral. That had been the best way to respond to her foster father's tirades, if escape wasn't an option.

"I asked for nothing," she said. "I'm very happy in my position."

"And well you should be." Mrs. Dunworthy approached in a rustle of lustring that somehow sounded menacing in the otherwise quiet room. "I knew of your unfortunate circumstances. You explained how you fled Mr. Fredericks's employ, how you feared he might pursue you here. What did I tell you?"

Emma's mouth felt dry, and she licked her lips. "You

said that I would be safe in this house so long as I gave good service." She knew the woman would likely take a direct look as a challenge, but despite herself, she turned her gaze to meet Mrs. Dunworthy's. "And I have given good service, madam. I love Alice, and she loves me."

Mrs. Dunworthy held up one finger, and Emma snapped her mouth shut and her gaze back to the wall.

"Do not for one moment think your affections for my niece nor hers for you will sway my opinion," the woman insisted. "I expect unswerving loyalty and uncompromising duty from each of my staff. Fail me, Miss Pyrmont, and you will be gone with the light."

"Yes, Mrs. Dunworthy," Emma murmured. What did the woman want her to do, beg for her position? Promise Emma would never gainsay her? She wasn't sure that was the truth. She already questioned some of Mrs. Dunworthy's rules, like the way she sometimes treated Alice more like a pet spaniel than a beloved child.

Father, help me. You know I've done nothing wrong. You protected me from Mr. Fredericks. I need Your protection now, too.

"Listen closely," Mrs. Dunworthy said, voice firm with conviction. "I will ask you a question, and I want an honest answer. Are you throwing yourself at my brother-in-law?"

Emma recoiled. "No! I would never presume—"

"Quite wise of you," she interrupted, eyes narrowing to slits. "Nicholas Rotherford could do far better than an orphan who is not even acknowledged by her foster family, long before his work earned him a knighthood from the crown. It will take a queen to replace my sister in his affections, certainly not his daughter's nanny."

Emma felt as if her heart wilted at the reminder. What, was she hoping Sir Nicholas might think otherwise? That the next time he touched her he would press a kiss against her knuckles like the courtiers in the books she read? Natural philosophers didn't react that way from what she'd seen. Besides, she didn't want to marry someone who had to be coaxed away from his work, who had to be reminded that he had a daughter. She thought perhaps he was changing, but he was not the man she'd read about, she'd dreamed of.

"Of course, madam," Emma murmured with what she hoped sounded like respect.

Mrs. Dunworthy regarded her another moment, aristocratic nose pointing in accusation. Then she straightened and turned back toward her desk.

"So," she said as she took her seat once more, "if you are not attempting to catch his eye, what am I to make of his sudden interest in you?"

Would the truth be enough to allow her to keep her position? She could think of no other way to phrase it. "It's not me he's interested in," she confessed. "It's Alice."

Mrs. Dunworthy waved a hand. "Doubtful. He has done little for Alice since the day she was born."

Which hurt just to think about. "All the more reason she needs her father," Emma persisted. "I simply thought that if I could bring them together more often, he'd realize what a darling girl she is. He'd want to spend time with her."

"I see," Mrs. Dunworthy said. She rubbed one finger against her nose. "So you would have it that all this attention came about because you wished to make Sir Nicholas a better father, perhaps have him be the father for Alice you wished you had had."

The statement opened old wounds, made her feel raw. Yet she could not deny it. She wanted Alice to have better than she'd had. She wanted the little girl to have the best.

"I suppose so, madam," she said. "I'm sorry if that was overstepping my bounds."

Mrs. Dunworthy lowered her hand. "It was entirely beyond the scope of your duties, but I cannot disagree with your approach. He should give Alice more attention. If that is the goal of your campaign, Miss Pyrmont, you have my unqualified endorsement and everlasting gratitude."

Chapter Eight

He was avoiding his work. Nick could not deny it. First he'd lingered over breakfast with Alice yesterday, and today he'd done no more than peruse his notes before discovering a fervent desire to speak to Charlotte about Miss Pyrmont's gowns. Her gowns, for pity's sake! That appeared to be the best he could do by way of the present he'd promised Alice he'd find her nanny. Was there ever a man more intent on malingering?

And why? Had he truly begun to believe the accusations leveled against him?

He could still see their faces, his colleagues who had decided to make themselves magistrate and jury. As one of a team of philosophers working to develop a safety lamp, he'd felt his own contribution to be regrettably small, merely the calculation of the heat efficiency of the material. But their leader, Samuel Fredericks, had disagreed.

"My lords, gentlemen," he'd said as he'd stood in front of the table over which their president, Sir Joseph Banks, presided. "I have studied our approach, gone over our calculations with exacting concentration. I simply could not understand how such a mistake could have been made."

Behind him, the society members seated on their hardwood pews were as stern-faced as the men in the gilt-framed portraits crowding the walls. The high-ceilinged room used by the society for its deliberations had never felt so confining.

"Nevertheless, Mr. Fredericks," Sir Joseph said on the other side of the table, leaning forward from his padded chair that Nick had always thought resembled a throne, "four people are dead. I am all for scientific progress, but not when it exacts such a toll."

His round face was solemn, his silvery hair sticking out on either side like handles on a pot. The men around him murmured their assent.

"I cannot tell you how this accident grieves me," Fredericks had assured him, deep voice solemn. "But I am able to report that I discovered where we went wrong. I regret to inform this council that this experiment failed because of the gross miscalculations of Nicholas Rotherford."

Heads jerked in his direction, faces slack with shock. Nick had gripped the back of the pew in front of him to keep from rising. "That cannot be," he told them all. "I was careful in my calculations. I even had Davy review my work."

"He did indeed," the famed chemist piped up. "It seemed fine work to me, completely in accordance with the circumstances."

Fredericks's smile was hard. "Circumstances that had changed since I originally made those calculations. Oh, yes, gentlemen, it was easy for me to determine what had gone wrong once I recognized the problem. I accuse Nicholas Rotherford of plagiarism."

The murmurs grew in volume, forcing Nick to his feet. "I deny it. That was my own work, and it should have held up in the field."

"Certainly I do not make such an accusation lightly," Fredericks said, voice as ponderous as his look. "I have proof. I request that a group be commissioned to review the information objectively. And when that commission determines the truth, I ask that you not allow such an offense to go unpunished."

Nick had sat, unblinking, certain it was all a mistake. The commission would review his work, exonerate him, identify the true problem that had cost those miners their lives.

"These are serious matters," Sir Joseph had said, thick fingers bound around the arms of his chair. "You can be sure we will give them due consideration."

They had. It had taken the commission Sir Joseph had appointed a full week to order Nick from the society, to refuse to share any further information with him. Only Sir Humphry Davy had taken his side.

"This is a travesty, Rotherford," he'd said as he shook Nick's hand in farewell that day in London. "I'll keep pushing for a more thorough investigation."

Nick had heard nothing further in the four months since. It mattered not. He knew he hadn't plagiarized Fredericks's work. But the thought that his mistake had caused the accident haunted him.

So Nick had retreated. He thought at least a few said he was hiding. He had another reason for moving to Derby. The distance provided a buffer. With him more than a hundred miles away from Fredericks and any other scientist, no one could claim his work, or any mistake, was anything but his own.

Of course, first he had to actually achieve something

from the effort. It was one thing to work in theory—determine how a combination of liquids and solids might interact with the gaseous firedamp dozens of feet underground. It was another to combine those materials and test their efficacy without endangering others. So far, the results had been less than satisfactory.

Still, he kept at it that day and the next, until someone knocked at the door of his laboratory.

Nick pulled out his pocket watch and consulted it. Not time for tea or for someone to remind him of a dinner he was about to miss. Ears attuned for any other sound, he glanced out the window. No one seemed to be calling for help on what appeared to be a sunny day. Surely his staff knew he was not to be disturbed.

Someone knocked again.

He should ignore it. It was an interruption, a distraction. He had more important things to do. He enjoyed confronting impossible problems, failing to find solutions. In fact, failure was his bread and butter lately.

Nick rose and opened the door. Alice clutched a bunch of lavender in her tiny hand. "We picked flowers for your laboratory, Papa. Miss Pyrmont said they would make it smell better."

Miss Pyrmont would certainly have some knowledge of smells, given the way she'd recently rescued him. "How thoughtful," he said. "Unfortunately, it's rather important that I know how my work smells. That's one of the ways I can be certain I've combined the chemicals properly."

Alice's face folded in on itself as it was wont to do when she was unhappy about something. "Don't you like flowers, Papa?"

Flowers had rarely appealed to him, but he liked less that look, particularly when it was directed at him.

"I think perhaps they would be better suited to his study," Miss Pyrmont said.

Nick blew out a breath. The woman had an uncanny ability to smooth things over. "Excellent suggestion," he said and was relieved to see Alice brighten again.

It took so little to change her mood. Ann had been the same way. He and his wife had gotten on well when they were younger, but once they were married, he'd never been certain which word or gesture of his would set her spirits plummeting. It had made conversation difficult.

"We were just going for a walk in the woods," Miss Pyrmont said. "Perhaps you'd like to join us."

Alice nodded eagerly, free hand reaching for the closest of his. He felt his work pulling from the opposite direction.

"I regret that matters require my attention," he tried.

This time Alice ignored him, fingers wrapping around his.

"A shame," Miss Pyrmont agreed, moving to take Alice's hand. Nick could feel his daughter slipping away and had to fight the urge to pull her closer. "Remember, we don't want to stand in the way of your father's progress, Alice."

Once again Alice did not look nearly so sure.

"Actually, there isn't a lot of progress being made this afternoon," Nick admitted. "I seem to have stumbled to a halt."

As Alice gazed up at him, Miss Pyrmont smiled. "Perhaps you need a change of scenery. I read somewhere that fresh air can be conducive to clearing the mind."

Alice glanced between the two of them. "Are you coming after all, Papa?"

Her high voice vibrated with an emotion he'd all but forgotten: hope. Truly, would a few more moments away hurt anything? His chemicals would still be sitting there, refusing to ignite. His problems weren't going anywhere. It might help to forget about them for a time.

"Yes, Alice," he said. "I believe I will. Thank you for inviting me."

Emma wanted to shout in triumph, but she settled for a smile as they returned to the house long enough to leave the flowers in Mrs. Jennings's care.

She still could not believe her luck. First Mrs. Dunworthy had encouraged her to bring Alice and her father closer together, and now Sir Nicholas had agreed to walk with them. Add that walk to the moments spent at breakfast yesterday morning and dinner tonight, and he would have spent more time in his daughter's company this week than in the previous three months of Emma's employment.

Of course, not everything had gone well. Mrs. Dunworthy had been popping in to the nursery more frequently yesterday and this morning, as if suspecting that Emma had somehow been neglecting her charge. Today, for example, she had arrived just as Emma and the little girl were sitting on the carpet, dressing Lady Chamomile in a fresh outfit.

"And what is the occasion?" Mrs. Dunworthy had asked, smiling down at her niece even as Emma stood out of respect. "Tea with the queen, perhaps?"

"No, Auntie," Alice had giggled. "Dinner with Papa! Lady Chamomile is looking forward to it."

Mrs. Dunworthy shook her head. "Lady Chamomile has not been invited. Dolls are for the nursery, Alice, not a fine table where grown-up ladies eat."

Emma felt her muscles stiffening. Didn't Mrs. Dunworthy know how much Alice depended on the doll? Surely if Lady Chamomile was allowed to come once or twice, Alice would feel comfortable enough going on her own in future.

"Then perhaps I'm not so grown up," Alice said, lower lip quivering.

Emma knew she should be silent when her mistress was addressing Alice, but she couldn't bear to see the little girl unhappy for such a trivial thing.

"But you are growing up, Alice," she said, kneeling so that she could look the girl in the eye. "See how tall you are now! You can't give up eating dinner with your father. I know you're looking forward to it, too."

"But who will keep Lady Chamomile company?" Alice protested.

Mrs. Dunworthy took a visible breath before patting Alice on the head. "It is sweet that you are so devoted to your doll, dear, but there are times when we must put such childish things behind us."

"But Papa wouldn't mind," Alice insisted. "He likes Lady Chamomile."

"Your father," Mrs. Dunworthy said, voice hardening as she drew back her hand, "does not run this household. He has left such matters to me. I will not spend my dinner with a doll. I shall expect to see you tonight without it." She picked up her skirts as if the nursery floor had dirtied them and swept from the room.

Once again, Emma had to still her trembling, but this time she knew it wasn't fear but anger that caused it. She understood the need to guide children. The Bible said children should be raised properly so they would not depart from that path as they grew older. But did it follow that children should have their spirits crushed, their imaginations stifled, for them to become good members of Society? She had been subjected to such treatment, and she didn't see that it had done any good.

Anything good I learned from You, Father!

"It will all come out right, Alice," she had promised her charge, who was blinking her eyes as if fighting tears. "Just think, if Lady Chamomile cannot join us, you'll have grand stories to tell her. And I'll ask Mrs. Jennings to make something special, just for her."

Now as Emma, Alice and Sir Nicholas started across the lawn behind the Grange, she considered asking him for permission to bring the doll to dinner tonight. As easily as he'd interacted with Lady Chamomile, surely he wouldn't mind if it sat at the table. But after his altercation with his sister-in-law earlier, she couldn't help thinking that she'd only be borrowing trouble, for her and Sir Nicholas both.

Then, too, his mind already seemed to be wandering. Though he walked beside Alice, his head was bowed, and Emma didn't think the grass they were crossing was occupying his thoughts.

But the greenery did give her another idea on how to draw him out.

"Do you know anything about the flora and fauna here, Sir Nicholas?" she asked as Alice swung her hand back and forth and hummed to herself.

His head came up, and he regarded the trees they were approaching. "My forte is the physical properties of materials, not botany, I fear. But my father brought me up here every summer when I was a child and on school holidays afterward, so I learned something about the area."

He nodded to the woods as branches wove their way above them. "These oaks, for instance, are not native to the grounds but were planted by the original owner for future firewood."

Emma glanced at the trees, their limbs drooping heavily, their tops filtering the sunlight in shafts of gold. Birds flitted through the light, calling; butterflies danced on the air. The breeze set the leaves to chattering, brought her the scent of water. She could imagine one of her favorite heroes, Robin Hood, leaping across the path.

"A shame to think of cutting these down," she murmured.

"They would make a very big fire," Alice said.

"I quite agree," her father said seriously, "but perhaps we should keep them standing for a few more generations."

Emma saw the smile tugging at the corner of his mouth, but Alice's tug was more insistent, and Emma released her to allow the girl to skip ahead on the pebbled path. How she would have loved such freedom when she was Alice's age. She'd already been set to scrubbing floors in the asylum, and the streets of London weren't as friendly as the Grange woods.

"Is she truly lonely?" he murmured.

Emma regarded him in surprise. His gaze had followed his daughter, his steps had slowed. The fingers of one hand were tapping at the side of his trousers, as if keeping time with his thoughts. Could her seeds yesterday morning be bearing fruit already?

"I believe so," Emma replied. "You may have noticed that she is rather dependent on the good graces of a certain doll."

"The capricious Lady Chamomile," he surmised. "You said you'd dealt with other children. Are Alice's affections for the doll typical?"

She didn't want to give him cause to be concerned. Fear was no way to motivate a father, or anyone else, she knew from experience. "Given that she lost her mother so young and suddenly finds herself in new surroundings, I think she's coming along marvelously well. So long as she knows you love her, she will flourish anywhere."

He puffed out a breath through his nose as if he doubted that. "Love, eh? A questionable quality. I have not found it to be particularly reliable as a predictor of success."

Emma frowned. How could he say that? True, she had had little human love growing up, and some would say she had made a success for herself. But she knew that her success came from God's love. He had been the one to look out for her when others hadn't. He'd been the one she'd run to when she'd been afraid. If Alice had her earthly father's love as well, what more could she want?

"I think love is the most important emotion," she said. "Perfect love is the pinnacle of human achievement."

He shook his head. "In my experience, the ideal is rarely achievable."

"That doesn't mean we shouldn't try!" Emma protested.

He raised a brow at her vehemence, and she nearly sighed aloud. There she went again, voicing an opinion when none was wanted. It seemed because she'd kept her opinions inside for so many years they must find voice now. Yet she couldn't help wondering at his insistence. What made Sir Nicholas think love was so unattainable?

Mrs. Jennings had said that he and his late wife had

been in love. What if she'd been wrong? Did the noted philosopher truly know nothing about the tender emotion of love? Was that why he had held his daughter at arm's length?

He stopped in the middle of the path. "Forgive me, Miss Pyrmont. My conversation wasn't very astute or useful. I fear I'm not particularly good company today. Perhaps you and Alice should continue on alone."

She should probably have pity on him, but she was loath to let him escape so easily. Surely, the more she teased him into Alice's company, the more he would enjoy being around his daughter.

"I'm sorry your progress doesn't please you," she ventured as Alice skipped back toward them. "No one's mentioned seeing smoke coming out of the doorway of your laboratory. I was hoping that was a good sign."

"You would be mistaken," he replied. "Now the material won't catch fire at all, and I can't determine what I'm missing."

He sounded so dejected that Emma couldn't resist helping. "I was always told fire requires three things," she said, eying Alice where she'd stopped to gaze at a passing butterfly. "Heat, fuel and air. Vary any one, and you control the flame."

"Indeed," he said. "I understand the basic principles, Miss Pyrmont."

She thought she'd overstepped her bounds again, but he continued as if they'd just met and were having a conversation at a fine ball in London. "The heat appears to be constant, despite my best efforts to vary it. At the moment, we have only certain types of fuel—tallow, whale oil and the like. And of course we know that air can vary belowground."

"Some of it being flammable," Emma agreed.

He eyed her, black brows raised, and she realized she'd blundered. Nannies did not understand the changes in oxygen levels underground when those changes had only been discovered a few decades ago. Women who had been raised in the household of a natural philosopher just might.

"I read about it in the *Times,*" she hurried to add, "when my previous master had finished with it. Terrible accidents have been caused by flammable air!"

He seemed to accept her explanation, which was the truth. She had read about it in the *Times,* but only after learning too much about it during her residence in the Fredericks household.

But his concern, for once, was not his work. He nodded to the path ahead. "Is it wise to let her do that?"

Alice had strayed from the path in pursuit of the butterfly, her blue skirts brushing the sparse undergrowth. Emma hurried forward and called her back. She didn't know of any dangers in the woods, but it wouldn't hurt to keep the girl to the path.

Just as Emma needed to mind her path if she was to ensure Sir Nicholas and Alice's future together without revealing her own past.

Chapter Nine

When Nick finally bid Alice and Miss Pyrmont good afternoon, he was in a thoughtful mood. He'd tarried with them in the woods for longer than he'd originally intended. His mind had felt clearer, as Miss Pyrmont had predicted, but he wasn't certain the fresh air had caused the change.

Something about being with the nanny and her charge invigorated him.

He had several hypotheses for the phenomena. It could have stemmed from the enjoyment of explaining his actions to an interested audience. It could have been the congenial surroundings of people who seemed to appreciate him. But he suspected it had more to do with the wit and kindness of his daughter's nanny.

And why should that be? He had not known many women. His father and Ann's had been lifelong friends who had encouraged their children to unite the families in marriage. He and Ann had been companions since they were in leading strings. She was comfortable, consistent. The other young ladies he'd met in Society were far more unpredictable, with mad whims and bold laughter. Marrying Ann had seemed the logical course for his goals to pursue the career of a natural philosopher.

Miss Pyrmont was not comfortable. She challenged him to see things differently—Alice, his role as a father, even his work. But she did it all with a general good nature and pragmatic approach he could not refute. He found himself wondering how such a female had come into being.

He also found himself hungry, so on the way back to his laboratory he stopped by the kitchen for a snack.

This time, Mrs. Jennings was the only one in evidence, and she smiled at the sight of him. "Sir Nicholas. How might I be of service?"

"I thought a little something to sustain me until your excellent dinner," he confessed, venturing into her domain. He'd always liked the kitchen at the Grange. The copper pots hung from the far wall in graduated sizes. The fire at one side was balanced by the large window on the other. And while Mrs. Jennings's chemistry did not involve industrial materials, it certainly produced just as interesting results.

Now his cook's hands fluttered, reminding him of the birds Alice had spotted in the woods. "Of course! I'll have another batch of those cinnamon biscuits done cooking any minute. But you'll want something more substantial with them. Shall I put together a tray and have it brought to your laboratory or will you wait?"

He should probably have the food delivered so he could return immediately to his work. But he didn't think it particularly healthful to mix materials he intended to consume with materials he intended to ignite, and it struck him suddenly that he might find more answers to his other line of inquiry if he stayed.

"I am quite content to wait on your good pleasure,"

he assured his cook. He pointed to the stool beside the worktable. "If I may?"

"Oh, of course." She hurried to dust off the seat with a towel. He nodded his thanks and sat while she bustled around the kitchen.

His feet touched the floor easily. He remembered other times when it hadn't been so. The kitchen had seen more of him than he'd seen his mother or father. They had never seemed sure what to do with him.

His parents had been married for many years, his mother approaching forty, when he'd been born. He had always wondered whether his advent into the world had been a surprise, and a not-too-pleasant one at that. Either way, his father had made it plain that ladies were far above the inquisitive, occasionally messy pastimes of young gentlemen, and his father had other matters to attend to. That these matters were more important than Nick had been too evident to question.

So Nick had been left mostly in the care of men—a tutor before Eton and then a manservant whenever he was home from school. But when he'd been lonely or concerned about anything, which was admittedly rare, he'd found his way to the kitchen and Mrs. Jennings's company. She had never failed to provide wise and caring counsel.

Her hair was white now, her girth broader. But she still exuded something he could not name. All he knew was that it brought him a certain peace.

"I understand we're to have the pleasure of serving little Alice and her nanny at dinner tonight," she said, returning to the table. She lay a plate before him with slices of fresh-baked bread dotted by butter, pieces of the Dale's tangy cheese, cold chicken breast and a bowl of pitted cherries.

"I'd like them to join us every night," Nick confirmed, reaching for a slice of the bread.

"So Mrs. Dunworthy said," she replied with a nod. "She already consulted me about the menu."

He was glad to hear her call the discussion a consultation. In his experience, Charlotte tended to be more forceful than that. "Then I take it you approve of the change," he said before biting into the cheese.

"Not my place to approve," Mrs. Jennings said as she went to pour him a glass of lemonade. When she returned, she grinned at him. "But yes, I'm glad you let the little one join you."

"And Miss Pyrmont?" he asked, keeping his gaze on the cherries, which somehow reminded him of the nanny's blushing cheeks.

"Her, too. A fine addition to the household. Clever, well educated, and she positively dotes on little Alice."

He wasn't certain what constituted doting, but he knew his daughter was pleased by it. Alice seemed to like attention more than he and Ann ever had.

"I wonder why she chose to be a nanny," he mused, popping a cherry into his mouth.

"She's naturally good with children," Mrs. Jennings insisted. "Kind, warmhearted, a fine Christian lady."

She made Miss Pyrmont sound perfect. He had never achieved perfection, despite the urgings of his father and Ann.

"So it would seem," he replied, finding the cherry hard to swallow.

Either his manner or his tone must have sought reassurance, for she hastened to comfort him. "Now, then, you mustn't worry you'll lose her. She seems quite happy with her position. She never talks of missing London." She bustled back to the hearth to check on her biscuits. The scent of cinnamon wafted through the room.

And why didn't Miss Pyrmont miss London, he wondered as he sipped the tart lemonade. Though he treasured the quiet of Dovecote Dale, at times he missed the opportunities London afforded—ready access to materials, the massive libraries of past research, easy consultation with colleagues. Of course, it was the last that had resulted in his exile.

Had some tragedy forced Miss Pyrmont north, as well? What sort of evidence would corroborate that hypothesis? He'd seen no melancholy, little talk of her previous homes. In fact, she seemed loath to speak of London at all. Was that the evidence he sought?

"And here are your biscuits," Mrs. Jennings proclaimed, setting a plate down on the table in front of him with a flourish. He could feel the steam rising from the little crescent-shaped delicacies, and with it their heavenly scent. His hand was reaching for one before he realized conscious effort.

"So Miss Pyrmont is content to be Alice's nanny," he said after eating two.

"For now," his cook replied with a nod. "Of course, children outgrow their nannies. And I expect some of the gentlemen in the area may wish to have a say in her future."

Nick frowned as he picked up the third biscuit. "I don't follow your logic."

Her skin tone approached the color of the cherries. "Begging your pardon, Sir Nicholas. It was only a flight of fancy. I have no call to be telling tales, and baseless ones at that."

Nick set the biscuit down uneaten. "If you know

something about Alice's nanny that might affect her ability to honor her position, I need to know."

She dropped her gaze, plump fingers tugging at her apron string as if it had suddenly become tighter. "Miss Pyrmont is the sort to give her work her very best, sir. But you're quite right—a pretty young lady of her talents is a bit wasted in the role of nanny to only one child. If the butler Mr. Hennessy in the Earl of Danning's household doesn't steal her away from us to work in their nursery, which he hopes will expand once the earl chooses a wife, I wouldn't be surprised if one of his footmen didn't make her a life offer. She could do worse than to marry a fine strapping fellow with ambitions."

And she could do a great deal better.

Nick blinked at the thought and was relieved he hadn't said it aloud. Miss Pyrmont was a member of his staff. Her matrimonial prospects were none of his concern. Even her future was not his to command.

Mrs. Jennings was right. In a few years, Alice would graduate from a nanny to a governess. Though Miss Pyrmont seemed to have an enviable education, she would not have the knowledge of Society Alice would need to be successful in her Season. Ann had started planning for that day the minute Alice had been born. She would certainly not have approved of Miss Pyrmont as a governess.

Or of Nick thinking about the lovely Miss Pyrmont as anything more than a nanny.

Emma had Alice ready for dinner a few minutes early that evening even though the little girl squirmed through her dressing. Emma found herself almost as eager for the meal. Though she'd always believed herself good enough to sit at the table, at least now she fancied she looked the part, as well.

Mrs. Dunworthy had sent Ivy up with an apron dress late that afternoon. Though the cotton gown would generally be considered a day dress, Emma thought it would do quite nicely for dinner with the family. The gown was printed with blue squares surrounding yellow flowers and had a fuller skirt that swung as she walked. The long sleeves ensured that her burn was out of sight. Best of all, the way the bodice tied in place under the bib front allowed her to size it to her figure even though it had plainly been designed for a more ample lady. It was the least worn and prettiest dress she'd ever had.

"Like springtime you look," Ivy had assured her before hurrying back to her other duties.

Emma felt like springtime, full of hope, full of light. When she'd dined with the family earlier, she'd been worried for her position. Now she merely wanted to further Alice's position with her father. Perhaps tonight would lead to greater success in her campaign to court Sir Nicholas for his daughter.

The gentleman and his sister-in-law were already waiting in the beautiful salon when Emma brought in Alice. Mrs. Dunworthy seemed to have felt compelled to dress for the occasion, for her auburn hair was piled up high on her head, and she'd left off her cap for once. Her carmine satin gown bared her shoulders. What was undeniably a ruby gleamed on a golden chain about her neck. Perhaps it was a family heirloom. Hadn't Emma heard that the lady had been destitute when she had come to live with the Rotherfords?

Sir Nicholas, on the other hand, looked less affluent. He still wore the tweed coat and brown trousers he'd had on during their walk in the woods. His only concession to fashion was that he'd changed his boots for evening pumps and then, Emma thought, only because Mrs. Dunworthy would not have allowed the mud of the field to touch her polished floors.

"There you are, Alice," Mrs. Dunworthy said as if Emma and her niece were late instead of early. "What a pretty dress you have on this evening."

Alice clutched the blue satin of her skirts and lifted them on either side so that the lace on the hem brushed her stockinged ankles while she twirled. "I like blue, too." She dropped the material and gazed up at her father. "Do you think it a good color for me, Papa?"

"An excellent color, Alice," he assured her with a bow. "Perhaps we should conduct our experiment on you some time, though, to confirm that."

Alice nodded eagerly. Emma made a note to remind him of his suggestion. But Sir Nicholas wasn't finished. He strolled closer as if regarding Alice's gown, then bent his head to Emma's.

"And I see that Alice and I were correct," he murmured. "You look very well in blue."

She could only hope she looked good in pink as well, for that was surely the color her cheeks were turning.

"I believe dinner is ready," Mrs. Dunworthy said, though Emma could see by the ormolu clock on the mantel that it was still ten minutes before the hour. The lady held out her arm. "If you would be so kind, Nicholas."

With a look to Emma that seemed to be apologetic, Sir Nicholas went to join his sister-in-law, leaving Emma to follow with Alice.

She couldn't mind that she wasn't walking on Sir Nicholas's arm this time. She was here for Alice, after all. And walking behind Sir Nicholas gave her a chance to appreciate the way the candlelight glowed on his raven hair.

Oh, this would never do! She dropped her gaze to the marble floor until she reached the dining room chairs, where she helped Alice into her seat next to her father.

"And how is Lady Chamomile this evening?" Sir Nicholas asked after the first course had been served. Emma wasn't sure what Mrs. Jennings had been thinking, for the food before them included a platter of smelt, the small black fish staring up at them from a bed of sautéed onions. Alice returned their stares, her back pressed so hard against the wood of her seat that her satin skirts nearly slipped from beneath her. And the spicy mulligatawny soup that accompanied the smelt made Alice wrinkle her nose.

"Lady Chamomile is hungry," Alice said, letting her spoon fall into the soup with a splash that dotted the white tablecloth with gold.

Mrs. Dunworthy eyed Emma as if she had chosen the food or should have been hand-feeding Alice to prevent such a thing.

Sir Nicholas did not seem to mind. "After all those cinnamon biscuits?" he challenged with a smile. "I find that hard to believe."

Alice brightened. "I like cinnamon biscuits."

"Entirely too much," Mrs. Dunworthy said. "It seems a family trait." Now her disapproving eye settled on Sir Nicholas. Though Emma felt for him, she was glad for the respite, using the moment to direct Alice's attention to the crusty bread that had been served with the soup.

"I'm certain there must be a limit to the number of biscuits one should consume a day," Sir Nicholas said, digging into his smelt with an enthusiasm Emma could not muster. "Happily, I have yet to reach it."

Emma hid her smile. "Perhaps that should be your next experiment, sir."

His chuckle was as dry as his wit, but it warmed her heart nonetheless. "I shall leave that experiment to you and Alice."

"How very kind of you, to be sure," Mrs. Dunworthy said, daintily lifting her spoon. "And how is your work coming, Nicholas? Are we any closer to saving humanity?"

His look dropped to his soup and darkened with his tone. "It isn't the sum of humanity that concerns me, madam, but the men laboring in my mine. And the solution to the problem remains unknown."

He sounded so frustrated, Emma could not keep silent. "But not unknowable, surely. Every advancement had setbacks. I'm certain that I read that Mr. Dalton had to study many gases before he could determine their properties. Some inventions required a number of trials before success. So long as you persist, you cannot be beaten."

"What an excellent sentiment, Miss Pyrmont," Mrs. Dunworthy said, although her tone implied otherwise. "A shame it's too long to be embroidered on a pillow. Alice, darling, do try to sit up when you eat."

Emma pressed her lips together as she turned to help Alice settle back onto the chair. What, had she let a pretty dress go to her head? She had to remember her place! Her opinion on any matter was no more welcome here than it had been in Samuel Fredericks's home. She might actually be seated at the table this time instead of standing along the wall, but she was still not a member of the family.

"Thank you for your encouragement, Miss Pyrmont," Sir Nicholas said in the silence. "I assure you, I am not giving up. You were quite right about that walk this afternoon. It did wonders for clearing my mind and showing me what was most important."

She chanced a glance at him. He was regarding her steadily, as if making sure that she heard what he said. She'd heard him. She could tell that what he'd said mattered to him. She had only one question.

Was it his work or something else he meant?

Chapter Ten

Nick knew he lacked a complete understanding of human behavior. It was not, after all, his chosen course of study, and the reactions of some of the people with whom he had engaged had proven that he was not particularly adept at the analysis. Chemicals were far more consistent. He had high confidence that the boiling point of water was two hundred and twelve degrees according to the Fahrenheit scale and would remain so tomorrow and the day after.

Unfortunately he also had high confidence that Charlotte's boiling point was far lower, and by the flaring of her nostrils and the height of her color, she was rapidly approaching it. The reason appeared to be that Miss Pyrmont had an opinion on a matter Charlotte generally preferred to ignore: his work.

Such a response defied logic. Miss Pyrmont certainly had sufficient education with which to form an opinion. And denying one's staff the right to share their knowledge seemed to him both arrogant and foolish. Science certainly benefited from the sharing of information!

So, although he generally tried to tolerate Charlotte's

rather narrow view of the world for Ann's sake, he could not help furthering the increase in her temperature.

"I wonder, Miss Pyrmont," he said, leaning forward over his smelt to look around Alice, "if you and Alice would care to join me for a time in the salon after dinner?"

He would have thought the footman had lit three more braces of candelabra by the way her face glowed. Alice was nodding eagerly, as well.

Charlotte, however, raised her chin, and her shoulders were suddenly above the top of the chair by at least an additional inch, he would have estimated.

"How kind of you, Nicholas," she said, although her own tone would not have ranked high on the scale of kindness, he thought. "However, I'm certain Alice has a routine, and we would be wise not to abuse it further. Besides, I had plans to read to her tonight."

Miss Pyrmont's smile seemed to have frozen in place, and she shifted on her own seat. Something was clearly troubling her, but asking her for her opinion on the matter could only get her into more trouble.

As if she knew it as well but had made a decision, she too raised her chin and met his gaze. "I'm sure Alice would enjoy reading with her aunt, but a routine that never varies can be quite dull indeed." She smiled at Alice. "Would you like to spend time with your papa first, Alice?"

His daughter ducked her head and peered at him through the screen of her lashes. "Yes?"

He smiled at the question of an answer. "Then it's settled. I think we have a game of ninepins about somewhere. Have you played before?"

Alice shook her head, eyes once more wide. "But pins stick."

"Not these pins," Nick promised her.

Charlotte rose and dropped her napkin on the table. "Clearly you have no need of me. I have household matters that require my attention. I will expect Alice in my chambers by half past eight."

Nick wasn't sure who she was addressing, him or Miss Pyrmont, but he stood, as well. "You needn't rush off, Charlotte. You're quite welcome to join us."

"Most considerate of you," she said, "but I've never been terribly good at games." She strolled from the room, but the way her skirts were swinging implied an excessive amount of energy about the action. He considered begging her pardon, but somehow he thought it would do no good. The older sister, Charlotte had never thought him the proper fellow to marry her precious Ann. Five years later, he found he could not argue with her on that score either.

"You asked after a game of ninepins," Miss Pyrmont said, rising. "I may know where it is. If you'd escort Alice to the salon, I'll attempt to find it."

"Done," Nick said and held out his hand to his daughter.

As always, the feel of those little fingers in his hand nearly felled him. They reminded him of his duty as her father, to help her grow into the woman she should become.

But how did one assist in the growth of a child? His parents had not been overly instrumental in his maturity, but somehow he felt as if he should be doing more for Alice. He simply didn't know what. Perhaps when he'd completed his work on the safety lamp, he could research the latest child-rearing strategies. Surely with children being the next generation someone had determined how best to raise them. Miss Pyrmont must have opinions in that area, as well.

He found himself missing her as he walked with Alice from the dining room, taking slow steps so his daughter could keep pace. Miss Pyrmont always seemed to know what to say and how to say it: to him, to Alice. Of course, not to Charlotte, but he thought few people had success there.

And how odd that he was expected to call Charlotte by her first name but not Miss Pyrmont. A decided lack of economy, certainly. How much easier to call her Emma.

He smiled at the thought, then realized that Alice was humming to herself. The tune was soft and lilting and seemed designed to fit his mood. My, but he was in a fanciful frame of mind this evening!

"I like the sound of that song," he said as they reached the entryway and turned for the salon.

"Nanny taught it to me," Alice said and proceeded to launch into the words:

"Since God regards the orphan's cry

Oh, what have I to fear?

He feeds the ravens when they cry

And fills his poor with bread.

If I am poor He can supply

Who has my table spread."

Her high voice carried such emotion, as if she understood the meaning of the song, as if she'd doubted her table would be supplied with good food or she had needed to cry to God for rescue. He had never had to worry about food. And he had never thought to ask for rescue.

Had Emma?

"I like the song," Alice finished as they entered the

salon, skipping a step as if to prove it. "So does Lady Chamomile. She likes Nanny, too."

"Very wise of Lady Chamomile, to be sure," Nick agreed, leading Alice to the sofa and helping her sit.

He wasn't sure how else to make conversation with his daughter, but Alice kept up a steady stream of questions that ranged from why the sun went to bed at night at different times to what color would look best on Lady Chamomile. Still, he felt a distinct sense of relief when Miss Pyrmont returned a short time later with the footman.

Charles carried the game of ninepins, and she carried a ball of yarn and several long, thin, pointy rods. While Nick set up the game on the drum table, she settled herself on the sofa nearby and began looping the yarn around the rods. Her fingers worked deftly, quickly, two rods holding her creation, the other weaving in and out to form a tiny tube that was rows and rows of tight loops. He could not conceive the purpose.

"What do we do now, Papa?" Alice asked, reminding him of his promise to teach her the game.

"We have a very important task before us," Nick told her, nodding toward the board as he knelt beside it. "These pins stand tall and proud, but it is our duty to knock them down."

Alice raised a hand as if to do just that.

He heard Emma's chuckle even as he caught his daughter's hand. "Not so easily, Alice," he told her. "It's a game of skill."

She frowned as he released her.

"I think your father means that you have to practice to get it just right," Emma explained, fingers pausing.

Nick nodded. "Exactly. The idea is to swing the ball at just the right angle, with the right amount of force and the right speed to knock down as many pins as possible."

Alice nodded solemnly. Nick handed her the ball, but she glanced at Emma first.

"Go ahead," Emma encouraged her. "Pull back on the chain and give the ball a swing."

Such a little thing, yet Alice needed her nanny's approval to try. He couldn't remember looking for such approval. Studies had come easily, and he'd always known that his tutor and valet served at his father's behest, not from any devotion. Emma made it seem as if Alice was the world to her.

What would it be like to be someone's world? To bask in the approval of someone respected, beloved? And why did his chest hurt as he even considered the matter?

Alice pulled back on the chain and swung the ball forward. Two of the pins toppled. She glanced up at Nick expectantly.

It seemed his opinion mattered, as well. Tears pushed at his eyes. "Very good," he assured her, blinking them back in surprise.

She beamed and reached for the ball again.

"I think," Miss Pyrmont said with a smile, "your father gets a turn now, Alice."

"Oh!" Alice handed him the ball. "I'm sorry, Papa!"

"Quite all right," Nick said, taking a breath to still his emotions and accepting the ball from Alice. "Why don't you put those two pins back in their places? Then we'll see what can be done."

As her little hands worked to set the polished wood pins into the precise spots, Nick found his gaze wandering back to Emma. She had apparently finished one of the tubes she'd been creating, for it lay in her lap.

Another was growing from her needles. He craned his neck to watch more closely.

"What is that you're doing?"

She glanced up to smile at him. "I'm knitting, Sir Nicholas." She stopped long enough to hold up the thing she'd finished. It resembled nothing so much as a tiny, holey teacup. "Lady Chamomile needs a new pair of stockings."

"To keep her feet warm," Alice agreed as she worked.

Emma laughed as she set the doll's stocking back into her lap and took up her needles once more. "Yes, well, I'm not sure how these will do against the cold, seeing as they are made of cotton and rather lacy. She's more likely to give off heat than retain it."

Heat. Nick stared at the stocking, and the ball fell from his fingers. He didn't even hear it strike the pins.

"That's it!" The knowledge thrust him to his feet, and he seized Emma by the shoulders and drew her up as well, tumbling the ball of yarn, the needles and Lady Chamomile's stocking to the floor. "That's perfect! Emma, I could kiss you!"

Emma stared at him. His face was alight with joy, softening the angles of his features, brightening his eyes. His hands on her shoulders positively trembled. With his mouth less than a foot from hers, he could have kissed her easily. It sounded wonderful and terrifying at the same time.

And had he just called her…Emma?

"You missed the pins, Papa," Alice said. "But don't worry. You'll do better next time."

As if awakening from a dream, Sir Nicholas released Emma and stepped back. She could see the effort he was making to calm himself, standing taller, rearranging his face into its usual more serious lines.

"I do beg your pardon, Miss Pyrmont," he said. "I had no call to lay hands on you. Please forgive me."

"No harm done," Emma said, though her heart persisted in beating faster. "May I ask the occasion?"

"A sudden inspiration," he said, and a smile popped into view a moment. "I seem to have those more often when I'm with you and Alice."

Was that the reason he was spending so much time with them, to ward off a lack of inspiration? The disappointment was stronger than it should have been. Perhaps she should simply be grateful he was here and not question the reason.

"I am very clever," Alice agreed, and she let fly the ball. Five of the ninepins went down. She nodded with satisfaction.

Sir Nicholas bent to gather up Emma's knitting. "You are very clever indeed, Alice. I haven't felt nearly so clever recently. I've been struggling with how to resolve the problem from a chemical perspective, but I suddenly realized that it may be a material problem."

Emma accepted the knitting back from him, all tumbled now. She'd have to pull out the stitches and start over. Thank goodness she was only knitting a doll's stocking!

But Sir Nicholas kept the stocking she'd finished, turning it over in his hands as if studying it from all angles.

"More porous materials, more oxygen," he murmured. "It might be the thing." His look speared Emma. "Could you create something to my precise specifications?"

She felt her fingers tensing on her bundle. Her foster

father had flown into a rage if she so much as breathed wrong near his work. That's how she'd earned the burn on her arm. She hadn't been paying sufficient attention to the reactions of the chemicals he'd set her to watching, and he'd tossed the oil of vitriol at her in punishment. The pale yellow acid had quickly eaten through the wool of her sleeve, but she'd managed to wash most of it off her skin before the burn grew to any size. Still, the pockmark reminded her every time she looked at it of what she must not forget: to protect herself.

But protecting herself did not mean that she shouldn't help others where she could. And Sir Nicholas, she was learning, was not Samuel Fredericks. How could she refuse his request and douse the light in those dark eyes?

"I could try," she offered. "What did you have in mind?"

He was staring at the stocking, already absorbed. The fingers of his free hand tapped on his thigh as if making calculations. "It would have to be longer, say five or six inches, perhaps two wide, to fit the current design. Or should the dimensions be modified to take advantage of the material?"

Alice was frowning up at him. "I knocked down five pins, Papa," she said as if afraid he hadn't noticed.

Emma was certain he hadn't noticed.

"Yes, Alice, very good," he murmured, gaze on the stocking. "And cotton? Perhaps silk or wool? I'd have to recalibrate…"

"Sir Nicholas," Emma interrupted.

"I wonder how the wick would change given the more porous material?" he continued undeterred. "Would I need to amend the fuel? Perhaps coat the yarn?"

"Nicholas Rotherford!" Emma insisted.

He blinked as if seeing her for the first time in minutes. "Yes, Emma?"

Emma again. Surely he understood that first names were only used for family, close friends or minor servants. Which did he count her?

"I do believe you are in the middle of a most pressing game of ninepins, sir," she reminded him. "Perhaps this analysis can wait until tomorrow."

He glanced at Alice, who had set up the pins and now held the ball out to him. Yet her face was already puckering as if she knew his refusal was coming.

"A very important game," he assured her, "but I truly must work out these calculations."

Emma felt her temper rising. She pried the stocking from his grip. "Of course. Alice is expected upstairs soon in any event, and work of a scientific nature must always take precedence over a promise to a lady."

His head whipped back toward her, and she could see him frown. One of the fingers of his free hand was still moving, but this time she wouldn't have been surprised to find he was calculating the exact response to her comment.

"A faulty assumption," he replied. "A lady should always take precedence, particularly when that lady is my charming daughter. Please return to your knitting, Emma. I'm certain Lady Chamomile will miss her stockings."

He bowed to Emma, and she curtsied in response, as if they were about to begin a set in a dance. But perhaps they had been dancing, within the confines of the roles placed upon them.

After he straightened, he knelt again beside his daughter. "Is it my turn or yours, Alice?"

"Yours," Alice said, face glowing. "But I'd be happy to take another turn if you like."

"Hand your father the ball, Alice," Emma said, returning to her seat with a smile. "He's already made enough concessions tonight."

Chapter Eleven

Emma went to bed that evening thoroughly satisfied with the day. Nicholas was coming around. She could see it. Surely they had turned the corner, and he would continue toward becoming the father Alice needed. All Emma had to do was encourage him.

That should not be hard, she thought as she snuggled beneath the covers in the room next to Alice's. She could see that he wanted to love his daughter. Indeed, his kindness to Alice, his willingness to take time to explain things in terms she'd understand, all said that he cared. That's the sort of father she'd always dreamed was possible, even when she had no firsthand experience, except one.

Thank You, Father. You showed me what a real father should be like—loving, caring, guiding, comforting. Help Nicholas become that for Alice.

But though she went to bed happy, the next day proved that her goal was not yet in sight.

It seemed that night had been the last concession from Nicholas. Indeed, Emma wasn't even sure he slept. Ivy reported he had been found in his study the next morning, still dressed in the clothes he'd had on the previous evening, hair disheveled, chin grizzled, head bowed over his calculations. He did not join Emma and Alice for breakfast or tea, and Mrs. Dunworthy sent word that their dinner would be served in the nursery that night.

Emma had one thought about the change. Unacceptable. She had begun to hope, and she wasn't about to let Alice's chances get swallowed by the ravenous maw of Madam Science. She and Alice had drawn him out once. They could do so again.

Accordingly, she set Alice to a task that afternoon, and by four they were out on the lawn in front of the Grange with a skeptical Ivy.

Dovecote Dale never ceased to delight Emma. After the lifeless stone walls of London, everything looked vibrant, from the grasses stretching across the fields, to the stream tumbling over stones on its way down the dale, to the trees edging the hills. The London buildings had towered over her. The hills and peaks made London seem pitifully small. In London, the mists had been tainted with sulfur from the many coal fires. Here they clung to the river, cool and moist and smelling of summer. London sounded of the rattle of tack from the carriages and lorries, the shout of the street vendor. Here she was greeted each morning by the coo of the dove.

Even with a leaden sky that threatened rain, there was something clean and bright about the dale. The beauty around them was one more thing she wanted Nicholas to appreciate, and this experiment of hers should help.

"Hold it up, like this," Emma instructed Ivy, lifting the maid's arms where she cradled a lopsided kite.

Alice was fairly bouncing in her leather half boots, her cotton day dress covered in a fitted pelisse of a violet that matched her eyes. Her velvet-covered bonnet wrapped her dark curls and dwarfed her face.

"Will it really fly?" she asked, gaze on the cloth they had latched to a frame built with kindling from the kitchen fire.

Emma had never flown a kite. She had never been to a park in London big enough to fly a kite unless she had been walking as chaperone to the Frederic19kses' daughters. Certainly those girls would have turned up their noses at the idea of such a childlike pursuit. But Emma had read about kites, and the principle of their flight seemed easy enough to master.

"It most certainly will," she promised, playing out the twine from the ball they'd borrowed from the gardener. "Let me show you."

She backed away from the kite and cast a glance toward the Grange. She'd chosen a spot directly opposite the windows of Nicholas's study. With the day overcast, she could see into the room easily.

He was at his desk, head still bowed, hand jerking across the page as he scribbled. Books were piled so haphazardly around him she wondered they didn't tumble to the floor. Surely he had a crick in his neck by now. Surely he needed a breath of fresh air. All it required was a little noise to entice him out to join them.

"When I say go, release it," she told Ivy.

Alice clapped her hands, eyes shining.

Emma took off at a run, one hand raising her brown wool skirts above her ankles, the other clinging to the twine. She felt the tug from the kite. "Go!" she shouted.

Alice's squeal of delight told her the kite was airborne.

"Cheer it on, Alice!" she cried, and Alice began calling out to the kite, encouraging it to climb, to soar. Emma's spirits soared with the sound.

She slowed, turned, played out the twine a little more. The kite was actually up in the air, dipping in the gray sky. She beamed at the sight as Alice ran to meet her.

"You did it! You did it!" Already the little girl's hands were reaching for the ball of twine. "Can I do it?"

"Of course." Emma handed her the ball, showed her how to hold the twine firmly. "You see, the wind's caught our kite now. We have to hang on, or it will get away."

Alice sobered. "I won't let it go."

Emma patted her shoulder and released the kite to her control. Alice stood, feet planted on the grass, hands steady, gazed fixed on her charge. Dedication and determination were written in every line of her little body. How could her father fail to appreciate such a sight?

Because he hadn't seen it.

That fact was all too evident as Emma watched him through the glass. Despite the noise outside his window, he hadn't moved from his spot at the cluttered desk. She could imagine the tension in those shoulders, the pressure of the chair at his back. The safety lamp was certainly important, but to the exclusion of all else? She'd thought she'd shown him how delightful his daughter's company could be, how much Alice needed a father. Didn't he care? Was he incapable of caring?

"Oh, no!"

Alice's cry brought her back to the moment. The kite had tumbled. Emma could see the twine strung across the ground and up the side of the Grange. She shook her head. It would have to be the roof, wouldn't it?

"It fell!" Alice cried, dashing up to Emma. "I didn't take care of it!"

Emma bent to put her gaze on a level with the girl's. Already tears were brimming in Alice's eyes.

"I'm sure you took good care of it, Alice," she murmured. "Kites can be willful things. Let's go ask Mr. Charles how to reach the roof. We'll fetch it right down and show it the error of its ways."

Alice caught Emma's hand. "We should be nice to it. It's probably lost and very afraid."

Emma gave her hand a squeeze. "We'll make sure it's brought safely home."

Ivy hurried up to them. "What should I do, miss?" she asked, eyes wide as if she feared she'd be blamed for the kite's loss.

Emma smiled as she straightened. "Please take a message to Sir Nicholas. Tell him his daughter needs his assistance in solving a problem involving the precise calculation of leverage. She'll be waiting for him on the roof."

Nick set down his quill and rubbed his eyes. So many variables made the ratio of space to material difficult to determine. The wick's ability to burn under the right conditions could be affected by the type of oil, the width of the yarn and even the dye used. He'd thought he could apply his knowledge to devise the correct dimensions, but it began to appear that experimentation would be required. That meant he'd need several of the little stockings, perhaps many of them. He'd simply have to conscript Emma.

Charlotte would protest. He could deal with Charlotte. Emma would likely protest, as well. She seemed uncommonly devoted to Alice. Of course, she had proven last night that she could knit while keeping an eye on his daughter. Perhaps it wouldn't be such an imposition. In other circumstances, he thought she might enjoy helping further the cause of science.

Someone scratched at his door, and he called permission to enter before eyeing his crowded sheet again. Perhaps if he eliminated the dye from consideration. It should be possible to procure yarn that had yet to be colored. Certainly some of the Duke of Bellington's tenant farmers had sheep. Perhaps Charlotte would know a way to contact them.

"Excuse me, sir."

He glanced up to find the maid who generally assisted in the nursery standing before him, hands clasped in front of her apron. She had some sort of plant name if he recalled. Daisy? Laurel?

"Yes?" he encouraged when she said nothing.

She bobbed a curtsey, and the compression of her lower lip suggested she was biting it. "Miss Alice has need of you on the roof. Miss Pyrmont said it was a matter of leavening."

"Leavening?" His frown must have been more fierce than he realized, because she scuttled back from the desk. "Do you mean leverage?"

"Very likely, sir." She visibly swallowed. "Will that be all?"

"Yes, thank you." Nick nodded his dismissal, but she was already fleeing. Was it a matter of such importance, then? Had the maid garbled the message more than he'd realized? He went over the pertinent facts again.

Alice. Roof. Leverage.

Had something happened to Alice?

He was on his feet and striding around the desk a second later. Snatching his coat off the chair by the door, he shrugged into it as he headed for the stairs, taking them two at a time. Up through the chamber story, up past the little rooms where his staff lived, to a door at the end of the corridor, a door that stood ajar as if waiting for him.

He had discovered the steep set of stairs that led to the roof when he was a child. The flat expanse of gray tile was covered with chimney pots, like a forest high above the ground. He'd been particularly partial to the corner pointing down the dale, for it had been the perfect place to mount a telescope so he could observe the stars.

He followed that path now and burst through the door onto the roof, looking in all directions for any sight of his daughter. He didn't see her at first, but he heard her. She was sobbing.

The sound cut into him, forced him forward, weaving around the chimney pots, searching. His boots slipped on a puddle, but he managed to keep his feet. The frantic pounding of his heart nearly eclipsed Alice's cries. He came around the last pot and skidded to a stop.

Emma was down on her knees on the tiles, skirts pooled about her, arms around Alice, who was crying against her shoulder, her bonnet fallen behind her. Nick strode to their sides, knelt as well, lay a hand on the silk of his daughter's hair.

"What's happened, Alice? Are you hurt?"

Emma's head came up, and she stared at him. "Oh, Nicholas, you're here."

An obvious observation. Surely she'd been the one to call for him. Did she think he'd refuse to come? Did she think him a monster that he'd be immune to his daughter's pain?

Apparently Alice did, for she looked equally surprised by his presence. Then she wrapped her arms around his neck and buried her face in his cravat.

"Oh, Papa, I killed it!"

"Oh, darling, it wasn't your fault!" Emma assured her, patting her back, her own face stricken.

What on earth was going on? Nick gently pulled his daughter's arms off his neck and drew her back so he could look at her. The dust from the roof had merged with her tears to form dark tracks down her cheeks. But he could see no sign of injury, no laboring of her breath.

He glanced at Emma. What he had taken for concern seemed to be dissipating, as if his presence had brought her comfort, as well. Her hair was coming free from the braid in which she usually kept it, creating a nimbus of pale gold around her face. She didn't seem physically hurt either.

"Emma," he said, "perhaps you'd be so good as to explain why I should find you and Alice on the roof."

Her voice trembled just the slightest, suggesting she was as distraught as Alice, but there was that light in her eyes again, as if even on a gray day they were capable of sparkling.

"I fear we've had a mishap," she said. "It seems Alice's kite was introduced rather abruptly to a chimney pot, and the two did not agree." She nodded to a heap of cloth lying nearby.

A kite? Alice was sobbing about a kite? He'd left his calculations for a kite?

"I killed it, Papa," Alice said with a sniff. "It got away, and it died."

Nick drew a deep breath as he released her and stood. "Kites are not alive, Alice. You didn't kill it."

By her frown, he could tell she didn't believe him. Why should she? She must have seen the thing soar as easily as a bird. She was too young to understand the difference. And the kite appeared to be as important to her as his calculations were to him.

Nick managed a smile for her sake. "Let me take a look. There may be a way to save it."

"Oh, Papa!" Now her eyes were shining, full of faith in him. And he knew in that moment that he would do whatever was necessary to save the silly kite.

He went to the jumble of materials, lifted them gingerly. The struts were inferior pieces of wood, rough, uneven. Under the strain of flight, they had snapped and poked through the fabric. The twine was a tangled mess. In short, the thing was a loss.

"Ah, yes," he said, tucking it under his arm. "A simple matter. We'll have it put right by dinner."

Alice rushed to hug him, further squashing the kite against him. But it was Emma that held him captive.

Her eyes were pooling with moisture, as if his gesture had touched her. Her hands were pressed together and up against her lips, as if to thank the Lord. It was the look of complete approval, of supreme appreciation. More, it spoke of something he hadn't known he could recognize.

Love.

Something poked at him inside, whispered that such a look was dangerous. Love was messy, unpredictable. Love had a way of interfering. Love meant compromising, ceding another point of view. He wasn't good at that. The reactions of his parents had suggested as much. His inability to see Ann's illness before it was too late had proved the point. The very thought of the tender emotion made him consider thrusting the kite at Alice and dashing for the safety of his laboratory.

But it was just a kite. Making it fit for its purpose did

not mean he was pledging himself to anyone. He could fix it for his daughter, and if fixing the kite pleased Emma as well, that was all to the good. He'd need her help in his experiments, after all. He had no other reason to wish to see her smile at him like that again.

Or so he assured himself as he escorted her and Alice back to the safety of the Grange.

Chapter Twelve

Emma's heart was swelling as she watched Nicholas help Alice down the stairs, the mangled kite tucked under his arm. Her foster father and brothers would never have taken such care of a makeshift kite. If they'd found her crying over it, they'd either have laughed at her for taking the thing so seriously or scolded her for wasting precious time. Precious time, ha! What was precious was spending time with Alice. Surely Nicholas was beginning to understand that.

He escorted them all the way back to the nursery. Alice ran to the table. "Come on, Papa! Let's fix it now."

"I fear it will take more than the work of a moment, Alice," he said. "Let me see what I can do and return it to you." He bowed to his daughter, then to the doll propped up on the chair next to hers. "And a very pleasant day to you, too, Lady Chamomile."

Alice gave him an approving nod. "You can stay for a biscuit, Papa."

The hope in her voice touched Emma. But if Nicholas felt a similar longing, he didn't show it. "Not right now, Alice, but thank you. Emma, may I have a word?" He nodded toward the door, and Emma moved to join him.

"Will she be all right?" he murmured in the doorway, gaze on Alice where she was telling her doll about their adventure.

"Most likely," Emma assured him. "So long as you keep your promise."

He inclined his head "I'll do my best. But I will hold you to your promise, as well." His gaze met hers, dark, probing, as if he would learn her deepest secrets.

Emma licked her lips. "Promise?"

"To help me with my experiment."

His experiment. Of course. Always it came back to that. Her smile felt stiff. "Certainly, sir. I'd be delighted to help, so long as it doesn't affect my other duties."

He nodded and excused himself, but she wasn't sure he'd actually agreed with her. Well, if he thought she was going to put his work before Alice, he had better recalculate.

She smiled to herself as she helped Alice out of her pelisse and half boots and into slippers for the evening. What would her foster brothers think if they saw how bold she had become, telling the master the error of his ways! She had never dared argue with Mr. Fredericks. None of them had. She still remembered the first time Jerym, the oldest of her foster brothers, had talked back.

Jerym had been ten when they'd all been sent to live with the Frederickses and already big for his age. He'd been assigned footman duties, fetching and carrying for the household from before dawn until after the family had retired for the evening. One night Mr. Fredericks had finished in his laboratory late, leaving a simmering batch of materials that stank.

"See that you clean that up before you go to bed, boy," he'd ordered Jerym.

"I wouldn't know how, sir," he'd sneered. "Me being a stupid orphan boy and all."

The blow from the back of Fredericks's hand had dislodged a tooth; the fall had strained a muscle in his leg. Emma hadn't known how to save the tooth when her foster brother had limped into the attic room he shared with the other boys that night. Little Barty had come to fetch her. She'd cried to see the bloody hole in Jerym's mouth.

His grin had still been cocky. "It's all right, Emma," he'd said. "I was never all that good-looking to begin with. One less tooth isn't going to hurt matters."

The memory now pulled the smile from her face. They had all suffered under Mr. Fredericks. Boys eager for love and approval had become sullen, fearful or resigned. She'd been the only one to escape when she'd reached her majority at twenty-one. If only her foster brothers had left, as well! They had ended up believing Mr. Fredericks that life anywhere else would only be worse. She wished she knew how to prove otherwise, but not everyone was cut out for service, and certainly Mr. Fredericks would never have given them any kind of reference to obtain another position.

I know You can reach them, Lord. Help them find a better way!

She had hoped the kite would take first priority that evening with Nicholas, but his calculations must have proved too tempting because dinner arrived with no further sign of him. Emma shook her head as she sat at the table with Alice. What would it take to get through to the man? She clasped her hands and said the blessing, then began serving up the ragout of lamb Mrs. Jennings had sent up with fresh-baked bread and butter.

As if she knew Emma was fuming inside, Alice

reached out to pat her hand. "It's all right that Papa didn't come, Nanny," she said, little face serious. "He must be still working on our kite."

Emma smiled at her. "I'm sure you're right, Alice. I was just hoping your father could join us for dinner."

Alice gave a gusty sigh. "Me, too." She glanced at Emma through her thick lashes. "I wanted to play more games with him tonight. I'm good at games."

"Yes, you are," Emma agreed, smile deepening.

Alice appeared about to say something more, but she looked up, and her face brightened. "Papa!"

Emma stiffened, then pasted on a smile and turned for the doorway, as well. Nicholas was striding toward them, but the look on his angular features was more determined than welcoming. In his arms he held a kite. Unlike the kite Emma and Alice had made, this one was constructed of a blue fabric bowed over its struts. Emma wouldn't have been surprised to find that every angle had been precisely calculated.

Alice slipped out of her chair with a cry and ran to meet him.

He stopped just short of the table to avoid a collision. "Good evening, Alice, Emma," he said with a nod. "I believe the kite is ready for its next flight."

Alice bounced on the balls of her feet. "Can I have it?"

"In a moment." He bent to show it to her. "I made a few changes," he explained as she gazed longingly at it. "See the wood here? Mr. Wilson, our head gardener, located it for me. It's willow, light and supple, less likely to snap. And Mrs. Jennings supplied a few more rags for the tail. That ought to help keep it away from chimney pots."

"Oh, Papa!" Alice said breathlessly. "It's beautiful!" She grabbed his hand. "Let's go try it now!"

He chuckled but didn't allow her to tug him toward the door. "I'm afraid we'll have to wait at least until tomorrow. That's no wind for one thing, and for another I need to talk to Emma."

While she knew it was too late to go fly a kite, Emma still wasn't willing to let him retreat again so soon. Perhaps if she kept him talking, she might think of another way to connect him with Alice that evening.

"Come finish your dinner, then, Alice," Emma said, patting the seat. As Alice hurried back to the table, Emma turned to Nicholas. "And what did you wish of me, sir?"

He set the kite on one of the chairs and fished in his waistcoat pocket to draw out a scrap of parchment which he offered to Emma. Easy enough to take it, but easy was too good for him. She eyed the paper, then returned her gaze to his, brows raised in question.

Alice wiggled into her seat. "What is it, Papa?"

"My specifications for a very special wick to use in my lamp," he replied, gaze on Emma's. "I need your nanny to create something to these precise dimensions."

Emma laughed despite herself. "I fear you have never knitted," she said. "It may not be so precise an art." Still, she took the paper and began to review the numbers on it.

"Then you can't do it?"

His disappointment shouted from every syllable. Glancing up, she saw that his mouth had sagged. So had his shoulders. Odd. She'd never known even her foster father to put so much hope into his work.

"I didn't say it was impossible," Emma hedged,

glancing down at the numbers again. "Simply taxing. Do these dimensions have any tolerance?"

His fingers were tapping at his thigh again, a tattoo that had a distinctly militant air. Perhaps the movement helped him think. There were times she was certain she thought better with her knitting needles moving in her fingers.

"Perhaps an eighth of an inch in either direction," he said.

Emma clucked her tongue. "You set a high standard, sir. How many of these will you need?"

He rocked to the heels of his boots and back. "A dozen to start."

A dozen? That might take her a few hours. Very likely she could work on the things in the evenings while Alice played with Lady Chamomile, but she'd have preferred to spend her time reading with the little girl. If Nicholas wanted that much of her time, it was only right that he give his daughter the same amount.

"And have you the appropriate yarn available?" she asked, making sure that Alice was eating her dinner.

"Charlotte assures me she can supply your every need," he replied, taking a step back from the table as if the matter was settled. "Now, if you'll excuse me."

Oh, no. She was not about to let him get away. If he'd been so busy with the kite and his calculations, he likely had foregone dinner, as well. Food had helped them once. Why not try again?

"But I have questions about your dimensions," she said, pushing out one of the chairs with her foot. "Why don't you sit and help me understand?"

He returned to sit with a sigh, as if resigned to his fate. "Very well. What more do you need to know?"

Emma lifted the lid of the tureen, which was still

half full, and let the savory aroma of the ragout waft toward him. By the flare of his nostrils, she knew he'd caught the scent. He leaned closer.

"An interesting set of dimensions," she said, giving the ladle a stir. "However did you devise them?"

He scooted the chair closer to the table. "It was a matter of fuel and oxygen, just as you surmised. Would you have any extra of that?"

"Oh, I'm certain we have a bowl around here somewhere," Emma said. She rose to go fetch one from the cupboard. "So am I making the fuel?"

"Its conduit, to be sure," he said.

"Bread, Papa?" Alice asked, offering him the basket.

He smiled at her, and she glowed. "Thank you, Alice." He selected a piece and took up the knife from beside the pat of butter to begin spreading the creamy yellow on the bread.

"So I'm making the wick," Emma said, returning to the table with a porcelain bowl. She began ladling the ragout into it.

"Exactly," he said, watching her. Indeed, his gaze made her aware of every movement, every breath. When she handed him the bowl, her fingers were trembling.

"Thank you," he said, and she wasn't sure whether it was merely the food he meant. As if he realized the tension in the air as well, he dropped his gaze to his bowl and continued his explanation.

"I believe by varying the width and length of the material, I can keep the lamp burning brightly enough to shed sufficient light but not so hot as to ignite the flammable air."

"How interesting," Emma said, pouring him a glass of lemonade. She followed with one for herself and kept her fingers against the cool of the glass.

"What's flammable air?" Alice asked.

He spent the next bit explaining the gas to Alice as they ate their ragout. Emma took a deep breath before sipping at her lemonade. Why had his glance so discomposed her? A brief moment in his company, and she was nearly giddy. She tried to focus on his words, the way he carefully defined the terms and used examples Alice would understand. But her gaze seemed to be fixed on his lips, moving slowly, surely.

She turned her head, smiled at Alice. That was where her mind should be, on this dear little girl. Alice was nodding earnestly, listening to everything her father said. Emma was certain she'd be hearing some of those phrases coming off the child's lips in the next few days. Alice soaked up knowledge just as she soaked up her father's attentions. Emma knew the same longing. How lovely to talk over dinner with a husband, her children at her side! To share confidences, hopes, dreams. To work together to make those dreams reality.

But not with Nicholas Rotherford. Even if she convinced him of the joys of spending time with Alice, he would not be the man for her. He was too cold, too calculating. He would never understand her dreams, and they could never be as important to him as his own. She would do what she'd come to do—be Alice Rotherford's nanny. Nothing more. She tipped back the glass and drained it.

Nick was surprised to find his bowl and glass empty. He'd only intended to remain in the nursery a few minutes to hand Emma her instructions and deliver the kite. He hadn't expected to prose on like an Eton don over lectures.

But Alice was an appreciative audience, and Emma

was an interested one. Dinner was surprisingly pleasant taken with the two of them. He was quite satisfied that he'd insisted on the matter with Charlotte.

But now there was work to be done. He needed to modify the lamp he'd devised to better fit the wicks Emma would be knitting. He should double-check the oil he meant to use, ensure that it contained no impurities that might affect the burning. He set down his spoon and rose.

"Thank you for dinner, Alice, Emma. When may I expect to see the fruit of your labors?"

Alice giggled. "Silly Papa! Nanny doesn't have fruit. Trees have fruit."

Emma smiled, and he felt the oddest sensation in his stomach, as if a muscle was spasming but far more pleasant.

"Ah, but your father expects me to bear fruit, too, Alice," she said. "Little white fruits made of wool." She turned her smile on him and that sensation intensified. Was this what people meant when they spoke of butterflies in the stomach? His seemed an uncommonly large variety and rather determined.

"To answer your questions," she said, "I believe I could complete six of the items a few days after I receive the yarn."

He felt his own face tightening. "A few days?"

Her smile seemed tighter as well, and the butterflies in his stomach appeared to have fluttered away.

"I'm afraid so," she replied. "My other duties must take precedence."

Nick was ready to argue. Oh, he had no doubt that her duties with Alice were important, but surely someone else could be found to help his daughter so that Emma had time to knit. But a movement in the doorway caught his eye, and he realized that Charlotte had arrived.

"Did I hear something about your duties, Miss Pyrmont?" she asked, moving into the room with that skirt-swinging walk of hers. He wondered that they needed anyone to clean the floors the way Charlotte was forever sweeping about.

"Sir Nicholas asked me to help him with his work," Emma explained, rising, as well.

Charlotte shook her head. "Really, Nicholas, must you conscript my staff? What a very good thing that I've hired another then."

For a moment he thought she meant that she'd hired another nanny. This time his stomach dipped, so low that he thought it might reach his knees, if that were possible. But the man following Charlotte through the door could not have been meant to raise children. He was tall, with shoulders that seemed too broad and a neck that seemed too short. With his close-cropped hair and bulging nose, he looked more like a pugilist than a footman. When he gave Nick a hesitant smile, Nick saw that his right incisor was missing, leaving a gap on one side of his mouth.

"This is Mr. Jerym Jones," Charlotte said to the room at large. "He will be assisting Miss Pyrmont in the nursery. I understand they knew each other in a previous post, so I'm sure they'll get along quite well."

Charlotte seemed confident in her pronouncement, as she usually was. For once, his sister-in-law's timing was perfect. Emma already had too much work seeing to Alice and keeping the nursery, and having some help would allow her to construct his wicks. And if she'd known the man before, his unconventional looks would likely not concern her.

But it was obvious that something about the new footman concerned Emma. Her face had lost nearly all its usual warm color, and she fell back into her seat as if the air was suddenly too thin to breathe.

Why such a reaction?

Immediately his mind began sorting the available data. Charlotte had said Emma had known the man previously, which would have to have been in London. Nick had considered the possibility that Emma had left London after some difficulty. Was this man the problem? Had he offended her, accosted her? If so, Nick would order him from the grounds this very minute.

He felt his shoulders rising, his eyes narrowing at the fellow, whose smile slipped off his face.

Nick turned to Emma. "Is there a problem?" he asked.

Emma's mouth worked, but no words came out. Nick returned his glower to the new footman.

Jones didn't quail under it. Indeed, there was almost a challenge in those gray eyes.

"I surely hope there's no problem, sir," he said respectfully enough. "My previous employer turned me out without a proper reference. Mrs. Dunworthy was kind to accept my application."

Charlotte managed a smile, but her gaze now focused on Nick.

"Yes, Mrs. Dunworthy has been considerably kind of late," Nick replied. That was odd enough. He knew Charlotte peppered each new staff member so thoroughly he wondered how they managed to find anyone willing to serve. Now she'd hired this Jerym Jones without having so much as a reference for his previous work.

"I merely know an exceptional staff member when I see one," Charlotte said, raising her chin. "But if you need further details, Nicholas, I can provide them."

"No need," Emma said, hands suddenly busy with the lid of the tureen. "Mr. Jones always gave good service in our previous post. I'm sure he'll do as well here."

The new footman nodded, sandy hair catching the light. "That I will."

"Excellent," Charlotte said. "If that's settled, I need your opinion on a matter, Nicholas. Miss Pyrmont, I leave you to acquaint Jones with the specifics of his post. I'll be back later to kiss you good-night, Alice. Now come along, Nicholas."

Another time Nick would have refused. He had never much liked being told how to behave. But he had questions for his sister-in-law, so he let the matter slide. Still, he paused before following her out the door.

Emma's head remained bowed, her capable hands moving as she tidied up the dinner table and stacked the dirty dishes on the tray. He would have thought it was the most important matter she would undertake all day, but he knew better.

"If you have any trouble, Miss Pyrmont," he said, "I want you to bring the matter directly to me. Do you understand?"

She glanced up and nodded solemnly. "Yes, Sir Nicholas. And thank you for your kindness. But I can take care of matters myself."

He could only hope she was right. But he vowed to keep an eye on the new footman, just in case.

Chapter Thirteen

Emma waited until Nicholas and Mrs. Dunworthy had left the room before turning to her foster brother.

Jerym grinned at her, showing his missing tooth to advantage. "Mr. Fredericks sends his regards."

Emma felt sick. When she'd first seen Jerym in the doorway, she'd feared this very thing—that, despite his tale of woe to Mrs. Dunworthy, he'd come on behalf of their foster father. Emma wasn't about to acknowledge that relationship in front of Alice, who was watching them, her eyes large and expectant.

She held up one finger to stop Jerym from continuing. "Not another word from you, sir. You have a position, and I expect you to fulfill it."

He shrugged. "I'm certain we can come to an agreement."

Did he think she'd be so delighted to see him she'd do his tasks for him? Or that she'd cower before him like she used to cower before Mr. Fredericks? Best to disabuse either notion now. She pointed to Alice's bedchamber. "No need for an agreement. You are to prepare the fire in Miss Rotherford's room, bring up fresh water from the kitchen and take back the dinner tray as you go."

That wiped the smile from his face. "No one said you were to be my supervisor."

"I'm the nanny, you're the footman," Emma replied tartly. "Who do you think orders your day? Now, hop to it!"

As soon as the words left her mouth, she regretted them. They were too much like Mr. Fredericks's favorite orders. As if her foster brother thought so as well, his shoulders went up and his mouth tightened. Still, he snapped a nod and went about the work she had set him.

She wanted to feel sympathy for him. But truly, the work she'd set out for him was expected of any footman. She couldn't favor him simply because he was her foster brother. Besides, if he had cut his ties to their foster father, then he should be glad for an honest position and willing to work hard to keep it. And if he was still doing Samuel Fredericks's bidding, he would get no mercy from her.

"Lady Chamomile doesn't like him," Alice announced.

"Lady Chamomile is a very wise person," Emma replied, returning to her seat. "But we'll need to become better acquainted with Mr. Jones before we make any decisions on whether we like him."

She had the opportunity to question her foster brother further after she and Ivy had settled Alice for bed. Jerym was cleaning up the nursery, and the maid kept casting glances at his tall form out the open doorway of Alice's bedchamber. Emma sent her back to help finish the kitchen work, which earned her a sigh from Ivy.

Emma returned to the nursery to find her foster

brother putting away Alice's toys in ill-disguised annoyance.

"Set those down a moment, and come talk to me," Emma said, going to sit in the rocking chair by the fire.

"Oh, but I couldn't shirk such an important duty," Jerym sneered.

Emma pointed to the chair opposite her, the one Alice usually perched on. "Sit."

Jerym let the blocks fall with a clatter and bowed. "Yes, your majesty, queen of the nursery." He took one look at Alice's padded chair and leaned against the mantel instead, crossing his arms over his chest and stretching the shoulders of his blue coat.

"Why are you here?" Emma asked.

He kept his head high. "My previous master discharged me without a reference. I heard you were working here and thought you might vouch for me."

Emma applauded quietly. "Excellent recitation. I always thought you'd do well on the stage."

He snorted, but he dropped his arms. "It's a poor story. That tight-faced housekeeper must be dim to believe it."

"Not dim," Emma assured him, thinking back to her dealings with Mrs. Dunworthy. "But perhaps too willing to trust when something meets her needs in other ways. You and I don't have that problem. We know trust must be earned. Now, tell me the truth."

He glanced at the door to Alice's room and leaned closer. The firelight danced in his smoky gray eyes. "Mr. Fredericks is none too sure of your employer, or you for that matter. He thought you might be telling tales."

Emma wanted to scoot closer to the fire, anything

to remove the chill that came over her. But she refused to let Jerym see the least sign of her distress.

"And what if I were telling people how I'd spent my life before now?" she replied. "I doubt any stories from me would affect him. You know many would say I was the fool for walking away. After all, I had a home, good food, decent clothes and an offer of marriage."

"Does seem a shame to waste," Jerym said, glancing around the nursery. He leaned back, nudged the fender a little straighter with one foot. "Wouldn't you rather be a wife with your own home than a servant in someone else's?"

"I'd rather be a servant than a slave," Emma countered. "That's all I was to Mr. Fredericks, and I can't believe it would have been any different with the man he ordered me to marry. At least here, I'm paid for my work, and I can leave any time I like."

"Lucky you," Jerym muttered, and this time there was no scorn in his voice.

Something tightened inside her. They'd all been orphans once, abandoned in the foundling home with no one willing to raise them. Samuel Fredericks with his ample girth, broad smile and friendly voice had seemed a Godsend. And even if they had known his true nature, they couldn't have refused. Orphaned children didn't get to pick and choose who adopted them, where they went to live.

But adults did.

"You don't have to obey his orders," Emma said. "You can break away, start your own life."

Jerym waved around the nursery. "Be king of all this, you mean? Fetch and carry and scrape and bow for pennies and what, a half day off once a month? The kick out the door if I'm old or injured? No, thank you. I'll take my chances with Mr. Fredericks."

"Then you might as well leave now," Emma scolded. "I haven't said anything that would embarrass him. You have nothing to report."

Jerym straightened away from the fire to tower over her. "That's not his concern. He wants to know what you told Rotherford about his studies."

His glower was meant to intimidate her. It had worked on the younger boys once. Then they'd all learned there was someone far more powerful they had to fear.

Now Emma rose as well, gaze meeting Jerym's in challenge. "*His* studies? I promise you, there is nothing he's doing that is so very innovative. Sir Nicholas is miles ahead of him."

"Is he now?" She could hear the calculation in her foster brother's voice. "What line is he pursuing?"

"Nothing that need concern you," Emma said, hands on her hips. "Or Mr. Fredericks. Leave now, Jerym. You'll only make trouble for yourself if you stay."

He narrowed his eyes and lowered his head to meet her gaze. "It's you who should worry about making trouble, Emma. I could tell Mrs. Dunworthy all about you."

Oh, but he'd learned well. Fortunately, so had she.

"She already knows," Emma retorted. "I told her about my connection to Mr. Fredericks when I took the job. She knows about me running away from an unwanted marriage, about being an orphan. You have nothing to hold over me, Jerym."

He frowned, straightening. "If she knows all that, why would she accept my Banbury tale about us working together at another house?"

"Perhaps she assumed you meant Mr. Fredericks's," Emma said, dropping her hands. "I told her I'd worked there overseeing the children. It was only the truth. I might not have been paid, but I took care of his daughters."

"And us, too," Jerym agreed. He smiled then, his first true smile since he'd walked in the door. "We've missed you, Emma. Little Mother, Frank used to call you. I wasn't sure Barty would ever let go of your hand. He sends his love."

Emma couldn't help smiling, too, remembering her youngest foster brother. He'd been Alice's age when they'd all gone to live with the Frederickses. Of any of them, he'd seemed to need love and assurance the most. If her actions had given him that, she was glad.

"And Frank?" she asked.

Jerym's gaze fell. "He's not up to talking right now. There was another accident in the laboratory."

Emma felt the familiar tightening in her stomach. "Bad?"

Jerym shrugged. "He mistook a direction and ended up splashed with some chemicals."

Mistook a direction. That was Jerym's way of saying Frank hadn't followed Mr. Fredericks's instructions fast enough or accurately enough and had been doused with the mixture as a punishment. Her scar ached as she remembered.

"Hands or feet this time?" she asked, almost afraid to know the answer.

"Neither." Jerym's voice was tight. "Peeled the skin right off his face, and I'm none too sure about his right eye."

Anger surged up inside her. "You see! You have to

leave him, Jerym, all three of you. He doesn't care about you. He'll kill you all!"

"Hush!" Jerym grabbed her arms and held her still as if even the movement of her hand would bring their foster father down upon them. "It's food and clothes, a roof over our heads and easy work, most days. Who else would take us on?"

"Mrs. Dunworthy," Emma protested. "She hired you with no more reference than a word from her nanny. There must be others like her, willing to overlook our circumstances. Good people, kind people, ready to give us a chance."

Jerym released her. "Good old Emma, always the dreamer. You seem to have found a nice place here, but don't think it will be the same for the rest of us." He tweaked her cheek, and she jerked away. "We don't have pale gold hair and a winsome smile. Barty's got a hump in his back from carrying things when he was too young. Frank won't be turning any heads after this accident, unless it's to look away in revulsion. No house will hire us to mind the babies or do anything else for that matter."

She didn't want him to be right. Outer beauty wasn't what was important. It was a person's heart that mattered. And she knew their hearts—Barty with his shy laugh and clever hands, always trying to please; Frank with his quick calculations, ready to get the job done; even Jerym, looking for the easiest, fastest way to reach a goal. They were men with potential, with capabilities. Someone besides her had to see that!

You must see it, Lord. You made them. Surely there's a place in this world for them better than with Samuel Fredericks!

"I think you're wrong," Emma told him. "You may

not like being servants, but there's honest work to be done. Better than what you have now."

"Maybe," he said, but she could see he didn't believe her.

"So what will you do?" Emma challenged. "I won't have you spying on Sir Nicholas."

Jerym raised his thin brows. "Won't? That's a strong word, Miss Pyrmont."

Emma held her ground. "Won't, Mr. Jones. I'll tell Mrs. Dunworthy why you're here. I'll tell Sir Nicholas."

He puffed out a sigh. "Mr. Fredericks won't like that."

Emma patted his arm. "Ah, but he'll be angry with me, and I'll be over a hundred miles away."

"Won't stop him from taking it out on those closest."

She nearly shuddered. He was right there. She had to give him something to report that wouldn't get him into trouble.

"Just tell him the truth," she advised. "Sir Nicholas is examining the problem from a material perspective and seems to have exhausted his knowledge for now. He is no closer to a solution than Mr. Fredericks was when I helped with his research. That should satisfy our foster father for the moment."

Jerym nodded and went to retrieve the building blocks. "I'll be gone in the morning, then. And I wish you luck, Emma. It would be nice to think that you at least found a place to call home."

Emma went to put a hand on his arm, heart hurting. "You could, too, Jerym. I know it. Think about what I said."

"I will." He shot her a smile. "Now, if you'll excuse me, Miss Pyrmont, I really should see to my duties. It's the least I can do after all you've done for me."

* * *

Nick strode back to the nursery later that night. Charlotte's questions had been no more pressing than his preference for beef or lamb at dinner. It was almost as if she wanted to leave Emma alone with this new footman. Nick knew he couldn't rest until he was certain all was well in the nursery.

But when he entered, he found the space empty. A quick glance in his daughter's room showed her sleeping soundly, Lady Chamomile pressed against her. Emma must have gone to bed, as well.

For a moment, he considered confirming that hypothesis, but peeking into her bedchamber, even to ensure her safety, seemed wrong. Instead, he located Charles, who was putting out the corridor lamps for the night.

"Watch the new footman," he ordered. "Tell me if you see anything of concern."

Charles snapped a nod. "Very good, Sir Nicholas."

Hoping he'd done enough to protect Emma, Nick retired for the night. He woke the next morning determined to put his calculations to the test. All he needed were those wicks from Emma. If the new footman did his job well, surely she would find time to create the wicks to his specifications. He shaved and dressed and went to the kitchen to forestall the delivery of his breakfast.

"I intend to eat with Alice this morning," he told Mrs. Jennings, who beamed at him so broadly he could only wonder how wide a person's face would stretch. Was it a matter of emotion or muscle? Another question for his colleague studying anatomy.

Alice was equally delighted to see him, if the squeal she uttered was any indication. Had anyone determined the exact pitch that would shatter crystal? Alice had very nearly reached it, he thought, and he was rather proud of his daughter.

Emma seemed nearly as pleased to see him, further assuaging his concerns about the new footman. She was dressed in the blue gown again this morning, the one that made her eyes match the color of the sky over the peaks on a summer's day like today. He felt his spirits lifting just by looking at her. But then she lifted the lid on the porcelain bowl in front of her where she sat at the nursery table, and he was dismayed to see the familiar gray and lumpy material inside.

"Porridge," she explained as if she'd noticed his look.

"It's yummy, Papa," Alice assured him. "Lady Chamomile loves it."

"Perhaps I should give her my share," Nick said, but he sat beside Alice and bowed his head as his daughter said grace.

"Bless us, dear Lord, and these Thy gifts which we are about to receive through Christ our Lord, amen."

Glancing up into her smile, Nick felt himself blessed indeed. *Perhaps You'll accept my thanks, Lord, if nothing else.*

The next thing he knew, Emma had set a china bowl in front of him. The porridge was surrounded by fresh cream, the color making the meal look more golden, as well. Two currants had been positioned equal distance from the edges of the bowl near the top, and a dribble of honey had been curved around near the bottom. Was he mad to see a face grinning back at him?

"Stir it all together, Papa," Alice encouraged him, "like this." Her tongue poking out of her mouth, she swirled her silver spoon around the mixture.

Nick did as she instructed and discovered more currants waiting under the surface along with nut meats and something more. A bite of the fruit confirmed it.

"Where did Mrs. Jennings get the pineapple?" he asked.

"I believe she said it's from the Duke of Bellington's conservatory," Emma replied, spooning up some of her own porridge. "She received it from the cook there. All the servants in the great houses of the dale seem to talk to each other."

He could imagine they would have many tales to tell. The Earl of Danning was an avid angler, he knew, escaping to the river whenever he could. Bell rusticated here when Parliament was out of session. And John Lord Hascot seemed to have found his calling with his riding horses.

"Alice thought to try the kite again tomorrow," Emma ventured across from him, "if there's a bit of wind. Perhaps you'd like to demonstrate."

Nick was surprised to see how quickly the porridge was disappearing from his bowl. "Another time, perhaps. I hope to work on my experiment then." He glanced up at Emma. "How is the new footman coming along?"

She was busy spooning up another bite of porridge. Funny that it would take such an act of concentration.

"Lady Chamomile doesn't like him," Alice said.

Nick raised a brow and turned his gaze to his daughter. Alice wore a deep frown, and he felt a sense of foreboding. "And why would Lady Chamomile take him in dislike?"

"He says mean things to Nanny," she replied, giving her porridge a whack with her spoon for emphasis.

Emma's cheeks were darkening again. "He was

merely questioning me about his role in the household, Alice. No harm done."

No harm done? That made it sound as if harm had been attempted. Nick raised his head. "If he questioned your authority in the nursery, he's a poor choice for the position," he said, feeling the prick of anger. How dare the man raise his voice or say anything unkind to Emma! "I'll speak to him myself."

"No need," she said with a cheery smile that did not seem commensurate with the tone of their conversation. "He is no longer employed here."

"What?" Nick set down his spoon. "Do you mean he quit?"

She nodded before dropping her gaze to her breakfast once more. "It seems he decided he liked London better after all. I understand he gave his notice this morning."

Nick shook his head. "Unacceptable. You require a footman."

"Alice and I will be fine," Emma replied with a look toward his daughter.

"Untrue," he returned. "You should not be doing heavy lifting as required by carrying these trays, bringing up the coal for the fire. And I need your help."

"Oh, yes, my help." She smiled to herself as if she'd somehow forgotten all about his request. "I'm afraid the wicks will have to wait."

He'd thought her outspoken from the moment they'd met, but such a bald refusal seemed too much even for Emma. "If you have no need for a footman, why are you unable to complete my commission?" he challenged.

"Because," she said, rising, "today is Sunday. We have services this morning and more contemplative pursuits planned for the rest of the day."

"Your knitting seemed entirely contemplative," he insisted, standing, as well.

"It can be," she acknowledged. "But not when I'm trying to help Alice. I'm sure her spiritual development must be just as important to you."

Certainly it was. In fact, given his inability to address the Lord since his fall from grace with the Royal Society, someone else must be Alice's example. "Very well," he agreed. "Tomorrow then."

"Ah, but tomorrow I fear I will be too busy showing Alice how to fly a kite properly. We wouldn't want another mishap with a chimney pot, particularly after you worked so hard to fix our construction."

"No, we would not," Alice agreed, scraping the bottom of her bowl.

"Besides," Emma continued before Nick could protest, "there is quite a science behind kite flying, you know—air pressure, weight, balance."

She glanced at him, and he could see that the light was back in her eyes, as if a candle was flickering in the blue-green. As before, he found the look challenging, demanding a response from him. And it suddenly struck him that the minx was manipulating him!

"Now see here, Emma," he said, drawing himself up once more. "You cannot barter for my time."

She widened her eyes. "Heaven forbid, sir. Besides, I hardly think you'd want to be a father who had to be cozened into spending time with his daughter."

Was that her game? The hypothesis encouraged additional examination. Her appearance outside his door, always with Alice in tow and with fanfare that required his involvement. The changes in his food that had landed him in the nursery for breakfast twice now.

Even his idea that they join him for dinner. She was trying to keep him from his work.

For Alice's sake.

How could he fault her? It was her job to see to Alice, and he could tell that she took the position seriously. She sincerely cared for his daughter. If she coveted Nick's time for the girl, she was only trying to help. She didn't know the harm that might befall others if he wasn't successful. Very likely she saw the construction of his wicks as another of his mad whims.

But if being with Alice would win him his wicks, he was all for it.

"Very well, Emma," he said. "This afternoon I will attempt some contemplation myself, and tomorrow Alice and I will go fly a kite. But I expect a reward for our efforts."

Chapter Fourteen

Sunday passed peacefully enough, but Emma had to smile when Nicholas presented himself in the nursery at precisely one minute after noon on Monday.

"Oh, is it afternoon?" she asked, rising from the table as Alice ran to meet him. "Wherever did the time go?"

"It passed more slowly than usual from what I can tell," he said, and she hoped some of his impatience had to do with boredom. Being with Alice was seldom boring.

She made sure her charge was dressed for the weather, for the day was cooler with a breeze blowing, and then sent her and Nicholas out to the yard, watching from the window until she sighted them below. Alice looked so tiny from this vantage point, but Emma could see that Nicholas was holding her hand and moving at her pace.

Thank You, Lord, for this opportunity. Help me make the most of it.

She started knitting, sitting in her rocking chair by the fire, but she finished two of the wicks to Nicholas's specifications within the hour. It would have taken even less time if she hadn't ripped out her stitches twice trying to make sure she had the right gauge. Still, she tarried in the nursery awhile longer, hoping to give Alice as many moments as possible with her father.

After all, Emma might not get another chance to further her goals for Alice. It was clear Nicholas was on to Emma's game. She'd seen the moment his brow had cleared yesterday, his eyes brightened as if he'd made a tremendous discovery. He knew she was trying to manipulate him, even if it was for an excellent cause.

At least he'd been a good sport about it, she mused as she descended the stairs for the ground floor, her gray wool cloak draped about her day dress. Her foster father would never have entertained her foster brothers or his own daughters for that matter to give her time to complete some task he'd set her. He would have expected his work to come first and for Emma to still get everything else done, even if it cost her sleep.

Nicholas seemed to care. Oh, he was insistent on hiring a footman to give Emma time to assist him with his experiments. But he'd suggested the footman before he'd ever known she could be useful to him. He'd noticed she needed support, and he'd taken steps to meet her needs. It was more than most people had ever done for her.

The kite was high in the sky when she located Nicholas and Alice on the side lawn. The day was overcast again, silvery mists rising into the sky. A breeze brought cool air down from the peaks, making Emma glad for her cloak.

Alice was standing on one edge of the lawn, holding on to the kite string. Her little head was tilted so far back to watch the kite that her bonnet had fallen behind her and clung to her neck by its blue satin ribbons.

Nicholas stood nearby, arms crossed over his chest, coattails flaring in the breeze.

He was watching just as fixedly, but his gaze was on Alice. The pride and love in his look froze Emma's movements.

That was the look of the father she'd dreamed might exist, the father she'd hoped Nicholas might become.

That was the look of a man she could love.

A man she could love?

As if the Lord had other thoughts, there came a deep boom, like a giant hammer striking far beneath the ground. The earth shook, and Emma nearly lost her balance. Above her, the glass rattled in the windowpanes.

"Papa!" Alice cried, dropping the string and running for him.

Nicholas caught her and pulled her close, but his gaze had turned to the hill behind his laboratory. The kite came plummeting down into the woods.

Emma knew where her duty lay. She hurried to Nicholas and Alice, put a hand on Alice's shoulder. "What was that?"

"Very likely an explosion at the mine," Nicholas said, and she marveled that he could state the matter so calmly. "They'll require help." His gaze jerked back to her, dark, unfathomable. "Are you opposed to nursing, Emma?"

"No, not at all," she assured him. Did he expect so many injuries then, perhaps even deaths? She felt a tremor run through her and knew it wasn't from an explosion this time.

"Take Alice to her aunt, then," he instructed, prying Alice's fingers from his legs. "Tell Mrs. Dunworthy to send me every servant who can be counted on to think logically in a crisis. I'll see Mr. Dobbins about a wagon."

Who was this dispassionate person? Where was the caring man she'd seen moments ago? Emma took Alice's hands into her own, gave them a squeeze of encouragement. "At once, Sir Nicholas."

"Papa?" Alice piped up, raising her head to meet his gaze before Emma led her away. "What about my kite?"

His face was set. "I can make you another kite, Alice. Right now, there are other papas in great danger, perhaps injured. I need to see to them first. Please go with your nanny. I'll return to you when I can."

A very short time later, Emma found herself up on the box of the estate wagon, the coachman Mr. Dobbins at the reins beside her. Charles, the footman, the grooms and gardeners and Dorcus huddled in the bed, along with all the blankets, sheets and water buckets Mrs. Jennings could muster on short notice. Already Dorcus was working with Charles to cut the sheets into the bandages they expected to need on arrival.

Nicholas rode beside them up the wide dirt track that wound toward the top of the hill. His face remained set, his gaze narrowed on their way as the mists darkened around them. Emma's stomach turned as she considered what they might find ahead.

Please, Lord, protect the miners. Bring everyone out safe.

The scene was as bad as she'd feared. The mine lay just over the hill from the Grange. Several tunnels had been dug into the hillside, the gaping holes held open by solid timbers. The undergrowth around them was coated with black dust. Between the tunnels, the ground had been scraped flat, crossed with the tracks of horses, mules and wheeled vehicles. Carts and wheelbarrows lay scattered on their sides, the black rocks spilling in piles from them as if a child had overturned them all in a fit of pique.

On either side of the clearing lay winches and smoking towers. From snippets of conversation she'd overheard between her foster father and his colleagues, Emma was certain the machinery was used to force clean air deep underground and pump out the water that frequently flooded the tunnels as well as to refine the coal before it was shipped to market.

Below them, she could see the road continuing down to a village where the miners must live. Already women and children had come out of their homes and the church to gaze up the hill. She didn't have to see their faces to know how frightened and worried they must be for their fathers, husbands and brothers.

Several men were crowded around the entrance to one of the tunnels. A man wearing a coat and trousers that had once been rather fine, Emma thought, separated himself from them to come striding to meet Nicholas and the wagon.

"Mr. Jennings," Nicholas greeted him, reining in his white horse and nodding to Mr. Dobbins to bring the wagon to a halt, as well. "I see there's been an incident. How can we help?"

Jennings? Related to Mrs. Jennings perhaps? Emma struggled to see the cook's warm welcome in the man's haggard face. She thought his hair might have been blond under the black of the coal, his eyes blue within their reddened rims.

"Good of you to come, Sir Nicholas," he said. "We can use all the help we can get. We've no news of deaths yet, thank God, but we've a dozen injured and one still trapped."

"Take me to him," Nicholas ordered. Though his face was calm, his horse turned in an agitated circle as if sensing that the philosopher's underlying emotions were darker than he displayed.

As Charles helped Emma down from the wagon, Nicholas rode to the mine entrance nearest them where the others were clustered. Rocks had fallen, obscuring the mouth of the tunnel, and a beam stuck up at an odd angle. With no one to direct her, Emma wandered closer.

"We can hear him tapping at the other side," Mr. Jennings, who must have been the mine manager, was saying. "But we can't reach him. Even with your men, there's no way to lift this rubble without risking another cave-in."

Emma could see Nicholas's fingers tapping at his thigh. "Have you any more beams waiting to be used?" he asked Jennings.

"Several," the mine manager confessed, eyeing him. "What did you have in mind?"

Nicholas pointed in rapid succession. "Place one of the larger rocks here and here and put the beams on top. Wedge one end under those two rocks. You should be able to lift the mass enough to allow the miner to escape, or someone to go in after him."

Mr. Jennings stared a moment as if trying to picture the arrangement, then shouted at his waiting men. "Well? You heard him! Fetch me those beams!"

As workers scattered in all directions, Nicholas dismounted. "I've brought Miss Pyrmont and Miss Turner to help with the injured."

Jennings turned and looked surprised to see Emma

standing nearby. He managed a weary smile as he gave her a nod. "Prettiest sight they'll have seen in some time. They'll be overjoyed to see you, miss."

Emma blushed. "How can I help, Mr. Jennings?"

In answer, he waved her toward a narrow metal-sided building a few yards away from the mine entrance. "We put the worst of them in my office. But they're a grim sight. Perhaps we should leave it to the fellows."

She could see Nicholas frowning. Did he think she would quail, as well? How was he to know she'd spent more than her share of time nursing others who had been injured? She could not tell him about her foster brothers, or the man who had repeatedly injured them, all in the name of scientific progress.

"I'll be fine, Mr. Jennings," she assured the mine manager. "I'll get Miss Turner, and we'll see what can be done."

The mine manager nodded his thanks, but Nicolas moved to her side, hands on the reins. "Thank you, Emma," he murmured. "If you're certain you'll be all right, I'll see what else can be done."

Emma smiled at him. "We'll be fine."

He nodded as well and set out. Emma went to find Dorcus.

The maid was less sanguine about their usefulness when she carried pails of water behind Emma to the manager's office.

"Eh!" she exclaimed, dropping one of the buckets with a splash to cover her nose with her sleeve.

A dozen men sat or lay on the rough plank floor of the office, their backs braced against the metal siding. Their faces were black with coal dust, their clothes blacker. Some clutched at legs, cradled arms. The pain and bewilderment on their faces were all too familiar to her.

Worse were the two boys waiting with them. At first, Emma thought they must be sons come running to help their fathers. But the amount of coal dust on their clothes and their injuries told her they actually worked in the mine. By his size, she'd have guessed one was no more than six.

Nicholas had been right—boys did need his safety lamp.

She handed Dorcus a piece of the sheet the maid had torn apart on the way up the hill. "The first thing we do is clean off this filth. Then we'll know what else needs to be done."

Dorcus looked doubtful, but she wet the rag in the bucket and knelt by the first man to swab off his face. Emma went to work on the littlest boy.

Within a half hour, she had determined that most of them had minor injuries—scrapes, cuts, bruises. She was thankful none showed burns, for those were still the most difficult for her to treat with equanimity, given her own history. One of the remaining six men seemed to have a concussion, for he was disoriented and dizzy. Barty had had one once after Mr. Fredericks had broken a glass over his head to see if the material could withstand such an impact. That was one of the few times she'd been able to prevail on her foster father to send for the physician.

How long would it take for the physician to reach them this time? Were her skills enough to help these men, these boys?

I never thought I'd be grateful for learning to nurse, Lord, but thank You for the knowledge. I believe I finally understand why Nicholas is so determined to solve the problem of firedamp. Show me how I can help.

Outside, Nick watched as the last miner was dragged to safety. The man's friends clasped his hand, touched his shoulder, murmured words of encouragement as he attempted to stand and took a few hesitant steps. A cheer went up when he gave them all a toothy grin.

A shame Nick couldn't save more lives as easily.

"Well done, Sir Nicholas," Jennings said, trotting toward him. "I received word the physician is on his way now. Will you join me in my office?"

Nick nodded and fell into step beside him.

He wasn't sure what to expect when he entered the single-roomed building. Certainly Emma had proven efficient and effective when dealing with Alice. But caring for grown men, perhaps badly injured, was something else. Charlotte would have recoiled in horror. Ann would have fainted long since. His mother had never so much as visited the mine.

The sight inside brought him to a stop. Instead of filthy, distraught faces and moans of pain, a dozen men and two lads leaned against the walls, calling encouragement to the maid Dorcus, who was sitting next to a fellow with a dazed expression on his face and singing at the top of her lungs.

"That's it," Emma was saying, waving her hands as if directing a choir. "Don't let him fall asleep."

Jennings strode forward, and his men lapsed into silence, heads ducking in respect. He knelt beside the maid, who snapped shut her mouth, as well. One look in his man's eyes, and he raised his head to Emma. "Concussion, eh? Nicely done, Miss Pyrmont. Carry on, Miss Turner."

Dorcus grinned at him and launched into the next verse.

"It was all I could think of," Emma said to the mine manager over the noise. "I knew we couldn't let him close his eyes."

"You're right there." He nodded at the others. "What do you make of the rest of them?"

Emma glanced at Nick as if begging his pardon. "Most have only scrapes and bruises. We've cleaned them up as best we can, but a cake of soap or two would not be remiss."

Jennings chuckled. "Always a challenge at a coal mine."

"What about those two?" Nick asked, noticing two men with their legs straight out in front of them strapped to what looked like pieces of wood as rough as the struts on the first version of Alice's kite.

"Broken legs," Emma reported with a sympathetic look to the men. "They'll need more than my skill to set. The best I could do was splint them with sheeting and some kindling from the hearth to immobilize them. I'm more concerned about them." She nodded at three men near the back of the office. Nick could hear their labored breathing from where he stood.

"Coal dust," Jennings said with cheerful disregard of his men's condition. "It can eat through the lungs. This explosion didn't help."

Emma's face tightened. "Can nothing be done?"

Jennings shrugged. "Part of the job, miss. You take the dangers with the pay. If you'll excuse me a moment, I'll go see if the physician has arrived yet."

Emma nodded, and he left the office. She stepped closer to Nick. "Is everyone all right out there?"

"Yes," Nick told her. "We were able to rescue the last man."

She smiled at him. "Because of your quick thinking. I'm sure he's grateful."

Nick would have been more grateful for a moment alone. The office walls seemed to be closing in, the air becoming more dense. Any second and his lungs would be laboring, too.

"Now," she continued, "if only science had an answer for their breathing problems."

Nick felt as if she'd stuck him with a pin. "Science isn't God, Emma," he managed to say, "and even He seems to have some limitations. Excuse me."

He shoved out of the office, strode away from the confining walls, the choking memories. Each step brought him closer to the road home, farther from his nightmares. He put his back to the mine works, stared back down over the hill to where the chimneys of the Grange were just visible.

It took no great hypothesis to determine the source of his reaction. The explosion reminded him of his previous failure. And the miners' raspy breathing reminded him of his worst failure, for it was too much like Ann's painful gasps. The sound still made him break into a cold sweat.

How had he missed her illness until it was too late?

How had he so badly miscalculated to cost four people their lives?

Why couldn't he find a solution to this problem of firedamp?

Was he good for nothing?

"Nicholas."

Emma had followed him from the office. Now she put a hand on his arm, her touch gentle, calming. "They will all survive," she assured him. "I know they're thankful you brought help."

Nick drew a breath. "Thank you, Emma. But you must realize it was the least I could do."

"More than most," she insisted. "I've heard Lord Hascot's horse farm isn't far from here, yet he didn't send aid. Servants at the duke's estate must have noticed something, as well."

"They wouldn't know the source," Nick said, feeling compelled to exonerate people he respected. "The mine's been on my family's land since my father was a boy. But our profit should not be another man's pain."

Her eyes widened. "You blame yourself for this? It was an accident!"

"An accident I could have prevented, if I'd just finished that lamp!"

Her mouth was a stern line. "Nonsense. As you pointed out, science cannot solve every problem."

"And I suspect you will tell me God can," he retorted.

Her smile was sad. "I could tell you that. I believe it. But I don't think you'll believe me."

He wanted to. For the first time in a long time, he wanted to believe in a God who gave His children everything they needed. Who forgave His children when they made mistakes, even ones for which forgiveness was otherwise impossible.

"Pardon my mood, Emma," he said. "I'm simply troubled to think men might have died, working to supply my family with income we scarcely need, providing our nation with fuel we all too often squander."

"I suspect they would say they were only doing their jobs," Emma returned. "That they were thankful for a way to support their families. Though I was troubled to see the children. Is it necessary for them to work?"

He'd actually envied the boys when he'd been younger—crawling around in the tunnels, exploring places no one had ever seen before. Then he'd learned how hard they worked, and he'd pitied them.

"Sometimes they are the support of their families," Nick explained. "A father dies, a mother is left with many children and no source of income. I don't like it, but I respect the boys for trying to help."

By the way her eyes dipped at the corners, he surmised that she was not comforted by the fact. "Your lamp will be the greater help," she said. "I must be satisfied with that, for now."

If she dreamed of finding a way to improve the conditions for those boys, he would not stop her. He had insisted on humane treatment at his mine, with limited hours and clean food and water. He knew conditions at other mines were far worse.

Nick took her hand, bowed over it. "Thank you for your concern, Emma, and for always seeing what might be instead of what is before us. You would make a marvelous natural philosopher."

He had intended it as a great compliment to her logical mind, her optimism. She snatched back her hand as if he had burned her.

"Thank you," she said, but her tone implied she was more hurt than pleased by his praise. "Now let's see what more we can do to help."

Chapter Fifteen

It was late when they returned to the Grange. The physician had arrived at the mine and dealt with the injured men, thanking Emma and Dorcus for their help. Mr. Jennings, the mine manager, also thanked them as well as Nicholas.

"I'm working on a new design," Emma heard Nicholas say to the man. "I hope you'll be willing to give it a try when it's ready."

"And can you tell me this one will work?" he'd challenged, shoulders stiffening.

"I won't bring it to you until I've tested it myself," Nicholas promised as Emma and Dorcus settled into the wagon with the rest of the Grange staff.

"I'll see if I can find you a volunteer," Jennings had said, turning away. "But I won't make any of them risk their lives again."

Emma thought she understood his concerns. The men and boys had talked with shudders about the firedamp that choked their breath, set off explosions with no warning. Now they used candles or open-flame lamps that were no proof against the stuff. They needed that safety lamp.

She was beginning to understand why Nicholas was so set on fixing the problem. While her foster father and his colleagues saw developing the safety lamp as an interesting pursuit, and a potentially lucrative one, he took the matter more personally. This was his land; these were his people. He wanted them to be safe. Having seen the consequences of an explosion firsthand, so did she.

Still, she felt sorry for Alice, for it was clear by the set look on Nicholas's face that it would be all work from here on out.

Perhaps that was why, after checking that Ivy had settled Alice in bed and someone had returned the kite to the nursery, Emma took the wicks downstairs and knocked on the door of his study.

When no one answered, she tried again. Had he gone to the laboratory after such a long day? By all accounts, he'd had little sleep the previous few nights. Had he passed out in exhaustion? Concerned, she turned the handle and opened the door.

The room looked different here than it had when she'd been peering through the window the other day. Between the fire and the lamp on the desk, the space was warm and bright. Crowded open bookshelves covered every swath of wall, from floor to ceiling, even over the tops of doorways and around the fireplace. More books were piled on side tables, with a particularly large stack beside the sofa that faced the fire.

Leather folios, parchment spilling from them, were stacked just as haphazardly on the end of the sofa, the floor and most of all the desk. Indeed, there was only a tiny space in the center of the desk for Nicholas to write.

He was seated there now, head fallen and pillowed by

his arms. His fingers were threaded through the raven strands as if he would pull them out.

Leaving the door open behind her, she tiptoed to his desk and laid the wicks beside him.

He sighed in his sleep, as if even in dreams he struggled to find answers. A shame she couldn't stroke his hair, which looked as smooth as satin, find some way to comfort him. But that was not her right.

So she closed her eyes a moment and helped him the best way she knew how.

Dear Lord, I was wrong about him. He is capable of caring, deeply. He genuinely wants to help those miners. You know the dangers they face better than any of us. Won't You help him find the answer?

The peace that usually accompanied her prayers flowed through her, and she opened her eyes. Nicholas was gazing up at her, as if arrested by the sight.

Emma felt her face heating as she took a step back. "Forgive me. I didn't mean to disturb you."

He flexed his shoulders as if to loosen stiff muscles, but with his coat off, she was suddenly aware of the breadth of those shoulders, the strength in his body.

"Has something happened to Alice?" he asked, rising.

"No, she's fine." Emma found herself retreating further and drew herself to a stop. She had nothing to be ashamed of, no reason to fear. "I finished two of the wicks," she explained. "I thought you would want them."

He stared down at his desk as if noticing the tiny pile of wool for the first time.

"Those should get you started," Emma said. "Now that I know the proper gauge, I can knit others in less than a quarter hour each. It may take longer if you vary the dimensions or the material."

He dropped his hand to finger the wicks. Then he glanced up at her. His eyes were heavy, his face worn. Again she wished she knew how to take some of the burden from him. Surely it was not his task to single-handedly save the world.

That's Your work, Lord! Help him to remember that and lean on You.

"Thank you," he said. Still he didn't move away from the desk. She'd thought surely he'd dash off to his laboratory, wicks clutched in one hand. The accident at the mine had obviously taken a greater toll on him than she'd thought.

She ducked her head so she could meet his downturned gaze again. "You are very welcome. After today, I can't deny your work is needed. I'm sure you'll solve the problem soon."

His fingers closed on her gift. "Not soon enough. Rest assured, I will put these to good use. Could you have two more ready by noon tomorrow, just in case?"

"It would be my pleasure," Emma replied. "I ask one favor in return."

He frowned as if he couldn't quite grasp the meaning of her words, and she knew what she was about to do was right.

"Favor?" he asked.

"Yes." Emma approached him and held out her hand, palm up. "Leave those wicks in my keeping, and get a good night's sleep. I'll return them to you with the others after you've rested."

It was the boldest thing she'd ever done, and he would have been well within his rights as her employer to refuse. He'd have been within his rights to discharge her for such impertinence!

He eyed her a moment, but the finger tapping against his leg told her that his reasoning ability was still functioning. "Do you use such tactics on Alice?" he asked.

Her cheeks felt hot. "When needed. Forgive me, Sir Nicholas. I know you're not a child. But someone must care about your health, especially if you won't."

His smile was grim as he handed her the wicks. "You are a very good judge of character, my dear."

She exhaled a breath she hadn't been aware she was holding and curtsied to him. "Good night, then, Sir Nicholas. Pleasant dreams."

His smile softened. "Dreams, eh? No warnings about bugs and fleas?"

Emma returned his smile. "And where would they possibly find room among all this knowledge?"

He inclined his head. "Good night, Emma, and thank you again."

She turned for the door, but she felt as if invisible hands were tugging her back to his side. She had no reason to stay, less reason to offer to help him, yet she longed to do both.

What must it be like, to have a calling, to have a vision that compelled you to stay up long into the night to achieve it? Of course, her work with Alice took all her time, and she knew she'd be proud to see the girl grow into the woman she could become, if Emma was given that chance. But his work could save the lives of hundreds, earn him the praise of a nation. Small wonder he was so devoted to it.

Just as Mrs. Jennings was devoted to her work. That was evident when Emma stopped by the kitchen in search of some food before retiring. The cook was waiting for her with a tray of cold beef and cheese. "Just rest a moment and catch your breath," Mrs. Jennings said, pulling out the stool by the worktable before going for the teakettle.

"Thank you," Emma said. She climbed onto the stool and reached for a slice of the cheese.

"Was it bad at the mine?" Mrs. Jennings asked, returning to pour Emma a cup of tea. Her face sagged with sorrow, as if she expected the worst.

Emma nodded but managed to swallow her mouthful. "More than a dozen injured, but no one killed, thank God."

"Oh, thank God, indeed," Mrs. Jennings said with a relieved sigh. The dying fire cast shadows on her cheeks. "Such difficult work, coal mining."

"It seems to be dangerous," Emma agreed. "The coal dust, the firedamp, cave-ins. I don't know how they do it, day after day."

"They are only doing their duty," the cook said with a nod of approval. "And bringing home an income for their families."

Her words reminded Emma of what Nicholas had said.

"There was a Mr. Jennings up there, the mine manager," she remembered. "Is he a member of your family?"

"Mr. Jennings's brother Evan's son," Mrs. Jennings said proudly. "He was raised in that mine."

And she'd thought her upbringing difficult. "He's safe," she assured Mrs. Jennings. "And the physician said the others would mend."

The cook blew out a breath. "Thank the Lord for that, as well. Last time I thought poor Sir Nicholas would rip out his heart he felt so responsible."

"But that's not fair!" Emma protested, setting down the cup of tea with a clatter. "He isn't there to direct their work. He can't be held responsible for a pocket of flammable air."

"Flammable air?" Mrs. Jennings wrinkled her nose. "Is that the proper name of the firedamp?"

Emma nodded. There she went again—all but proving she knew more than she should about the matter. "So I've heard."

"Flammable air." The cook rolled the words around on her tongue as if tasting her latest recipe. "Nasty stuff. You're right the master can't be held responsible for when and where it appears. But he blamed himself for the last explosion, that's clear as day. All on account of some calculations that went wrong."

Emma frowned at her. "His calculations?"

Mrs. Jennings shrugged her solid shoulders. "So the papers said. And those other philosophers at the Royal Society thought so, too. A team of them had built a lamp, you see, and they brought it up to our mine to test. But it didn't work properly, and the men who tested it were killed."

Emma pressed her fingers to her lips. She knew the story too well. How her foster father had railed about being accused of negligence in his work.

"They'll not blame me," he'd warned his wife over dinner while Emma had stood along the wall waiting to clear. "They'll not catch Samuel Fredericks in a mistake."

Had he made it look as if Nicholas had made the mistake instead?

"Now then," Mrs. Jennings said, reaching out to pat Emma's free hand where it lay on the worktable. "I've upset you with such talk. Forgive me, my dear. I just wanted you to understand why the master frets about the matter."

She understood. Nicholas blamed himself for the explosion gone wrong, and it seemed the Royal Society blamed him, as well. It was possible they were right, and he had made a fatal error, but Emma thought it more likely her foster father had made it appear Nicholas had miscalculated to cover his own ineptitude.

Should she tell Nicholas?

There would be no proof. Her foster father would have seen to that. And if she told Nicholas how she knew Samuel Fredericks could be so devious, she'd have to explain how she knew the natural philosopher at all.

If Nicholas realized she'd been raised by the man who'd ruined him, she could lose her post, be forced to leave Alice. She'd see the admiration she so appreciated in his gaze turn to disgust. Yet how could she watch him suffer when she suspected he was innocent?

Emma pushed the tray away, appetite forgotten, then slid from the stool. "Thank you for the food, Mrs. Jennings. It seems I'm not as hungry as I thought. I'll be down in the morning for Alice's tray."

"All right, dearie," Mrs. Jennings said, capable hands reaching for the tray. "Sleep well."

Emma returned the sentiment, but she doubted she'd sleep at all that night.

Nick actually managed a full night's sleep for once and woke ready for the day. With Emma's wicks, he had an opportunity to right his wrongs. He wasn't about to waste another moment. She must have anticipated his need, for Charles delivered the set of four wicks as Nick was shaving. Cramming one of Mrs. Jennings's cinnamon biscuits into his mouth, he took everything to his laboratory and went to work.

Because he had only four of the wicks, he decided to forego chemical testing. Instead, he set to work inserting one of the wicks into the lamp he'd designed. He had several sets of the chimneys and bases, but he expected some revision might be needed for the device to work at peak efficiency and safety. This version would give him at least an indication of whether his approach was valid.

He had already constructed a test box—a metal frame with glass inserts, all wrapped in metal shielding that could be lowered on hinges as needed to monitor the processes inside. A bladder of flammable air gathered from a nearby swamp was connected on one side, with a bladder of oxygen on the other so he could vary the atmosphere. Now he lit his lamp and placed it inside the box, sealing the device inside. Turning the valve, he let in the flammable air.

The box shook with the explosion, and he heard the tinkle of breaking glass.

Nick shut off the gas and sagged, but only for a moment. No! He knew he was on to something. The problem must lie in the oil.

Someone tapped at his door, but he told them to leave. He wasn't ready for company, had no need for food. He had work to do.

He spent the rest of the day varying the mixture. He replaced the glass in his box time and again. His eyes were soon gritty. His back ached from stooping over his worktable. With one wick left, he calculated and recalculated, forward and back to make sure he'd forgotten nothing.

Dawn was breaking by the time he thought he had it

right. His hands shook just the slightest as he fashioned another lamp and inserted Emma's wick. Carefully, he placed the device into the box and sealed it in. Hand on the valve to release the flammable air, he stopped.

Alice and Emma believed in going to their Lord in times of trouble. Indeed, when he'd woken from dozing at his desk the other evening to find Emma standing near him with her eyes closed, he'd known what she'd been doing. She'd been praying, for him, her devotion shining through her upturned face. The look called to him, reminded him of a devotion he'd forsaken.

Perhaps it was time he prayed for himself. Perhaps, knowing Nick's intentions, the Lord would listen to him again. He took a deep breath, closed his eyes.

Lord, I haven't come to You in months. I've felt unworthy of Your notice, and I know I don't deserve Your help now. But those men at the mine, the men working in mines all over England, I know You care about them. Show me how to solve this problem. Let my work be right this time.

Swallowing his fears, he turned the handle and let in the gas.

The box sat silently.

Nick stared at it. Could it be? Was the wick burning or had it sputtered out? Carefully, he lowered the metal shield on one side of the box. Behind the glass, the lamp glowed in a sea of flammable air.

He'd done it.

Thank You, Lord! It worked!

"Nicholas?"

He hadn't heard the knock on the door. Hadn't noticed the tap of her feet on the marble floor. All he knew was that Emma was beside him, more wicks in one hand. The slight frown on her pretty face suggested she wasn't sure he heard her even now.

"It works," he said, and the truth of the statement made his voice unsteady. He waved an equally unsteady hand at the box. "Your wick worked, Emma. We did it."

Her lips pursed in an *O* of wonder, eyes widening. It was the most natural thing in the world to bend his head and kiss her.

Joy and thanksgiving for having solved the problem had motivated him. A quick kiss to celebrate, to thank her, to acknowledge their shared victory had seemed only right.

But one touch to her lips, and he found he had no wish to stop. He still felt joy, but now it was the joy of having her beside him and the thanksgiving was for what she'd done to make his life complete. His arms came about her, sheltering her, holding her. He could feel her returning the kiss, trembling against him. It was as if she touched his very soul.

He'd faced the problem he had been attempting to solve. Now it seemed he faced another.

What should he do about these feelings for Emma?

Chapter Sixteen

Emma had dreamed of her first kiss, how it might feel, how it might make her feel. But the touch of Nicholas's lips to hers, the warmth of his embrace, was like nothing she'd ever imagined. Suddenly, for one moment, she was the most important person in the world, the center of his universe. Every sense, every breath, every heartbeat seemed attuned to his. She returned the kiss with equal measures of joy and thanksgiving.

He raised his head and gazed at her, smile tremulous, as if he'd felt the same way: happy and astonished and buoyant. Then he blinked, released her and took a step back.

"Forgive me," he said, straightening his cravat as if to erase any trace of their closeness.

It seemed the natural philosopher found it difficult to accept his own feelings. Emma smiled at him. "No need to apologize."

He ran his hand back through his hair, setting the raven strands on end. "I'm quite certain Society would disagree with you."

Very likely, but she couldn't care. Every part of her

seemed to be tingling. "You didn't take advantage," Emma assured him. "I'm not protesting."

"Perhaps you should be," he murmured, dropping his gaze.

No! She would not see shame in their kiss. She admired him, and she thought he admired her. There was nothing evil in it.

"That's quite enough," she said and was pleased to see his gaze come up as if she'd given him hope. "You were overjoyed that your lamp worked. It was only logical that such joy find expression." She bent to retrieve the wicks she'd dropped and closed the distance between them. "Perhaps you'd care to explain how you solved the problem."

She thought surely the appeal to process would bring him around, perhaps result in a quarter hour's lecture on the properties of flammable air, which would give them both time to regain some semblance of normal. She'd attempted to contact him yesterday, to tell him her suspicions about her foster father's role in his downfall. He'd refused to answer her knocks. She'd brought the extra wicks this time, hoping they might help make amends for what she had to tell him. She was only relieved that his success made her confession unnecessary. Surely if he'd proved his work, the other natural philosophers would realize that the original mistake had not been his.

But instead of discussing his work, he laid a hand on her cheek, warm, sweet. "Thank you," he said, and she wasn't sure if he meant for the kiss or the fact that she hadn't made more of it.

She knew she shouldn't refine on his touch. She'd clearly been correct in her assessment—the kiss had arisen from the emotions of the moment. Very likely he would have kissed Mrs. Dunworthy had she been standing beside him at the time of his triumph. And she certainly had no wish to marry someone with the emotional range of a teaspoon.

But, oh, for one moment, how she wished it were otherwise!

So she stood and listened as he explained the steps he'd undertaken to allow the lamp to burn in the presence of firedamp without igniting the gas. She tucked away her feelings, reminded herself that she had a purpose and a place for which to be thankful. Told herself not to wish for the moon.

"Would you be willing to call me Nick?"

Emma blinked. Had she imagined that? But no. He was looking at her, gaze serious.

"I beg your pardon?" Emma said.

He smiled. "I suppose it is unusual, but ours seems to be an unusual companionship. I simply thought it would be more efficient and edifying if you were to call me by my given name as I call you by yours."

Efficient? She saved a couple syllables. But he had also called the approach edifying, so apparently hearing her say a form of his given name pleased him at some level. Besides, she'd already been calling him Nicholas in her mind.

"Nick," she said, trying it out, and one corner of his mouth turned up. "Somehow that doesn't seem serious enough for a man of your studious pursuits."

He shrugged. "As I said, it's efficient."

She couldn't help her chuckle. "Very well, then. Nick it is. But not in front of the other servants. I wouldn't want them to think you favored me."

He took her hand, cradled it in his own, the touch pushing her emotions into the forefront once more.

"That's truer than you know," he said. "How could I not think of you kindly? You were the one who pointed me in the right direction. You were the one to create the proper wick. I could not have done this without you, Emma. Thank you."

Tears heated her eyes. Such a little thing, being appreciated—just two little words. Yet it seemed as if she'd waited her whole life to hear them said so warmly. "I'm glad I could help," she murmured.

"And Alice," he continued. "I understand what you've been trying to do there, as well. You've brought me closer to my daughter."

One tear trickled down her cheek. "She is the sweetest child. I knew it wouldn't take much for you to realize that."

"I only wish I knew a way to repay you," he said.

The answer popped into her mind as clearly as a scene from one of her beloved books: her and Nick standing before an altar, the vicar giving them his blessing. The vision stunned her. Marriage? Was that where he was leading? She reached for the comfort of her dreams of the perfect family, but the lines of that dream were blurring. It seemed she yearned to hear something more than appreciation for a job well done. Three little words:

I love you.

Nick dropped her hand. "I will think on it." He glanced at his lamp, still brightly burning inside the sturdy box. "Indeed, it seems I may have some time to consider other matters if this proves reliable. I'll have to complete a few more trials, send word to Mr. Jennings to arrange the test."

She'd lost him. Already his body was turning, his

hands drifting toward his notes on the table before him. She felt the tears coming faster.

"It was no trouble," she managed to say with a calm voice that betrayed nothing of her feelings. She set the wicks on the worktable. "I was simply doing my job."

When he only nodded, she turned and fled.

Outside the laboratory, she pressed her back against the sun-warmed stone of the building, gasped in a breath. Why had she thought he meant anything more than appreciation? Why had she thought he might be different? She'd set out to court him for Alice, and time would only tell if she had succeeded. She shouldn't expect him to lay his heart at her feet, as well. Much as she'd dreamed, much as she'd hoped, no one else ever had.

The men and women who had worked in the orphan asylum had been caring but always with the lingering sense that the children were there because of some deficiency. Even the name of the place—the Asylum for Deserted Orphans—suggested they were unwanted. If they had been loved—by a remaining parent, by a family member, by a friend of the family—they would never have been forced into the asylum. It had been as if, having no one to love them, they must therefore be unlovable.

Certainly Mr. Fredericks and his wife had gone out of their way to reinforce the notion with Emma and her foster bothers. They were less than the daughters born to the Fredericks; they were less than the few servants they had all but replaced. Certainly they were less important than the instruments and chemicals with which Mr. Fredericks conducted his experiments.

Her foster brothers' behavior stemmed from the belief. If they were unlovable, better to stay with Mr. Fredericks and be fed than to take their chances on the rest of the world.

But she'd rejected the notion. She wasn't unlovable. She was clever and kind. If no one had managed to notice, the worse luck them. Besides, she knew someone who loved her. She couldn't remember her parents well, but she remembered the stories they'd told about a loving God, who cared for all His children, regardless of family, face or fortune. A God who had died to see her saved. Knowing she had His love, why did she suddenly crave another?

Emma took a deep breath and wiped her tears on her sleeve. *Thank You, Lord, for loving me when it seemed no one else would. I know You have a plan for my future. Perhaps the perfect husband is waiting at my next post. Perhaps I'm not supposed to marry at all. Help me see Your path and follow, wherever You lead.*

Nick had a great deal to do to test the lamp. He started by making detailed instructions for the blacksmith and the glassblower and dispatching them to the nearest town for the pieces he'd need to test the lamp in the mine. He sent word to the house to take dinner without him. Then he compiled his notes into a single leather binder, suitable for review by others. He could hardly wait to prove that his ideas worked in a natural setting. Surely that would redeem him in the eyes of the Royal Society. In fact, he'd write to them that very day and invite them to send a representative to the mine to observe the test.

But first he needed to confirm a date. He could have written to Mr. Jennings as well, but he felt as if his body and mind were pushing him to move, to act. So, he had his horse saddled and rode to the mine.

Work had evidently returned to normal since Nick had last visited. Though one tunnel remained blocked, the miners streamed in and out of the others, and black smoke poured from the chimneys. Jennings must have seen him coming, for he met Nick part way and directed him to the mine office, which had also been returned to efficiency.

"I've a working prototype," Nick explained when the two of them were seated on either side of Jennings's squat desk. Nick took some solace in the fact that the surface was nearly as cluttered as the top of his own desk.

Jennings leaned back in his seat. "And I suppose you want to test it. We're still recovering from the last explosion. I don't want another."

"It will work," Nick promised. "I'll carry it into the mine myself."

Jennings raised his brows. "That sure, are you? Very well. What about this Thursday?"

Though Nick's spirits rose at the thought, he shook his head. "Too soon. I'm hoping to bring observers from London."

Jennings chuckled. "You are serious. A week from Thursday, then?"

"Perfect," Nick agreed. He stood and held out his hand. "I appreciate your faith in my work."

"Not so much your work as you," Jennings returned, rising and shaking his hand. "My men are still talking of the way you rode to the rescue after the accident." He dropped Nick's hand with a grin. "And more than one's been dreaming about your Miss Pyrmont unless I miss my guess."

Nick felt himself stiffening and forced himself to relax. Why such a reaction? Emma was a fine woman.

That other men had noticed only proved their intelligence. Yet he still remembered the feel of her in his arms, the warmth of her lips against his. Something about Emma—her encouragement, her challenges, her smile, the light in her changeable eyes—had called to him, from the moment he'd met her.

Still, his admiration of her did not give him the right to kiss her, he reflected as he rode back to the Grange. Certainly admiration didn't account for the joy he'd felt having her in his embrace. In the same circumstances, another woman could well have demanded an offer of marriage. Emma was more pragmatic than that, thank the Lord. Nick had not made a good husband before. He didn't think he had it in him to be a better one now.

Yet the desire to thank her, to show her how much he appreciated her efforts, persisted as he dismounted at the stables and handed the reins to a waiting groom. He seemed to remember his father giving out a gold coin to the staff at Christmas, but waiting six months was hardly satisfying, and he didn't think Emma was motivated by gain.

He wanted something grand, something a woman would enjoy, something that involved Alice as well, and by extension Lady Chamomile. Something that would brighten Emma's day, give her something to remember with pleasure.

Ah, yes.

The idea presented itself with clarity, and he strode toward the house, eager to get to work. To do his plans justice, he'd need some help. Convincing Charlotte might take a little effort, but he thought his best ally lay in another direction.

He headed straight for the kitchen to discuss matters

with Mrs. Jennings. He had no doubt his cook would know exactly how to achieve his ends.

But he couldn't wait to see how Emma liked it.

The next afternoon, Emma was seated in the rocking chair, watching Alice and Lady Chamomile play on the rug before the fire. She'd finished one more of the wicks and had started on another. It very much looked as if Nick would not need them after his success yesterday, but she wanted them to be ready just in case. She was a little disappointed he hadn't joined them for dinner last night or breakfast this morning, but she supposed it was understandable given the circumstances. However, if she hadn't seen him by dinner tonight, she would simply have to think about the next step in her courting campaign.

"Sit up at the table, Lady Chamomile," Alice said. "You are a fine lady. You want to make sure everyone knows it."

Emma smiled. "I think perhaps a lady is known for more than how she sits at a table," she suggested, starting on the next row of the wick.

Alice abandoned her doll to come hang on Emma's leg. "Is she? What else makes a lady?"

"A good heart for one," Emma said, fingers moving. "Kindness toward others, a ready smile to help someone else smile."

"You smile a lot," Alice said.

Emma's smile deepened. "I suppose I do. And why would I not smile being the nanny of such a sweet girl like you?" She bent and rubbed her nose against Alice's.

Alice giggled as she pulled back. "I smile a lot, too."

"Yes, you do," Emma agreed. "And I'm very thankful for that."

"Pardon me."

Emma looked up to find Charles standing in the doorway. Seeing that he had her attention, the footman kept his gaze high, his tread measured as he approached Alice and bent to hold out a silver tray on one gloved hand.

"An invitation for you, Miss Rotherford," he intoned.

Alice's eyes were huge, and her little fingers trembled as she plucked the folded note from the tray. "Thank you."

He straightened with a nod. "I was told to wait for a reply."

Alice stared at the parchment a moment before handing it to Emma. "What does it say?" she whispered.

Emma saw the same hurried scrawl she'd noticed on the notes on Nick's desk, and her heart started to beat faster. Why would he write to the child? Was he going away, perhaps to London to share his discovery?

Please, Lord. Let this be good news for Alice.

She broke the seal and read aloud.

"To Lady Chamomile and her delightful friend, Miss Alice Rotherford, my most sincere greetings. Would you two and your companion, Miss Pyrmont, do me the honor of joining me in the Green Salon for a ball in your honor this afternoon at five? Dinner to follow. Your humble servant, Sir Nicholas Rotherford."

Alice clapped her hands together and jumped up and down. "A ball! Oh, a ball! May we go, Nanny, please?"

"I'm certain we can find the time," Emma said, folding the note carefully. What a wonderful idea! Good for him for thinking of it. Alice would talk of nothing else for weeks.

"Then shall I tell my master you agree?" the footman asked Alice.

Alice stopped cavorting to nod. "Oh, yes, please."

He bowed. "Very good, miss." With a wink to Emma, he made his stately way from the room.

Emma glanced at the clock on the mantel. There was still an hour before they were needed downstairs, but she knew Alice would never be able to sit still. Emma rose and held out her hand. "Well, what are you waiting for, Miss Rotherford? Let's get you and Lady Chamomile ready for a ball."

It took more than a half hour to dress the bouncing Alice in her prettiest gown, a white satin dress with rosebuds embroidered around the hem, neck and puffed sleeves. Ivy arrived to help. Emma left the two of them to dress Lady Chamomile and went to her own room to tidy her hair. She thought she might change into the blue flowered apron gown Mrs. Dunworthy had found for her. It was hardly a ball gown, but it was certainly more appropriate than her brown wool.

But when she entered her room, she found another gown lying on her bed. The skirt and puffed short sleeves were of white crepe, the high bodice of velvet in a violet as deep as Alice's eyes, with similar velvet at the edge of the sleeves. The neck was trimmed in lace. Around the hem and up the front were a line of waves made from bluer chenille. She imagined they must move as she danced.

Danced?

Well, why not dance? She was going to a ball, after all!

"Isn't it beautiful?" Ivy asked, coming into the room. "It was made for Lady Rotherford, only she never had a chance to wear it."

How sad! Emma fingered the soft velvet of the bodice. "Perhaps I shouldn't wear it either then. I wouldn't want to bring up sad memories."

Ivy hurried to join her at the side of the bed. "Oh, please, miss, you must wear it! Mrs. Jennings said she's never seen the master so happy. And you'd set such a good example for Miss Alice."

That ache was rising inside her again. What would it be like, just once, to dress in something so fine, to act like the lady her parents must have hoped she'd be? She knew it was all just a game—she had no expectations that tomorrow would be different. She was generally very happy being Alice's nanny.

But couldn't she pretend to be a princess from one of her books, for one night?

"All right," she told Ivy. "I'll wear it. But you'll have to find me some gloves that will go at least to my elbow." That would cover any sign of her burn.

Ivy nodded eagerly. "Yes, miss! Anything else?"

"Yes," Emma said with a grin, "bring Alice in here while you help me change. I don't want to think about what she and Lady Chamomile can get up to left to their own devices and all this excitement!"

Chapter Seventeen

Emma and Alice stood in the doorway of the Green
Salon at the back of the Grange. She could see why it
wasn't generally used by the family. For one thing, the
room was too long for the current residents to sit com-
fortably and converse. For another, she suspected Nick
might not find it congenial.

The walls were paneled in emerald silk patterned
with scallops of white, like moonlight spearing through
the leaves of a garden. Each wooden beam overhead
and between the silken panels was painted white with
fanciful leaves and flowers weaving their way along
the length. On the mantel of the fireplace, huge vases
held sprays of lavender that perfumed the air. Even the
carpet in the center of the hardwood floor was woven
with curling, leafy fronds of green. The gilded chairs
appeared to be hugging the walls in self-defense.

So much imagination, so little geometric symmetry.
Alice was immediately entranced.

Her aunt looked as if she belonged in the space. Mrs.
Dunworthy was draped along a chaise lounge. Her ball
gown of embroidered net over spring-green satin made
her seem as if she had been planted in the garden. Mr.

Dobbins, who was seated in one corner with his fiddle, looked out of place, particularly dressed in footman's finery.

But more impressive was the gentleman waiting for them in the center of the carpet. Nick wore the black double-breasted cutaway coat of a London gentleman out for the evening. His cravat was elegantly tied, his cream-colored waistcoat shot with gold. The light from the crystal chandelier made his raven hair glow and set the pocket watch peeking from his coat to sparkling. She thought no duke or prince had ever looked better.

At the sight of them, he bowed.

"Ladies. Thank you for accepting my invitation." He held out his hand. "Miss Rotherford, would you favor me with the first dance?"

Alice glanced at Emma as if seeking permission. Emma released her hand and nodded toward her father with a smile. Handing Lady Chamomile to Emma, the girl scampered forward.

Mr. Dobbins began to play, and Nick guided his daughter through the steps. Emma moved along the wall to watch, holding the doll in her arms.

Mrs. Dunworthy rose to join her. "This was his idea, you know," she murmured. "It seems you achieved your goal."

Emma had the same thought. He was so patient, a smile teasing his lips, as he danced a minuet with Alice, that her heart nearly turned over in her chest. But what she couldn't understand was why Mrs. Dunworthy sounded less than pleased by the fact that Nick was finally favoring his daughter.

He brought Alice to their sides after the first dance and handed her to her aunt. "Perhaps you'd care to take a turn, Charlotte?"

"Delighted," Mrs. Dunworthy said with a smile to Alice. "Mr. Dobbins, another minuet, if you please."

"Yes, ma'am," the coachman said and began to play the stately music.

Nick held out his arm. "Would you partner me, Emma?"

Though she'd never taken the floor herself, she'd seen her foster sisters at lessons with a dance master. Surely if Alice could make it through the steps, then so could she. With a grin, she set Lady Chamomile on a nearby chair, put her hand on Nick's arm and let him lead her out.

It was a simple dance, slow, elegant. Alice moved hesitantly with her aunt. Emma was more aware of her hand on Nick's arm, his body moving with hers. She couldn't quite match his step at first, but then she caught sight of Mrs. Dunworthy's slippers as the lady moved beside them. Right together, left-right-left together. Two sets of that combination forward, two back, two right, two left.

Emma raised her head and danced, floating on the music, guided by the assurance of Nick's arm under her fingers. His face remained composed, dignified, but a smile graced his expressive mouth.

She didn't try to look composed. She was having too much fun. The lilt of the music, the swirl of her borrowed crepe skirts against her ankles as she danced, the scent of lavender clinging to the air and the admiration in Nick's gaze all combined to make the salon a place of fantasy, of dreams come true.

But the music faded, the dance ended. Nick bowed, she curtsied, and Alice ran to her, calling her name. The world settled in around them. She had her place, her duties. But Emma knew she would hold the memory of that dance in her heart for a long time.

She danced with Alice for the next song, and Nick partnered his sister-in-law. They moved elegantly to the music, with no hesitation, no uncertainty. But while they were a match in looks and demeanor, Emma couldn't help noticing they seemed remarkably stiff. Each time she glanced their way, Mrs. Dunworthy's gaze was steadfastly away from Nick. And Emma caught no hint of a smile from him.

Emma and Alice had no such trouble, giggling when they misstepped, hurrying to catch up with the more practiced pair. But by the time the dance was over, Emma was panting for breath.

"Another, another!" Alice begged, hopping up and down.

Nick nodded toward the door, where Mrs. Jennings, Charles, Ivy and Dorcus had been watching with grins on their faces. "I fear we have tarried too long. Dinner appears to be ready."

Mrs. Jennings reddened and shooed the maids out into the corridor. The footman clicked his heels together, head high as if he had intended on doing nothing but his duty all along.

"Ladies, Sir Nicholas, dinner is served," he announced.

"Oh." Alice deflated.

Nick took her hand. "We'll hold another ball soon," he promised. "Perhaps Lady Chamomile can be convinced to partner me."

Alice took his hand with a giggle. "Silly Papa. Lady Chamomile doesn't dance. She is a doll."

A doll? *Oh, thank You, Lord, for helping her see the difference between Lady Chamomile and the people who love her.*

"And a delightful one at that," Nick said. "Given that

she cannot eat either, let's go to dinner and retrieve her on our way back upstairs."

Alice seemed to accept that, taking his hand and allowing him to lead her from the room. Emma and Mrs. Dunworthy fell into step behind them.

"I trust you enjoyed the ball," he said to Alice as they started down the corridor for the front of the house.

"Oh, yes," Alice assured him.

He glanced back at Emma with a smile. "Excellent. Perhaps your aunt can locate a dancing master for you and Emma."

Emma laughed. "I think that's your father's way of telling us we need more practice, Alice."

He grinned before facing front again, but Mrs. Dunworthy fanned herself with one gloved hand as if the dancing had winded her, as well. "Emma, is it," she murmured. "Are you certain that's appropriate?"

Emma felt herself coloring. In truth, she hadn't given him permission to use her first name, but surely the rules were a little different between master and servant. The maids here were all called by their first names within the house, and her foster father hadn't bothered to call her foster brothers anything other than "You, boy!"

"I wouldn't know, madam," she said truthfully as they approached the dining room.

Mrs. Dunworthy dropped her hand. "About this dance master, Nicholas," she said, raising her voice. "Alice is a little young. Most girls don't require a dancing master until they are fourteen or fifteen."

"All the more reason for my daughter to be more accomplished," Nick said, and the pride in his voice made Emma's smile return.

"Well," Mrs. Dunworthy said, entering the room

and going to her place at his left as he led Alice to her place at his right, "if you're determined to advance her education, then I expect we'll need to hire a governess, as well."

Emma nearly missed her step as she came around the table. A governess? Once a girl had a governess she had no need for a nanny. Emma had hoped for at least two more years with Alice. If Mrs. Dunworthy hired a governess, would Emma have to leave?

The very thought hurt so much she could barely take her seat at the table. What was wrong with her? She'd known this day would come. Alice was growing physically. A day didn't go by when one of her articles of clothing didn't need to be let out or let down. And she was growing in accomplishments as well—sounding out her letters, playing at the pianoforte, now dancing. Emma didn't want to hand her over to someone else. She wanted to be there to see Alice become the lady she was capable of being.

Just as she wanted to be there to see Nick blossom into the father Alice needed.

Perhaps that was the thought that made Mrs. Jennings's excellent roast so difficult to swallow. When Emma thought of moving to a new household, new children, her losses seemed more important than her gains. She'd miss raising Alice. She'd miss Mrs. Jennings's counsel, Ivy's cheerful help. She'd miss walking in the woods and flying kites with the peaks behind her.

But most of all, she'd miss conversations with Nick, partnering on some activity for Alice, watching his eyes light at the sight of her in his laboratory doorway, hearing him explain the wonders of the world so patiently, so earnestly. She'd miss his reluctant smile, the way he tapped his fingers on his thigh, the touch of his hand, the sweet pressure of his lips on hers.

She felt as if she were leaving a part of herself behind.

How ironic. Mrs. Dunworthy seemed to be right. Emma had succeeded in capturing Nick's heart for his daughter.

And lost her own heart in the process.

Nick leaned back in his chair and smiled at the ladies on either side. Alice had arranged her peas in a precise four-by-four square that boded well for her mathematical abilities if not her artistic pretensions. Charlotte actually seemed in charity with him for once.

And Emma, well Emma had an exceptional amount of liquid in her eyes and a tremble to her smile that suggested she was pleased by his gesture. With his prototype soon to be tested and his notes compiled, he could not imagine a better end to his efforts.

As if Charlotte had read his mind, she raised her glass. "I understand you achieved your goal in your laboratory, Nicholas. Congratulations. To second chances."

"To success," Emma said instead, raising her glass. Alice mimicked her and drank along with the others.

"Thank you," Nick said as he lowered his glass. "But congratulations are premature. The device won't be tested in the mine until next week."

Charlotte shuddered as she set down her glass. "Surely you won't need to take part."

Surely he would. "I already promised Jennings," he replied. "I intend to oversee every aspect. Nothing will go wrong this time."

"I cannot believe those people at the mine will be receptive to trying again," Charlotte said with a curl to her lip. The look suggested contempt, but he wasn't sure whether it was the hardworking miners or his scientific pursuits that Charlotte found beneath her.

"After the recent explosion," Emma put in, "I would think they would be more eager to find a solution."

Nick nodded. Count on Emma to state the matter plainly.

"Indeed," Charlotte said in her usual detached way. "I imagine you have much work ahead of you then, Nicholas."

He nearly chuckled aloud. And count on Charlotte to bring him back to reality. "Actually, I am confident the device is ready. Thanks to Emma's excellent wick, it functions exactly as I had hoped."

"*Emma's* wick?" Charlotte turned her gaze on Emma, who blushed.

Nick would have sworn the emphasis in that sentence should be on the material, not Emma's first name as Charlotte had stated it. "Emma's *wicks,*" he said, deliberately shifting the balance. "She has this talent to construct various items out of loops of yarn. Ingenious."

"I knit," she seemed compelled to explain to Charlotte. "Socks, gloves, that sort of thing. Mrs. Jennings has been supplying me with yarn until you provided Sir Nicholas with undyed wool." She reached for her glass and took a deep swallow. Somehow he didn't think it was thirst that motivated her. Was she trying to avoid further speech?

"She made pretty socks for Lady Chamomile," Alice said with a nod. She selected one of her peas and popped it into her mouth, then frowned as if she noticed she'd destroyed the symmetry of her design.

"From socks for dolls to wicks for safety lamps,"

Charlotte said. "What a very versatile person you are, *Emma*."

Charlotte definitely had some issue with Emma's first name, but he didn't have enough information to determine a reason. "Yes, she is," he said, cutting off a piece of the roast. "We're very fortunate to have her with us. I commend you for recognizing her talent, Charlotte."

He'd thought the compliment might help counter whatever was troubling her. Charlotte merely smiled at him, with no warmth. "Thank you, Nicholas. But you have me quite curious now. I'd very much like to see this device of yours. Perhaps you'd be willing to show me and Alice after dinner."

"Delighted," Nick assured her. "You'll want to come too, Emma. I've made a few adjustments I think you'll find interesting."

Her eyes lit. Something inside him brightened, as well. It seemed a continuous phenomenon when she was near. With Emma at his side, challenges seemed surmountable, his skills sharper. Alice had benefited from the encouragement, as well. His daughter hadn't even questioned his suggestion that they leave Lady Chamomile behind in the Green Salon, when previously she had seemed more dependent on her beloved doll.

What would Alice do if Charlotte hired a governess and they lost Emma?

The very possibility seemed so dire he knew he must find an alternative. So as they finished the second course of apricots and strawberry ice, he put his mind to work on how to keep Emma at the Grange. She'd make an excellent assistant, but he knew too many would consider a man and woman working together alone to be scandalous. He could not see her serving elsewhere in the house. Indeed, the more he thought about it, the less he liked the idea of her serving at all.

But if Emma was neither servant nor staff, there was only one way for her to live in the same house with him. They would have to be family. If he wanted Emma to stay, he'd have to marry her.

"Sir Nicholas," Emma ventured. "Is something wrong?"

Nick blinked. Strawberry ice dripped off his spoon where the implement was poised halfway to his mouth. By the amount dripping, the warmth of the room and the state of remaining ice in the crystal cup in front of him, he'd estimate the spoon had been hanging that way for a good two minutes. Alice was frowning, Emma had her head cocked as if trying to determine what troubled him and Charlotte's mouth was set in an even sterner line than usual.

"Really, Nicholas," she scolded. "Was it too much to ask that you leave your work behind for one evening?"

For once he was glad his work was much on his mind, for if Charlotte had suspected the true direction of his thoughts her ice would probably be dripping, too, from the heat of her temper. She would never understand another woman taking Ann's place in his affections. And he could not tell her that his affections for Ann had been more about compatibility than romance.

Nick lowered the spoon and smiled by way of apology. "Forgive me. When you are all finished, I'd be delighted to show you out to the laboratory."

Charlotte sighed and returned to her ice and a conversation with Alice about the need for gloves when leaving the house or some such matter. Emma offered him a sympathetic smile before taking a bite of an apricot.

He could not ask her to marry him. Though marriage

to him would provide her with benefits—her own home, a reliable income, stability, she would have to give up something she found altogether precious: love. Their discussion in the woods last week had made her opinion plain. She had called love the pinnacle of human achievement. His skills in that area were considerably lacking, fundamentally inferior he felt.

She would never accept a safe, civil arrangement with no expectation of entanglements. And that was all he was capable of.

He had composed his thoughts by the time he led the ladies out to his laboratory after dinner. He would find some other way for Emma to stay with Alice, and he would continue his work. Though he held a conventional lamp to light their way, he had high hopes Mr. Jennings and the other miners would soon have a much safer light to work by. He threw open the door to his laboratory and set about lighting the lamps in the room.

"And where exactly have you hidden this contraption?" Charlotte asked, skirts lifted slightly to keep them from touching the marble floor.

"In the box on the table," Nick explained, finishing with the lights.

He turned to find them all frowning at the worktable. It was the cleanest it had been since he'd moved them all to the Grange.

Entirely too clean.

Nick stumbled forward, touched the scarred and stained surface. The box with his prototype, the binder with his notes, everything to prove what he'd done and how he'd done it, was gone.

Chapter Eighteen

Emma saw the change in Nick. One moment, he was smiling, his brow clear of its occasional furrows of concentration. The next, he had stiffened, and all pleasure had vanished.

"Did you ask someone to clean my laboratory, Charlotte?" he said. The tone was polished, curious, but tension gathered in the room as surely as the poisonous smoke she'd seen the day they'd first met.

"Certainly not," Mrs. Dunworthy declared. "Most of the staff are too afraid to even set foot in the place."

"Someone mastered that fear, then," he said, taking another look around the room as if expecting to find a servant cringing in a corner. "My work is not where I left it."

Emma glanced at the empty space on his worktable. The last she remembered, it had been filled with a large metal box, with the prototype safety lamp burning brightly inside. Now there was no sign of the box or the lamp, and the notes she generally saw scattered about his work area were missing, too.

Mrs. Dunworthy waved a hand to encompass the

crowded space. "And how would you know if you lost something in all this mess?"

"Because I know precisely where I leave things." As if he suspected she doubted him, he pointed to what appeared to be random piles in rapid succession. "That is Davy's alternative design for the lamp from two years ago. Those are my calculations on the properties of iron for use in industry that earned me the knighthood. That, to my sorrow, is what's left of the wool blanket Ann gave me our last Christmas together, and that—" his hand stilled over the yawning space on the worktable "—that is where I left the prototype and my calculations."

Emma's stomach threatened to rebel. No one on the staff, she was certain, would have moved his work. As Mrs. Dunworthy had said, none of them dared to so much as set foot in the laboratory. That's why Emma had had to be the one to rescue him nearly a fortnight ago. They would never have taken his work.

But she was afraid she knew who would.

What if Jerym hadn't left the area as he'd promised? Her foster brother could easily have slipped into the laboratory while everyone was busy at Alice's ball. With a fast team of horses and a good carriage, he could be miles away by now.

"It seems we have a thief," Mrs. Dunworthy said, voice gone colder than the night. "We'll search the house, Nicholas. The creature can't have gone far. Miss Pyrmont, return Alice to the nursery. I fear our pleasant evening is over."

Emma hesitated. She had no proof it was Jerym, no evidence he was anywhere in the area. Should she say something? Only Nick's previous success had kept her from mentioning her foster father the other day. But if she was wrong about Jerym, she would have to explain her relationship to Samuel Fredericks, and she wasn't sure how Nick would take it, particularly under the circumstances.

But before she could reach for Alice's hand, the little girl stepped forward and slipped her fingers into her father's hand.

"It's all right, Papa," she said. "I'm sure we'll find your special lamp to keep the little boys safe."

He gazed down at her, and his face softened. "Thank you, Alice. I won't let them down."

Alice pulled back her hand. "You should pray about it," she insisted. "That's what we're supposed to do when we're worried."

He smiled at her. "I have heard that, as well. Go along now. I'll see you in the morning."

Alice turned to Emma, who took her hand. Nick laid a hand on Emma's shoulder, stopping her.

"Thank you as well, Emma," he said. "For everything. When this is settled, I'd like to talk to you about plans for your future."

Emma's breath caught. Even in his distress she thought she heard a warmth in his voice. Only yesterday morning she'd thought he meant to propose and had her hopes dashed. If she told him the truth now, would he still be so willing to discuss a future together? And how would he feel if he learned the truth later? Would he think she'd hidden it from him out of loyalty to her foster father?

"I'd like to talk to you as well, Sir Nicholas," she said. "I'll settle Alice and then come find you. Excuse me." She took Alice's hand and hurried away before either he or Mrs. Dunworthy could question her. She needed time to think about what she would say and how she would say it.

And she could only hope that time would prove she was wrong about her foster brother, and someone would find the prototype tucked safely away in the Grange instead of on the back of a coach headed for London.

Emma stopped by the Green Salon to retrieve Lady Chamomile then returned Alice to the nursery suite and set about preparing the girl for bed.

"I don't want to sleep," Alice protested, wiggling out of Emma's grip. "I want to help Papa find his lamp."

"I know," Emma said, catching her close once more. "I want to help your papa, too. But the best thing we can do right now is to be very good and very quiet. Can you do that for him?"

Alice nodded, but the way her lower lip stuck out told Emma she wasn't pleased about the approach.

Luckily, Ivy came up to help.

"I could barely slip away," she confided to Emma as they helped the four-year-old out of her ball finery and into a flannel nightgown. "Mrs. Dunworthy has turned out the entire staff, from the stable boy to Mrs. Jennings. They're searching corners I didn't even know we had here."

Emma could imagine. Nick must be frantic thinking his work gone. She had to find a way to speak to him about it.

Lord, she prayed as she tucked Alice into bed, *You promised to give Your people the words when it came time to testify about You to kings and authorities. I haven't been called to testify about You in word but in action. I know You would not want me to be silent in this case. Please show me how to explain the situ-*

ation to Nicholas so that I don't diminish the feelings he has for me.

"Shall I help you change for bed as well, miss?" Ivy asked after Alice had said her prayers and they'd left her to sleep.

"Help me change out of this dress," Emma replied, heading for her room, "but into my day dress. I must speak to Sir Nicholas."

She didn't glance back to see if Ivy was following her. She knew she had to confide her suspicions. If Jerym had taken Nick's work on orders from Samuel Fredericks, Nick might still have a chance to catch her foster brother before he reached London.

She opened the door to her room and stopped on the threshold, staring at the large gray metal box sitting at the foot of her bed. She felt as if it reached greedy fingers toward her.

"What's that?" Ivy asked from beside her.

Emma swallowed. "That, I very much fear, is Sir Nicholas's prototype."

Ivy's voice fell to a frightened whisper. "You mean that's what they're all searching for?"

"Yes," Emma said, amazed her voice could come out more firmly. "Help me with it, if you will. We need to take this to Sir Nicholas. Now."

Nick knew his staff was searching the Grange. He could hear their feet on the stair, catch glimpses of them as they dashed past the withdrawing room door. He hardly attended to Charlotte as she paced about the room. His mind was already calculating, his fingers tapping at his black wool evening breeches.

"We will find your lamp, Nicholas," she assured him.

"No thief could have entered this house without leaving some trace."

"This isn't a random theft, Charlotte," he countered. "Surrounded by so many opportunities like vases and paintings, a common thief would never resort to a strange-looking lamp in a gray box and a leather portfolio of scribbled notes."

Charlotte stopped her pacing, her skirts swinging to a halt. "What are you saying?"

"Whoever took the box and my notes had to know the value," Nick replied. "And anyone observing the laboratory would quickly have discovered that I might be found there at any hour of the day or night. Determining the precise moment when I was occupied elsewhere would have required information from someone who knew us well."

Charlotte blanched. "To think one of the staff…"

"Ah, but we agreed that few on the staff understood my work," Nick reminded her. "If one of the servants stole the items or aided in their theft, it was more likely on the order of someone outside the house, someone who stood to profit."

Charlotte took a deep breath, as if relieved to find her staff at least partly exonerated. "Who would profit from the theft of a safety lamp?" she demanded.

His thigh protested, and he realized he'd been tapping rather mercilessly. He moved to the window, braced his hand on the molding. At least there his tapping would only be another noise along with the hiss from the nearby fire.

"I have several theories," he replied, gaze on Charlotte's reflection in the glass. She stood watching him as if unsure of his reaction. "The mining association is avid to procure a working lamp, but they'd have no reason to take it. Jennings must have told them I'd already scheduled a test."

"And what of your colleagues in the Royal Society?" Charlotte challenged. "They haven't been nearly so patient in their own work, if memory serves."

Nick shook his head. "Davy was working on his own approach. With Fredericks's disdain for my work, he'd be the last to seek to copy it."

"How naive you are, Nicholas," Charlotte chided.

Nick turned with a frown. Her lips were compressed as if she fought strong emotions.

"These colleagues of yours are men," she explained, "and thus prone to weakness. Perhaps they lacked vision and sought to steal yours. Perhaps they wanted the money that could come from manufacturing such a lamp. Perhaps they were jealous. Simply pick a motivation and you will likely find it true!"

Nick struggled to find the flaw in her logic. He didn't like seeing greed or jealousy among his fellow natural philosophers. They all held a common goal, after all, the betterment of the human condition through the expansion of knowledge.

From his youth, the parable from the Bible came to mind. The Lord had cautioned His followers not to attempt to gain the places of highest honor at banquets but to wait until they were invited to such seats. Nick had never sought the praise of his peers, only their respect. Was praise or income of more interest to one of his colleagues, no matter the cost?

Just then Emma and the nursery maid came through the doorway, balancing a load. He recognized their burden in an instant and dashed forward to meet them.

"What's all this?" Charlotte cried, following him.

"I believe this is Sir Nicholas's prototype," Emma said.

Relief washed over him. He'd known he could re-create his work, but the effort would have taken time, and more miners might die while they waited.

He took the box from her with a smile, but she did not return his look. Indeed, her face seemed smaller, as if it had been pinched with worry. Perhaps he should reassure her, and himself, that all was well.

He set the box on the drum table by the sofa and worked the clasp to lower one metal side. The glass chimney of the prototype winked back at him in the light of the wall sconce.

"It's intact," he told them all, closing the box once more. He felt as if his shoulders had somehow broadened, his lungs expanded. The very air tasted sweeter. "I'll need to check it more closely, of course, but it appears that no harm was done."

Charlotte put a hand on the chest of her green ball gown. "No harm done! How can you say that? Someone has abused your trust terribly." She turned to Emma. "Where did you find this?"

Emma met her gaze, chin high. "In my bedchamber, Mrs. Dunworthy. But I assure you, I did not put it there."

"Of course not," Nick agreed, running a hand over the box. "Perhaps the culprit thought it a safe place for the moment while the rest of us were busy with Alice. You had no reason to take it."

She drew in a breath as if she had been holding it and offered him a smile at last.

"Unfortunately," Charlotte said, "that isn't true. I am very disappointed in you, Miss Pyrmont. I knew about your background, and I chose to offer you an opportunity. This is how you repay me?"

Nick pulled his hands from the smooth surface of the box. "What are you talking about, Charlotte?"

His sister-in-law waved a hand. "Oh, open your eyes, Nicholas! She's obviously our culprit."

"Nonsense," Nick said, but Emma took a step forward, hands reaching out as if she were begging.

"I didn't take it!" she protested. "I would never do anything to hurt Sir Nicholas or Alice."

"It wasn't there when I helped her change for the ball," the maid put in, then cringed when all gazes swung her way. "I promise!"

Nick turned to his sister-in-law. "Stand down, Charlotte. Emma isn't our enemy."

"I think you will change your mind when you hear what I have to say," Charlotte insisted. She nodded to the maid. "That will be all, Ivy. You've done your duty. Go tell the others to call off the search."

Ivy started to back toward the door.

"But what about Sir Nicholas's notes?" Emma protested. "They weren't with the box." She looked to Nick. "You'll need those to prove your work."

Certainly he would, though he wondered how she knew.

"We can deal with that matter ourselves," Charlotte said. "Go about your business, Ivy."

With an apologetic glance at Emma, the maid fled.

Nick closed the distance between him and Emma. She was hunched, as if nursing some inner pain. He remembered Ann looking that way when the consumption made it hurt to breathe. The thought of Emma in such distress made him put his arm about her shoulders, drawing her closer to shelter her.

"Do not coddle her," Charlotte demanded. "Force her to tell us the truth!"

Force her? What, did Charlotte think he should strike

Emma? Lock her in a tower with only bread and water. Ridiculous!

"Be reasonable, Charlotte," Nick replied, tightening his grip. "I'm sure there's a logical explanation."

"Of course there's a logical explanation," Charlotte said. He wasn't sure of the entire spectrum of the human voice, but he was fairly sure Charlotte's approached the strident. "Only you are too much a gentleman to see it." She narrowed her eyes at Emma. "This woman came into our home under false pretenses."

Emma tensed in his arms. "That's not true! I told you everything about my circumstances."

"Oh, indeed you did." Now Charlotte's voice was more a sneer. "You told me all about your sad life, orphaned young, adopted by a prominent London gentleman. Did Samuel Fredericks put you up to this or was it your own idea?"

Fredericks? Nick was so surprised he stiffened, and his arm slid off Emma's shoulders. "What does Samuel Fredericks have to do with any of this?"

"Do you wish to tell him or shall I?" Charlotte challenged.

Emma met his gaze, her own tight and troubled. "I was on my way to tell you when I found the prototype in my room. Samuel Fredericks is my foster father, but I wish no part of him. He has nothing to do with my employment here."

He heard the words, but they made no sense. He knew Fredericks's family, had met his two daughters. Neither looked anything like Emma. "Samuel Fredericks, the natural philosopher?" he asked.

Emma nodded. "Yes. He adopted me and three boys from the orphanage. But I haven't lived in his house for more than a year."

Nick frowned at Charlotte. "You knew of this?"

She drooped as if she thought she had failed him. "I did. She seemed so sincere in her desire to leave London, to start fresh. How was I to know she was a cozening thief!"

"I'm not!" Emma turned to him, eyes wide. "Please, Nick, you must believe me! I've had no contact with my foster father since before I even joined your household."

"And how inconvenient for him," Charlotte said before Nick could respond. "Is that why he had to send your brother to pose as a footman? Is that why you sent Mr. Jones packing so quickly, so you could send word to Mr. Fredericks?"

"No!" Emma pushed away from him, each movement frantic. "I told Jerym to leave because I was afraid he was spying for Mr. Fredericks! I've only ever protected this family. Surely you see that!"

Everything inside him demanded that he defend her, despite the logic that aligned so neatly with Charlotte's accusations, his own calculations. He'd thought the culprit had to understand the value of his work. Raised in Fredericks's household, Emma could have known about the safety lamp and its importance, even before Nick had explained it to Alice in front of her. He'd thought the thief had to know his movements. Emma had been there when he'd made his discovery, was aware he'd be at the ball and dinner with Alice from five until at least eight. If Charlotte was right, Emma's brother could have waited for a sign from her and then taken everything from the laboratory.

Yet how could he doubt Emma? He'd seen her care of Alice, her delight in a new discovery, her patience with his inept ways of expressing himself. Jennings had told him about the gratitude of the men she'd nursed at the mine. He'd watched her smile, heard her laugh. He'd felt her body tremble in his arms. He didn't want those moments to be lies.

It was as if he'd been torn in two. Still, the logical, pragmatic part of him could look dispassionately at the emotions tumbling through him to the center of the tumult. It was very simple, really.

He'd fallen in love with Emma Pyrmont.

He'd come to love the clever, canny woman who cared so deeply for his daughter, for his well-being. It seemed some part of him longed to lay his heart at her feet.

And that would be the worst mistake of all. He wasn't good at love, was far too logical and preoccupied with his work to make a good husband. Hadn't Ann's death taught him anything? If he loved Emma, the best he could do for her was to ensure she had a safe, comfortable future and allow her to find a man who could offer her the love and attention she deserved.

"Leave off, Charlotte," he said. "Your hypothesis is flawed. I suggest you go apologize to the staff. In the meantime, I'd like a few words alone with Emma."

Chapter Nineteen

He believed in her! Emma wanted to throw her hands up in thanksgiving. Those accusations had had a horrible ring of truth to them, for all she knew them to be false. Trust a man of Nick's intelligence to see to the center of the issue.

But Mrs. Dunworthy was obviously unwilling to let the matter go. She drew herself up, eyes narrowed at Emma.

"I will not leave you alone with her," she insisted. "I was afraid she'd set her cap at you, but I said nothing to you, for Alice's sake. But when you insist on parading her in my own dear sister's clothes..." she choked. "I cannot sit silent."

"You seldom sit silent, Charlotte," Nick said, though not unkindly. "And while I have always appreciated your efforts on my behalf, I cannot allow you to continue to accuse Emma when she is innocent. I will not be swayed by her beauty or somehow forget my responsibility to my daughter and you because of her winsome smile. You know me to be a man guided by logic. Trust that and give us a moment of privacy."

Her jaw worked, but she picked up her skirts and swept from the room.

Nick watched her go. "I am very sorry you had to hear all that," he told Emma.

"I'm very sorry she felt the need to say it," Emma replied with a shudder. "I'm glad you believe in me. I would never do anything to hurt you or Alice."

"That is evident," he said.

He was so sure of the matter she wanted to hug him as tightly as Alice did. But with Mrs. Dunworthy's suspicions still hanging in the air, she refused to give him any reason to doubt her. She wrapped both arms around the waist of the soft ball gown. "What did you wish to say to me?"

He clasped his hands behind his back as if considering the matter. "I have a number of questions for you. First, did you see anything different in your room?"

"Besides a great gray box sitting at the foot of my bed?" Emma returned.

"At the foot of your bed, you say?" He dropped his hands, and one finger started a beat against his leg. "Odd place to put it if the thief was intent on hiding it or had dropped it on his way to escaping discovery."

Emma relaxed her arms. "I hadn't thought of that."

"And why divorce it from the notes?" He began to pace as well, striding past her on the carpet. "If someone were intent on taking the work as his own, he'd need those notes to prove the point."

"And so will you!" Emma reminded him, moving to intercept him. "You can't prove your efforts without them!"

He waved a hand. "The proof will be in the working prototype. I'll have to re-create my notes, but the observers sent by the Royal Society will have to determine the efficacy of my approach. In the meantime, I'd prefer to determine how this happened. You noticed nothing more that would give us a clue as to the reason for the theft?"

Emma shook her head. "No. I'm sorry. You are very welcome to check my room and the nursery, but I doubt you'll find anything useful."

"A necessary precaution just the same," he replied. He eyed her a moment. "Are you really Samuel Fredericks's daughter?"

She had not expected the question, but she answered it easily enough. "Foster daughter."

"Other than the issue of blood, I see no reason for the distinction."

She smiled grimly. "And that's where you differ from Mr. Fredericks. In his eyes, there is a great deal of difference between the two."

He frowned as if trying to see the matter from her point of view, and she hoped he wouldn't pursue this line of inquiry. She didn't want to spread gossip, or remember some of her foster father's worst moments.

"Such a great difference that he'd prefer you working as a servant?" he asked as if he could not fathom it. "You were raised as a lady, Emma. You should be a guest in our home, not Alice's nanny."

"I like being Alice's nanny," she insisted.

"Working from sunrise to long after sunset," he countered.

"Having a place where I am useful and respected," she argued. "There are worse things in life, believe me."

"Such has being accused of theft," he said.

Emma sighed. "You said you believed in my innocence."

His answer was immediate. "I do."

She couldn't resist asking the question. "Based on what evidence?"

His finger began moving again, as if he were calculating her worth. "You are strong and clever enough to have taken the prototype and my notes, you understand their value, and you are related to the man who wished to believe I wasn't capable of creating them."

Said that way, how could he believe her? "That is your evidence? Why did you support me to Mrs. Dunworthy!"

"That is only half of the equation," he replied, finger moving faster still. "I must also consider you as a person."

A novel approach, particularly for him. "Oh?" Emma said, raising her chin. "And what do you conclude?"

"I am not, perhaps, the best student of human nature," he admitted. "However, if I go by observation alone, I have seen you use your wiles to manipulate me."

"Oh!" Emma started, but he stopped tapping long enough to hold up one finger.

"I believe we have agreed that was your approach. You wished to make me a better father for Alice."

Emma deflated. "That's true enough."

He took no offense to her acknowledgment that he had been less than a perfect father. "So, you are capable of manipulation," he said, lowering his finger. "However, I have never seen you use it for your own sake. Indeed, everything you've done has been for Alice. Hurting me, even helping Fredericks, would not further that goal."

"All very logical," she agreed, but some part of her wanted more. She wanted to hear him say that he believed in her because he thought she was a good person, because he cared about her. It was obviously asking too much.

"Nevertheless," he said, brows still knit, "this incident changes things. I cannot in good conscience continue to employ you when I know you have better opportunities elsewhere."

Emma's head came up once more. "You know nothing of the kind."

His brows lifted, but Emma stalked up to him. "Let me make this perfectly clear to you. Your hypothesis is flawed."

"What hypothesis?" he asked, holding his ground.

"That my foster father would care that I work for a living. That he would somehow mind that I support myself rather than living on his largesse. You are wrong."

"I can see you feel strongly about this," he ventured. "But I find it difficult to believe that any man would see you struggling and turn a blind eye when he could help."

And there lay the difference between her foster father and Nick: compassion. Perhaps she'd always known it. Why else attempt to build his relationship with Alice? If he had been the monster her foster father was, Alice would have been better off being ignored. Nick actually cared about the well-being of those entrusted to him: his daughter, his sister-in-law, the miners, even Emma.

"You want to help me," she said, emboldening herself to take his hand and give it a squeeze, making sure his gaze was held by hers. "I know you mean it for the best. But most of my life I've been told how fortunate I was to be adopted by such a fine, upstanding gentleman. That was not my experience. I am thankful for the home he provided me, but I don't owe him my life or my future. If you will not believe that, discharge me so I can find work elsewhere, but do not presume you have done me some favor by reuniting me with Mr. Fredericks."

Now his brows came down in a frown, and she saw the telltale finger begin to tap. She had presented him with something he did not understand, and he would not rest until he had probed the matter to its depth.

"Don't start," she said, letting go and stepping away from him. "I am not one of your experiments, Nicholas Rotherford. Accept my word—I would be happier if I never met Samuel Fredericks again. So what will it be? Do I work here or not?"

His brow remained furrowed, but his finger stilled. He did not approve of the situation. Like his work, his world was ordered by rules and strictures, and she challenged them.

She thought he would argue, perhaps present additional evidence to change her mind. Instead, he reached out a hand and touched her cheek. "I would like to see you happy. I only wish I knew the best way to accomplish that."

With his hand warm against her cheek, his dark gaze searching hers, she thought she knew what it would take to be happy. More than being Alice's nanny, she wished she had his love. But a lady couldn't say such a thing to a gentleman, and certainly not to an employer.

As if he knew her thoughts, he closed the distance between them and lowered his lips to hers. He kissed her, gently, tenderly. Emma held herself still, drinking in the sensations surging through her. This is what it meant to be cherished. This, not the perfect husband, not the perfect family, is what she had been dreaming of her whole life.

He raised his head and gazed down at her, and she

gave him a watery smile, heart overflowing. He dropped his hand and stepped back. "Forgive me."

A laugh slipped past her warmed lips. "You truly must stop apologizing for kissing me, Nick. Either you want to kiss me or you don't."

His smile was reluctant. "Oh, I have no question on what I want. I merely question what is right. By kissing you, I undoubtedly raised your expectations, and now I must lower them. I should ask you to marry me, Emma, but I can't be the husband you need. That's why I apologized."

The warmth seeped away, leaving her chilled. "I see. You care nothing for me, then."

He took another step back, as if wishing he could escape. "What I feel is immaterial. My work takes all my time. You know I have neglected Alice. A wife, any wife, would get far less attention, and certainly less than she deserved. I'm sorry, Emma, but that is the way it is."

Nick watched as Emma's eyes turned a deep, implacable gray. Her lovely lips were nearly as tight as Charlotte's less appealing pair. Had she been one of his safety lamps, he'd have been concerned she was about to explode.

"That is the way it is?" she said. "Or that is how you insist on behaving? There is a difference."

She could not know how many times he'd wondered about the matter. "I have evidence to suggest that that is my nature," he replied.

She crossed her arms under her bosom. "Such as?"

Would she make him recite the litany of his faults? Surely after her experiences in this house she knew them as well as he did. "I was never close to my parents, and my first marriage did not end well."

Her arms fell, and her face softened. "She died of consumption, Nick. That was no fault of yours."

"She died because I failed to notice her symptoms." Saying it aloud brought the whole horrid matter rushing back at him, and he could not look at Emma. "I am knowledgeable enough to recognize the disease, having heard it discussed any number of times in proceedings of the Royal Society. I helped Davy with some of his calculations on the breathing apparatus that was to help people stricken with the illness. But I was too busy with my work to notice that Ann was suffering, until it was too late to help her."

He felt Emma's hand on his shoulder. "Was she simple, your wife?"

The question was so far from his thoughts, and reality, that he turned to face her. "Certainly not. Ann was well read, well educated. She would have been an outstanding natural philosopher had she set her mind to it."

"Then she was terribly busy raising Alice and managing your home," she said, hand falling to his arm.

"No," Nick replied, thinking back. "Charlotte had come to join the household by then. She was always more interested in the running of things than Ann was. And we had a nurse then for Alice."

Emma gave his arm a squeeze. "Then how is it your wife never noticed her own symptoms either?"

He stared at her. "I...I don't know."

She squeezed his arm again. "Perhaps something to consider. If she, educated, with time on her hands, didn't recognize the symptoms until too late, perhaps you are not to be blamed for failing to recognize them either."

The burden he'd been carrying since Ann's death eased, and he felt as if he'd grown two inches. "I will consider the matter further. Thank you."

"You're welcome," she said, withdrawing her hand. "And at the risk of sounding brazen, you might reconsider your stance on remarrying, as well. Alice could use a mother who was more involved in her upbringing."

He'd thought the same. Yet there went Emma again, considering Alice's needs before her own. "I fear you have just proved my point, my dear. In making my assessment of my matrimonial future, I thought only of myself. That is not the trait of a man who would make a good husband."

She puffed out a sigh as if he was vexing her. "But you've made progress," she protested. "Look at the ball today."

"A ball that resulted in the theft of my work," he pointed out. "That theft will require me to take the time to replicate my experiments and reconstruct my notes, time away from Alice, time away from friends and family. And when this is over, it will be something else. That's just the way I am, Emma."

Emma shook her head. "I can see that it is the way you have determined to be, and for that I'm sorry. I feared you would deprive Alice of a father. Instead, you've deprived yourself of love."

As if she'd realized what she'd said, she clamped shut her lips and turned away from him.

She loved him? The gift, the responsibility, was overwhelming. How could he possibly accept it?

"Don't love me, Emma," he murmured. "It will only bring you pain."

She turned back, managed a smile. "I'm afraid you haven't studied the vagaries of the human heart, sir. You cannot tell it when or whom to love. However, you needn't worry about me. I will do my job, as always. Provided that I am still employed in your household."

What could he say? Having her here, knowing her feelings, would make matters difficult for them both. He could discharge her, make sure she found another position. But if she was happy being Alice's nanny, then he could not gainsay her.

"Of course," he said. "Only know that you have my respect and appreciation, Miss Pyrmont." He bowed, deeply. When he straightened, she was gone.

Emma hardly slept that night. For one thing, her pillow kept getting damp despite her best efforts not to cry. She knew why Nick's dismissal hurt so much. She had begun to build dreams about him.

She'd had dreams fall down before—when she'd been adopted only to find she wasn't to be part of her new family, when she'd heard a gentleman was interested in courting her only to learn her foster father was using her as a bargaining ploy, pretending she mattered to him to ensure his colleague's loyalty. Those had been terrible disappointments, but the Lord had helped her through them, and she'd never stopped dreaming.

Oh, but Lord, this one hurts more!

She hadn't experienced the love of family, so she'd been able to persevere without it. She hadn't known the man who was interested in her, so refusing his courtship hadn't mattered all that much. Now she knew the challenge of Nick's company, the pleasure of his kiss, the joy of seeing him rise to the role of Alice's father. This time it would be harder to let go.

She also wasn't sure Mrs. Dunworthy would let the matter go. She'd been so sure of Emma's guilt, so positive that Nick was blind to it. How would the lady react when she heard Nick intended to keep Emma on as nanny?

Ivy evidently had the same concerns.

"I'm very glad to see you this morning, Miss Pyrmont," she said when she came to help Emma dress. "The Grange wouldn't be the same without you."

Mrs. Jennings said similar things when Emma came to fetch Alice's breakfast tray. The cook went so far as to enfold Emma in a hug. "Never you mind Mrs. Dunworthy," she murmured. "You are the best person to set foot in Alice's life in a good many years. I can see the difference you made in Sir Nicholas. Don't let that woman drive you away!"

Emma smiled as they disengaged, but it was harder to smile when Mrs. Dunworthy came to the nursery later that morning with Dorcus in tow. After greeting Alice, she left the maid to watch her niece then ordered Emma to join her in her suite for a private word.

Emma walked silently beside the woman through the main corridor of the Grange. She'd never thought such grandeur would be hers to manage, but the thought of leaving it behind under such conditions hurt. Mrs. Dunworthy led her into the suite, then shut the door behind Emma. Even Charles was absent, as if Mrs. Dunworthy wanted no witness to the conversation. She went to her desk and took her seat behind it, picking up her quill as if to note Emma's shortcomings on paper.

"I do not agree with Nicholas's decision to keep you on," she said to the paper. "What did you say to him last night?"

Too many things, though she regretted none of them. She only regretted his decision to lock away his heart.

"I merely explained my innocence," Emma replied.

The quill continued moving. "You told him everything? About your father, your experiences in London?"

Experiences? Emma sucked in a breath. She'd never

told anyone about her foster father's abuse. Had Mrs. Dunworthy somehow learned of it?

"Experiences, madam?" she hedged.

Mrs. Dunworthy waved her quill. "Your work there. Didn't Mr. Jones say the two of you had been involved in your father's experiments?"

She made it sound as if Emma had been a natural philosopher, too. Emma shook her head. "I don't know what Jerym said, madam, but I assure you I was little help to science."

"Do not attempt to sway me with humility." Mrs. Dunworthy raised her head and met Emma's gaze. "You owe your position to my good graces. However, if I find you have been derelict in your duty to Alice, you will be discharged immediately. Do I make myself clear?"

"Yes, Mrs. Dunworthy," Emma said, wanting to retreat and fight for her position at the same time. "I didn't take Sir Nicholas's work, and I'm glad for the opportunity to remain Alice's nanny."

"For now," Mrs. Dunworthy said, and she waved a hand to dismiss Emma.

Emma walked quickly back to the nursery. The woman obviously held her in contempt. Why else bring her all this way only to warn her? With Mrs. Dunworthy's enmity, the possibility of a governess and her own feelings for Nick, she would be wise to look for a new position. Yet she couldn't help feeling that, despite everything, her place was here.

If only she knew what place that was.

Chapter Twenty

Nick was almost glad when Charles came to his study that night to confirm that the staff had found no trace of his notes. Re-creating his efforts would take Herculean effort, but it might be the only thing that would keep him too busy to think about Emma. He'd hurt her badly; he could see that. But allowing her to think something further could come from their companionship would have hurt her even more. Better that she knew now and could find someone who would love her as she deserved.

However, the footman had other news.

"You asked me to report anything unusual about that Mr. Jones, sir," he said as he stood at attention before Nick's desk.

Nick leaned back from the piles of books and frowned. "Mr. Jones was a member of the staff for less than a day."

"Indeed, sir." Charles's face never changed, so Nick could not be sure whether the matter distressed or pleased him. "I was present when he tendered his resignation and Mrs. Dunworthy gave him a note to take back to London."

A note? Very likely a reference. Charlotte had been in a generous mood. "Then what is the problem, Charles?"

The footman went so far as to lick his lips. "The other day, when we were up at the mine, Ivy fetched Miss Rotherford's kite back from the woods. She told me she thought she saw someone out there. I wondered whether Mr. Jones actually left, sir, especially considering the theft tonight."

Charlotte had intimated as much. She seemed to think Samuel Fredericks, and by extension Emma, was behind the theft. Was it possible Fredericks had sent his son to rob the house, steal the notes? Why leave the prototype behind in the nursery? The pieces of data continued to multiply; they simply did not add up.

One thing Nick knew: his best defense against additional claims of plagiarism and miscalculation was to prove the worth of his prototype, before any other natural philosopher constructed one of his own. He would put his mind to re-creating his notes and try to forget about the woman upstairs who had captured his heart.

Emma saw Nick rarely the next few days, catching glimpses of him through the kitchen window. Alice continued to take dinner with him, though Emma was excused, and often he shared the evening with the girl. At least he still spent time with Alice. She'd been afraid he would corner himself in his laboratory until he'd completed documenting his work. Still, she found herself missing him.

The one time she saw more of him was at services that Sunday. As before, she made it a point to try to see him over and around the other parishioners. But the sight of him brought no comfort. His broad shoulders seemed to sag; his dark head was bowed. Was he speaking to his Savior about some worry, or had he lost hope?

Please, Lord, help him. You always gave me more to hope for, to strive toward. Show him how to resolve whatever is troubling him.

Unfortunately, she left the services feeling just as troubled. She had no doubt that, having solved the problem once, he could do so again. But she knew how important a natural philosopher's notes were to him. Without the painstaking documentation of trial and effort, it was more difficult to prove the advancement of knowledge. Certainly creating a paper to be read at a Royal Society meeting would be more challenging. Failing that, how would he regain his reputation with his peers?

He was so much on her mind that she could not be surprised when he showed up at the breakfast table in the nursery the following Wednesday.

"No biscuits today," Alice told him with a sorrowful face.

Nick's smile tugged on Emma's heart. "I'm sure whatever Mrs. Jennings sent up will be delightful," he assured her. "And I'm not here for biscuits. I thought you and Miss Pyrmont should know that my lamp will be tested tomorrow."

Emma's delight slipped out despite herself. "Oh, Nick, that's wonderful!"

His smile deepened as if he were as pleased by the matter, but she couldn't help noticing the circles under his dark eyes, the pallor of his skin. It seemed he'd been going without food and sleep again.

"May I come?" Alice asked.

Nick shook his head. "No, Alice. It may be dangerous. However, it appears that two of my colleagues from London will be joining us."

"Thank the Lord," Emma said, relief palpable. "You'll have your vindication."

He did not look nearly as glad. "I was hoping you'd still be willing to attend the demonstration, Miss Pyrmont."

He said it carefully, politely, but something in the way he held himself told her the matter was important to him. It was easy to answer him. She wanted to see him succeed, to have others acknowledge his worth.

"Certainly," she said. "So long as Ivy cares for Alice while I'm gone."

He took a deep breath as if she'd relieved a burden. But still his look didn't lighten.

"There is another matter," he said, body as stiff as his words. "And it may affect your decision. One of the members of the Royal Society who will be attending the demonstration and staying here at the Grange is your foster father, Samuel Fredericks."

Emma stared at him, feeling as if the chair had sunk under the table. "Mr. Fredericks, here?"

"Lady Chamomile doesn't like him," Alice said, though Emma was certain she'd never mentioned her foster father in front of the child.

"As I have said before," Nick replied to Alice, "Lady Chamomile is very wise. I'm not overjoyed by his presence either. However, we should let Miss Pyrmont decide whether she's willing to receive the gentleman."

Receive him? The familiar dread at the sound of his heavy footstep on the stair came back to her, the anger when she'd bandaged the latest burn or bruise on one of her foster brothers.

Yet she wasn't that little girl anymore. She had a position, a future that didn't revolve around her foster father. So long as Nick wrote her a good reference when she was finished here, and she continued to choose jobs outside London, Samuel Fredericks could only do so much to affect her life.

Thank You, Lord!

"If he asks after me," she said to Nick, "I will meet him. But please don't expect more."

He covered her hand on the table with his. Emotions flooded her, threatening to swamp her. She pulled back from his touch.

He rose, face all tight angles once more. "I'll send word when we're ready to leave," he said, and he left before she could think what to say. She only prayed that Fredericks would leave her in peace.

She couldn't help feeling some trepidation, however, the next morning. Knowing how Mrs. Dunworthy felt about Emma borrowing her deceased sister's clothes, Emma had returned the apron dress and the ball gown. So she was wearing one of her brown wool gowns that afternoon when Dorcus brought word Emma was wanted in the withdrawing room.

"Where's Ivy?" Emma asked quietly after making sure Alice was occupied with changing Lady Chamomile into a new gown Emma had made from fabric Mrs. Jennings had supplied.

"Pressed into service as a lady's maid," Dorcus griped. "Mr. Fredericks brought his wife, but no lady to attend her. Ivy must help her change for every occasion and see to her room between times."

Emma knew the pattern. What lady in London saw to the Fredericks women now that Emma was no longer there, she wondered. She instructed Dorcus about the activities she'd planned for the next few hours in case she was to accompany Nick to the mine immediately and made sure Alice was comfortable before going downstairs.

To her surprise, Nick was waiting outside the withdrawing room door. As on the day of Alice's ball, he was dressed like a proper gentleman in navy coat and fawn trousers tucked into polished boots. The memory of that day, dancing beside him, sent her spirits even lower.

As if he felt the same, he came to meet her at the bottom of the stairs. As when she'd last seen him in the nursery, his features were so tightly controlled she knew he was masking strong emotions.

"Fredericks insisted that I invite you down," Nick said. "I have done so. But that doesn't mean you have to face him. I can offer your regrets."

"I'm not so fainthearted," she assured him.

He nodded. One hand moved, as if he longed to reach out to her again, but otherwise he held himself still.

"Neither did I think you were," he said. "But your description of Fredericks seemed to imply that he had done you a disservice. It would be understandable if you preferred not to meet him."

Understandable but not the woman she wanted to be. "It's all right, Sir Nicholas. Thank you for your concern, but I'll be fine."

In answer, he held out his arm to escort her. His cocked head told her he wasn't sure she'd accept. Her hand did not tremble as she placed it on his. Together, they entered the withdrawing room.

Her foster father was seated on one of the upholstered chairs, his shoulders and paunch straining the fine fabric of his russet-colored coat and satin-striped waistcoat. Both hands were braced on the ebony walking stick planted before him. Her foster mother, in a demure muslin gown trimmed with lace, her graying blond hair set in ringlets, sat on the sofa next to Mrs. Dunworthy, who looked equally fashionable in her gray lustring gown.

Mr. Fredericks stood as Nick led Emma into the group. "Emma! How good it is to see you!"

Mrs. Fredericks rose as well and rushed forward to embrace Emma, pulling her away from Nick. "Oh, Emma, darling! How we've missed you!"

Emma held herself still, stunned. Tears glistened in her foster mother's blue eyes as she disengaged, and her usually rosy cheeks were pale. The woman who had spoken to her only when needed to issue commands seemed genuinely touched to see her. It made no sense.

Nick must have seen how shaken she was. "Won't you sit down, Miss Pyrmont?" he said, holding out a chair for her. Emma sank onto the seat and was glad when Nick stood beside her. Mr. Fredericks and his wife returned to their seats, as well.

"And how do you like these mountains, eh?" her foster father asked as if she'd merely gone on a sightseeing jaunt after leaving his household.

She prayed for the strength to be polite, as well. "The Grange estate is lovely," Emma replied with a look to Nick. "Alice and I love walking in the woods."

She turned back in time to see Mr. Fredericks frown. "Alice?" he asked.

"My daughter," Nick offered, laying a hand on Emma's shoulder as if to protect her. "She is very fond of Miss Pyrmont."

"And who isn't?" her foster father said, face brightening in a grin that widened his jowls. He thumped his walking stick against the geometric pattern of the carpet as if to prove it. "Very clever of you to steal a march on her other suitors, Rotherford, and invite her to visit. Nothing like keeping the belle of London all to yourself."

The belle of London? What was he doing? She'd never had a London Season. He hadn't even allowed her to accompany his daughters on their Seasons, as if she was an embarrassment to the family. Jerym must have told him she was working at the Grange, not lounging on the chaise comparing impressions of the latest styles with Mrs. Dunworthy.

That lady was quick to correct the impression. "Miss Pyrmont isn't a visitor," she said with a smile Emma thought to be as false as Mr. Fredericks's. "She is employed as Alice's nanny."

Mrs. Fredericks gasped and clutched her generous bosom. Her husband scowled. "I say, Mrs. Dunworthy, I know you and Mrs. Fredericks have been great friends since you were girls in London, but that's a rather poor joke, our Emma working."

Emma could stand it no longer. She rose, forcing Mr. Fredericks to his feet, as well.

"What must be more humorous to you, sir," she said, voice choking, "is that someone would actually pay me for an honest day's work after I served as a slave in your household for more than a decade. I wish you both well, and I thank you for giving me room and board. But please stop pretending I am more to you." Head high, she picked up her skirts, sweeping toward the door as elegantly as Mrs. Dunworthy ever had. It was a rather satisfying feeling.

Unfortunately, it was short-lived. Mr. Fredericks pushed past her to intercept her. "Emma! How can you say such things to your own mother and father?"

Blocked from the door, Emma met his gaze defiantly. Though his face was slack as if from great sorrow, there was no mistaking the cunning gleaming from his pale blue eyes.

What was he up to? Why was he so determined that Nicholas and Mrs. Dunworthy think Emma his beloved child? Was he afraid how his colleagues would react if they suspected his cruelty to the children he adopted? Before meeting Nick, she'd assumed they would have been in agreement with him: any sacrifice for the expansion of knowledge.

"My mother and father died when I was six," she replied. "I have repaid any debt I owed you a dozen times over. I won't hear otherwise."

"What did I tell you, Charlotte?" Mrs. Fredericks lamented, drawing out a handkerchief and dabbing at her eyes. "You see how stubborn she can be? Oh, the stories I could tell you, Sir Nicholas."

"Yes, your family seems particularly adept at storytelling," Nick said, going to join Emma. Everything about him was calm, composed, yet she could see the finger moving beside his thigh. What was he calculating now?

"But take heart," he continued. "It seems Miss Pyrmont learned well from her time with you. She's been wonderful with Alice and invaluable in my work."

"Your work?" Mr. Fredericks drew himself up, face reddening. "Emma, tell me you did not share my discoveries with this man."

That was it! That was her foster father's game. Whether through Jerym or some other servant, he must have stolen Nick's notes, and he intended to pass off the work as his own, claiming Emma had shared the secrets. And the worst of it was, Emma had shared information, the things she'd gleaned while working in his house. She'd been the one to direct Nick toward material properties, to create the new wick. If she was called before the Royal Society to testify, she knew how they'd rule on the matter. And Nick would never reclaim his reputation!

"I have nothing further to say to you," she answered, voice shaking. "I am a nanny in this house. Nothing more. Excuse me, sir, madam. I must return to my duties."

Emma was in pain. Nick wasn't sure why, but he could see the evidence—that pinched face, the pale skin, the tensed shoulders. The need to understand, to help her, drove him to her side. But Fredericks caught her arm, pulling her to a stop in the doorway.

"Not so fast, missy," he declared. "I came here to see a demonstration. Is it my own work I'll be seeing? Answer me!"

Emma's look flew to Nick's, and he knew anguish when he saw it. Did she think there was validity to Fredericks's accusations? Perhaps she had inadvertently told Nick things she'd seen. It didn't matter. His work was his own. He knew he'd solved the problem. What concerned him more now was that Emma continued to suffer for her kindness.

"If you have issue with the work, Fredericks," he said, "I'll be delighted to discuss the matter with you. Let her go."

Fredericks said nothing, but Emma winced. Nick did not think he'd said anything that ought to compel such a reaction. Indeed, there was only one explanation he could see. Fredericks had had the temerity to tighten his grip and hurt her!

He'd wondered at her antipathy for the man, but suddenly, all the things she'd said and the way she'd reacted made sense, and he knew why she so feared her foster father. Fredericks had abused her. He'd dared to raise his hand to a child, with such frequency and violence that she could not forget it as an adult. Nick had wondered what Charlotte's boiling point might be. It seemed he had discovered his own.

He took another step closer, forcing the man away from Emma. "I said let her go. Now."

"Nicholas!" Charlotte berated him. "You forget yourself."

He felt as if he had forgotten himself. Somewhere along the way, whether in his drive to succeed, Ann's death or the explosion at the mine, he'd lost Nicholas Rotherford, a man who stood up for his principles, a man who knew it was right to put the needs of others before his own. A man who protected those he loved.

Forgive me, Lord. I don't know how to reclaim that man, but I'll try. And I promise You I won't allow Emma to be hurt anymore.

His intentions must have been evident, for Fredericks dropped his hand. "No need to be difficult, Rotherford. I'm sure you'll agree it is a father's duty to discipline his child."

"A child surely," Nick replied, sickened by the sight of the man's gloating face. "A grown woman with a life she's chosen for herself, no. And I suspect we would disagree on the nature of discipline." He turned to Emma. "I'd still like you to attend the demonstration, Miss Pyrmont, if you're willing. Will you wait in the entry, please?"

Her jaw was set, but she nodded and left the room without another look at her foster parents.

"I think," Charlotte said, "you owe Mr. Fredericks and his wife an apology, Nicholas."

"Forgive me," Nick said with a bow, "for preventing you from doing Miss Pyrmont a further injury. It must have been a grave disappointment after the years of abuse. But I'm afraid I cannot allow such actions in my home. Excuse me."

"Nicholas!" Charlotte gasped, while Fredericks sputtered and his wife cried out in indignation. Nick ignored them all. He had more important matters to attend to.

He caught up with Emma in the entry. Someone had fetched her cloak and a plain straw bonnet. The gray wool hung from a form that seemed to be trembling, if the movement of her skirts was any indication.

"Once again you are treated poorly in my home," he said, anger at the injustice still burning inside. "I won't allow it to continue, Emma. I promise. Ride with me in our carriage. I'll let Fredericks take his own. Sir Humphry Davy, the other observer, will meet us at the mine."

But it seemed something else weighed heavier on her mind than her foster father. "I didn't betray you, Nick," she murmured, reaching out to lay a gloved hand on his arm. "Nothing I told you was pertinent to his work. He approached the problem from the chemical perspective, not the properties of the materials. Don't let him take your reputation, your work."

He laid his hand over hers. "I wanted as much to prove to myself I was right as to solve the problem, Emma. I've achieved both. That's what matters."

Her face was bunching again, as if something still pained her. "How I have misjudged you. I thought you would be like him, caring only for your work, willing to sacrifice others for it."

He shrugged and tried for a smile. "You had ample evidence on which to base your conclusion."

"Sometimes it takes more than physical observation," she replied, moving her hand to his chest and pressing against his waistcoat. "Sometimes you must trust your heart."

"A fickle organ," he countered, though he noted it had started to beat faster at her touch. "I have never been willing to rely on it."

She withdrew her hand. "Pity. I only hope someday you'll change your mind."

He could not promise that, although the smile on her face made him want to try. He offered her his arm, and together they went out to the carriage.

Charlotte joined them a short time later, taking the seat opposite them and glaring at Nick as if he had had any doubt as to her feelings on his behavior. Emma kept her gaze out the window. Despite everything, however, Nick felt his spirits rising. This time, he knew the lamp would work.

Davy was waiting at the mine. The chemist took his top hat from his wavy brown hair and shook Nick's hand.

"Delighted to be here for your triumph, Rotherford." He leaned closer and lowered his voice, blue eyes serious. "Forgive me for allowing Fredericks to tag along. I thought if he saw what you'd accomplished without him, he might rethink his accusations."

Given how Fredericks had treated Emma and Nick's suspicions that he had taken his notes, Nick doubted that. With a thanks to the chemist, he went to meet Mr. Jennings and two of his men, who stood waiting at the main entrance to the mine. All the other workers, Nick knew, had been told to go home this afternoon, for fear of what might happen. He wondered what incentives the two remaining men had received for being willing to stay. The entire area seemed too silent, the clouds hanging heavily. It was as if nature itself doubted him.

He didn't. The surety had been building since he'd prayed in the withdrawing room. Hands firm, Nick took out the lamp, waited while first Davy and then Fredericks examined it. The chemist seemed suitably impressed, but Fredericks's bulldog jaw was set and something moved in his eyes. Still he stepped back with a nod. "Let's see it work, then."

Nick picked up the lamp and carried it to Jennings. "Show me the way."

"Nick!"

Everyone turned at Emma's cry, and she blushed as she stepped forward. "You can't mean to go in there."

He offered her what he hoped was a confident smile. "These men are risking their lives. Should I do any less?"

"Step back and be silent, Miss Pyrmont," Charlotte murmured. "You are making a spectacle of yourself."

Emma's eyes flashed, but she stood her ground. "What about Alice?" she protested. "If something happens to you, she'll be an orphan."

In her eyes, he suspected, there could be no worse fate. He was putting his work before the well-being of his child. But he knew otherwise. He moved back to her side.

"Alice won't be alone, Emma," he murmured. "She has Charlotte and you. I'm not essential to her happiness."

"You're wrong," she replied, gaze brimming. "You matter more than you know—to Alice, and to me. Please, be careful."

"I will," he promised. He wanted to say more, to take her in his arms, to assure her all would turn out well. But he knew the chance he was taking. So did she.

He turned and retraced his steps to the mine entrance. "If you'd be so kind, gentlemen."

Exchanging glances, the two miners went to work the winch. Nick and Jennings entered the tunnel.

"You're a game fellow to come with me, Sir Nicholas," Jennings said as they stepped into the basket at the top of the shaft.

"It's my work," Nick said. "I stand behind it."

The mine was much as he remembered it as a child, all darkness and thick air, with a feeling that the weight of the world was above him. But as the black walls rose around him, Nick found his thoughts going to Emma. She could have argued further, pressed her case. Yet she had accepted his decision, trusted him. All she'd asked was that he look out for himself.

More, she'd said that Alice wasn't the only one who could be hurt by his untimely demise. She'd intimated that she'd be crushed by his loss. Could she still love him?

With a thump, the basket reached the bottom, and Jennings worked the gate to let them out onto the floor. The ceiling was low, forcing Nick to duck to move forward. He took a few steps into an adjoining tunnel.

"Sir Nicholas." Jennings's voice was thick. "Don't move."

Nick stopped. Ahead, it seemed the floor of the tunnel was moving, wavering in the light of his lamp as if something obscured the air. A flickering candle or older lamp might have made it invisible. He glanced back at Jennings.

The mine manager nodded to the way ahead. "That's firedamp, that is. Don't go any farther."

Firedamp, the miner's worst enemy, the problem Nick had sought to solve. A few breaths, and a man was likely to pass out cold. A spark, and he and his co-workers were doomed.

"Go back to the basket and signal them to haul you up," Nick said. "If there's an explosion, come back for me if you can." He waited until Jennings had retreated, took a deep breath and plunged ahead.

Chapter Twenty-One

At the mine entrance, Emma waited with Mrs. Dunworthy, Sir Humphry and the Fredericks. None of them paid her any mind. Sir Humphry was talking with the two miners while they waited for a sign from below. Mrs. Dunworthy and Mrs. Fredericks were chatting about friends they'd known years ago as if they were meeting over tea instead of in a great coal-dust-covered landscape. Her foster father was pacing from the winch to the entrance and back, boots crunching against the rocky ground. None of them seemed to care that Nick's life might be in danger.

That duty lay solely with her. Yet much as she worried about him, facing the firedamp hundreds of feet below the ground, she wanted to shake some sense into him! Everything she'd done, every change she'd seen in him, and still he didn't understand. Alice needed a father—a living, breathing, caring father. How could he jeopardize that by risking his life?

Yet he wasn't the man she'd originally thought him. In risking his life, he was putting the needs of others—Mr. Jennings, the miners, even the advancement of knowledge—before his own. He didn't act like the heroes in her favorite books, and he would certainly never be the perfect husband. But that didn't stop her from loving him.

The realization brought tears to her eyes. This was love—not the expectation of perfection but the care and joy in the face of very real flaws. That was the love her heavenly Father had offered her. How could she not offer the same to Nick?

A shout from below set the miners to hauling. Sir Humphry and Mr. Fredericks rushed to the entrance and peered inside. Mrs. Dunworthy and Mrs. Fredericks clutched each other's arms.

Emma could scarcely breathe. Was it over? Was Nick hurt? Was he dead? She pushed past the other ladies, every part of her trembling.

Nick walked from the mine, face blackened, clothes dusty. Though the two natural philosophers and Jennings hovered near him, his smile was all for Emma.

"We did it," he said, lifting the lamp, which was still burning. "It worked."

The miners who had manned the winch came running with a cheer, and Mr. Jennings went so far as to clap Nick on the shoulder, raising a puff of dust. Emma wanted to clasp him close and shout in triumph at the same time, but she couldn't help noticing her foster father's reaction. Mr. Fredericks beamed congenially at them all, as if this success was his. Very likely he was only biding his time until he could assert his claim on Nick's work.

She had to stop him. She knew the work was all Nick's. He'd pored over calculations, come up with the design, risked his own life to test it. Surely he deserved the credit and a chance to regain his reputation!

Nick stopped in front of her, his grin the cleanest

thing about him. There was even coal dust lodged in his cravat.

She couldn't help smiling, as well. "Congratulations," she said. "You solved the problem."

"We solved the problem," he corrected her. "I couldn't have done it without you."

"You'll have the thanks of every collier in the country," Mr. Jennings predicted, joining them.

"Every collier in the world, once this is manufactured in bulk," Sir Humphry assured them.

Mr. Fredericks's smile was smug.

Oh, no. She was not about to let her foster father get his hands on this invention. *Please, Lord, show me how to stop him!*

"We'll need to come up with a way to develop the wicks then," Nick said with a chuckle. "I doubt Miss Pyrmont will want to spend all her time knitting them."

"And I'm sure more than one gentleman might like to have her spend more time courting than knitting," Mr. Jennings replied with a grin to Emma. "I've already had three of the men you nursed ask your direction, Miss Pyrmont."

"Now, now, gentlemen," Mr. Fredericks said. "I expect a fine fellow to offer for my daughter, with a generous bride portion. I cannot see a miner in my family."

Jennings's smile vanished.

"I'm honored they would think of me that way, Mr. Jennings," Emma said. "They are fine men, doing dangerous work. They have my thanks."

Jennings nodded but turned away to speak to his men.

"I'll be sure to note Miss Pyrmont's contribution in my report to the Royal Society," Sir Humphry said, with a smile to Emma.

"Yes," her foster father encouraged, "you do that."

Nick looked thoughtful, and she saw his finger moving against the metal of the lamp. Did he understand at last the danger her foster father posed to his work? Did Sir Humphry?

Perhaps she should tell him.

Part of her wilted at the thought of having to expose the pain she and her foster brothers had endured. Yet she felt an urge inside, an encouragement, a courage. Nick had worked so hard for this. She couldn't allow her foster father to ruin it.

"I'd be happy to explain my contribution to you further, sir," she said to the chemist. "I see you brought an open carriage. Might I beg a ride home with you?"

Nick frowned as if he wasn't sure what she was doing. Her foster father seemed to think he knew, for he beamed at her.

"Excellent suggestion! Rotherford deserves a run for his money. You could do worse than to marry into my family, Davy."

Emma knew her face was crimson. She was only glad the chemist was too polite to respond to her foster father. Instead, he offered her his arm. "It would be my pleasure to drive you back to the Grange, Miss Pyrmont."

Nick took a step closer. "Are you certain, Emma?"

She knew by the way her foster father's face changed and Sir Humphry's arm stiffened that they had noted his use of her given name. She thought by the way Nick regarded her that he'd chosen to use that name for a reason. She hoped he could tell by her smile that she knew her mind.

"Quite certain, Nicholas," she assured him, careful to use his name, as well. "I'll see you at the Grange.

I can't wait to share our success with Alice and Lady Chamomile."

He smiled then, and she knew he understood that, whatever she intended, her feelings for him and Alice had not changed.

"Lady Chamomile?" her foster father asked, eyes lighting. "A new sponsor, Rotherford?"

Knowing Nick would now have to explain, Emma put her hand on Sir Humphry's arm and urged him toward his own carriage.

"Thank you for allowing me to impose," Emma told him as the open landau started down the hill. The cool breeze brushed her cheeks inside her straw bonnet, and she clasped her hands in her lap to keep them from trembling at what she must do.

"I would like to be flattered that you'd ask," Sir Humphry said. "But I sense you have something more to discuss than your contribution to the development of the safety lamp."

Emma nodded. "Very astute of you. And I made no significant contribution to Sir Nicholas's work, I promise you. But I'm very afraid Mr. Fredericks thinks otherwise."

"Ah." His brow cleared. He was a handsome man, with dark hair curling back from a boyish face. She could feel the energy radiating from him. "Allow me to assure you that your foster father's impressions will not sway my report."

"I wasn't concerned about that," Emma explained. "I fear he intends to claim Sir Nicholas's design as his own."

Now he frowned, fingers splayed on his trousers. "A serious accusation, Miss Pyrmont. What evidence do you have?"

Emma swallowed. Now came the hard part. "For one, I know that he sought to find someone to blame for the previous explosion. For another, I have reason to believe he stole Sir Nicholas's notes."

Sir Humphry shook his head. "My dear, you must know there's never been a hint of scandal involving Fredericks. I don't know what Sir Nicholas told you, but I have no reason to believe your father is anything less than a gentleman."

"Then you are greatly mistaken, Sir Humphry." Emma moved her cloak aside so that the sleeve of her gown was evident. Carefully, she pulled up the edge just enough to show him the pockmark on her skin. "I received that for failing to properly mind a mixture of chemicals. My foster brother Barty is deformed because of the weight he was forced to carry when he was young. I have it on good authority my other foster brother Frank may be blind now in one eye from being splashed with chemicals as a punishment. In short, Sir Humphry, Mr. Fredericks would never qualify as a gentleman in my estimation."

Sir Humphry leaned away from her as if somehow her story had dirtied him, and his face settled into lines too harsh for his youthful features. What had she expected? Her foster father had hidden his true nature too well. No one would believe he could be so cruel, so devious. She tugged down on her sleeve even as tears threatened.

You know the truth, Lord. Let it shine forth, for Nick's sake!

"Thank you for telling me this, Miss Pyrmont," Sir Humphry said quietly. "I can appreciate the courage it took to do so. I will see what I can do to protect Sir Nicholas from further accusations."

Emma drew a breath. "Thank you."

He nodded. "Indeed. And I will do something further. I am friends with a number of the fine gentlemen and ladies who serve as trustees for the orphan asylum, who also occasionally serve to fund our scientific pursuits. It might interest them to know the sacrifices its children have made for your foster father's discoveries."

Emma stared at him. "You'd tell them what happened to us?"

"In an oblique way, of course," he said. "But enough to ensure an inquiry is made. I only wish I could do more."

Emma leaned closer, heart lifting. "Perhaps you can. I'm ashamed to say I thought all natural philosophers would be so stone-hearted. Knowing Sir Nicholas, and now meeting you, I have revised my assessment. I wonder, would you know others, like you, who might need assistants? I can promise you my foster brothers learned their trade well."

"On penalty of death, it seems," Sir Humphry murmured. "Yes, Miss Pyrmont, I believe I could find a use for such men. Give your foster brothers my direction. I'll be happy to speak to them further about a change in position."

Emma pressed her fingers to her lips, heart swelling. "Oh, Sir Humphry, thank you!" *And thank You, Lord!*

He cocked a smile. "It is the least I could do. After all, it seems Sir Nicholas has indeed discovered more than how to design a safety lamp. He has quite a gem in you, Miss Pyrmont."

Emma blushed and was glad when the carriage pulled up before the Grange. Tea and cakes were waiting in celebration, but she managed to slip away. She had no interest in spending more time with the Frederickses, and after her confession to Sir Humphry, the nursery had never looked more welcome. She stopped by her room only long enough to hang up her cloak and set aside her bonnet.

But when she walked into the nursery, she found the maid dozing in the rocking chair.

"Dorcus!" she scolded, and the maid's head jerked up, eyes opening and mouth snapping shut.

"Where's Alice?" Emma asked, hands on her hips.

Dorcus covered her yawn with one hand and motioned toward the girl's room with the other. "Taking her afternoon nap, as she always does."

Emma moved to the door of Alice's room and peered inside. Though the covers on the bed had been disturbed, there was no sign of her charge. She felt cold all over.

As Dorcus rose from the chair, Emma strode to the center of the nursery and raised her voice. "Alice, dear Lady Chamomile, come out, come out, wherever you are."

No giggle greeted her call; no dark head popped into view. Dorcus stared at her, eyes widening.

"Find her," Emma ordered.

She and Dorcus searched the nursery suite, calling to Alice and Lady Chamomile, but to no avail.

"I only nodded off for a few minutes," Dorcus protested when they regrouped in the center of the nursery. "I promise!"

"Check the chamber story," Emma ordered. "Then go downstairs to the main floor. If you can't find her, tell Sir Nicholas."

Dorcus quailed. "Oh, not the master, miss."

"Yes, the master," Emma insisted, tugging her toward the door. "Alice is his daughter. He needs to know if she's missing. I'll take the servants' stair and check with Mrs. Jennings, then go out to the woods. Don't fail me."

The maid nodded and dashed for the main portion of the house.

Emma started down the stairs, heart pounding louder than her steps. Every turn, she hoped to find Alice and her doll playing, but every turn stood empty.

Please, Father, help me find her!

"I hear it was a great success!" Mrs. Jennings greeted her when Emma came into the kitchen.

"Yes," Emma said, "but that's not why I'm here. Alice has gone missing. Have you seen her?"

Mrs. Jennings blanched, hands braced on her work-table. "No. Oh, where could she have gone?"

"I doubt she slipped past you, but check the servants' hall, the larder and the laundry just in case," Emma said. "Dorcus is searching the main house. I'm for the woods."

"Of course," Mrs. Jennings said, hurrying off. "And I'll wave some of those biscuits about. That ought to bring her out of hiding!"

Emma wanted to smile at the reminder of how much Alice loved those cinnamon biscuits, but her laugh caught in her throat. The Grange seemed so large compared to the London town house where she'd spent most of her life. How much larger must it seem to Alice? Had she locked herself in a little-used room by accident? Fallen down a window well? Emma's mind conjured up a dozen ways a child of Alice's size and curiosity could get herself into trouble.

Once out the door, however, Emma saw that it had begun to rain, and her heart sank further. If Alice had gone into the woods alone in her muslin gown, she'd soon be chilled. Chills had been known to lead to pneumonia, and pneumonia could kill a young child.

Oh, please, Lord, protect her!

Refusing to take the time to fetch her cloak and galoshes, Emma hurried across the lawn, rain wetting her shoulders, grass wetting her hem. She could see nothing moving in the darkening woods, but as she passed the laboratory, a sound caught her attention. Was that Alice's voice?

"Sing a song of sixpence, a bag full of rye,

Four and twenty blackbirds baked in a pie."

Emma drew in a breath. That high piping voice could belong to no other at the Grange. She opened the door, ready to pounce on Alice for scaring her half to death. But when she peered inside, she felt as if her heart had stopped beating.

Nick must have returned his prototype to the laboratory, for Emma could see it sitting on the worktable. The fact that the lamps remained burning told Emma that he intended to come out and work later, as well.

In the golden light, Alice stood beside Nick's worktable, a glass flask in one hand, Lady Chamomile in the other. Emma recognized the oil of vitriol immediately by its pale yellow color. She knew the danger to Alice, had lived through it herself. Her arm still bore the brand. Just touching the chemical could burn the girl. Drinking it would be fatal.

"Alice," she said gently, moving forward carefully so as not to frighten the child, every muscle demanding that she move, she act. "Put that back on the table."

"Why?" Alice asked, giving the flask a shake. "It is very pretty. I want to do an experiment like Papa. And Lady Chamomile wants to take a sip."

Emma edged closer. "Please tell her ladyship it would make her very sick. Put it down, Alice."

Alice frowned, but she reached obediently toward the table with the vitriol. Then her face broke into a grin. "Papa!"

The bottle tipped off the edge, the spout turning toward Alice. Emma dove forward.

Nick stood in the doorway, terror holding him in place. There was Alice, gripping one of his most virulent chemicals. It seemed Emma had recognized the danger as well, for she had been about to talk Alice into setting it down. Then Alice started toward him, and the flask began to tip.

Nick ran.

He grabbed Alice with one hand and Emma with the other and pulled them both away from his worktable. The flask hit the floor, spilling the vitriol in all directions. He smelled the scent of burning leather from his boots. He scooped Alice up and drew Emma around the table and out the door.

Emma shut the door behind him and leaned against it, wide-eyed.

"I'm sorry, Papa," Alice said, lower lip beginning to tremble. "I made a mess of your laboratory."

"Oh, Alice." Emma knelt beside her and held her tight. "Please don't leave the house without me again. You could have been hurt so badly!"

Nick knelt as well, wrapping his arms around both of them. "It's my fault. I should never have parted the two of you. I should have locked the door, put the chemicals away. I…"

"Hush," Emma murmured, and he felt her hand stroking his hair as if in benediction. "It's no one's fault.

Accidents happen. Thank the Lord this time nothing bad came of it."

Yes, Lord, thank You. What would I do without them in my life?

His prayer brought tears to Nick's eyes. What a fool he'd been! All this work, only to lose those most precious to him—his daughter and the woman he loved.

Why had he thought he could be whole without Emma? She helped him be a better man, with Alice, with her. He was thankful for her patience when he struggled with concepts of forgiveness, particularly his own. When he'd seen that flask tipping, he'd feared for Alice, but he'd feared for Emma just as much. Emma had already been forced to sacrifice—her childhood, the chance for a mother and father who would have loved her. At that moment, he would have done anything to spare her more pain, even if it meant losing his own life.

"Nicholas!" Mrs. Dunworthy came running from the house, Charles dashing along beside her to hold the umbrella over her head. Nick blinked, feeling the rain on his cheeks for the first time, washing away his fears, his guilt and his tears.

Thank You, Lord. I can see You've been patient with me, as well. And You sent Emma to make sure I knew of it. I will honor You and her all the days of my life.

He gave Alice and Emma a hug before rising. "It's all right, Charlotte. Alice is safe, thanks to Emma."

"Thanks to Emma?" His sister-in-law stopped in the rain, head so high the footman struggled to keep her covered. "How can you say that? She has neglected her duty, letting Alice wander about on her own!"

"Emma was with us this afternoon, if you recall," Nick pointed out. "She is not to blame for this."

"There you go again!" Charlotte cried. "How can you continue to take her side after this? I will not have it!"

Emma rose, Alice held in her arms, the little girl's dark head pressed against her chest and Lady Chamomile dangling from one small hand.

"I must get Alice inside," Emma said, voice firm with conviction. "We can settle this later."

"How dare you speak to me in that manner!" Charlotte raged, but Emma pushed past her for the house. "Do you hear her, Nicholas?"

"Get out of the rain, Charlotte," Nick advised. "Give everyone a moment to calm. Then, I promise you, we will talk."

Chapter Twenty-Two

Emma dried Alice thoroughly and put her to bed with a warming pan at her feet. Very likely Mrs. Dunworthy would insist on discharging Emma, but she would not shirk her duty while it was hers. Besides, she was still worried about how Alice's little adventure would affect the girl.

"Your father works with some very nasty things," she explained to Alice as she sat at her bedside. "Because he is very clever, he knows exactly what to do with them. You will be as clever one day, but right now, you may only enter his laboratory if he is there with you. Do you understand?"

Alice nodded, dark hair splayed against the white of the pillow. "I'm sorry. I was just looking for him, and I thought I could experiment."

"Right now, experiments are a game to you," Emma replied. "But those chemicals aren't something to play with. They could make you very sick or hurt your skin."

As she had with Sir Humphry, she pulled up her sleeve to show Alice the puckered skin on her arm. "Here's what happened when I encountered one of those chemicals."

Alice put a finger on the skin, and her lip trembled. "Lady Chamomile was the one who thought of it."

It was one thing for Alice to use Lady Chamomile as she struggled to express her feelings. It was another to blame Lady Chamomile for her actions.

"You are responsible for Lady Chamomile," Emma countered. "You must explain to her what is safe. If she cannot understand, then I cannot allow her to leave the nursery."

"I'll tell her," Alice promised solemnly, hugging her doll close. "It was very bad of her to think about drinking Papa's mixtures. She may have no biscuits for a week."

"A fitting reminder," Emma agreed. "So long as you remember, as well."

"Perhaps we should all forego biscuits for a week," Nick said from the doorway. He had changed too and now wore a cinnamon-colored banyan over his waistcoat and trousers. His boots had been replaced with shoes, and Emma couldn't help wondering whether his former footwear had been ruined by the splash from the vitriol.

And if that had been Alice's skin... She shuddered just thinking about it.

"Were you naughty, too, Papa?" Alice asked as he came into the room.

"I have made quite a few mistakes," he qualified. "And you and Emma have been very patient with me." He pressed a hand against Emma's shoulder, the touch warm, kind. However, she saw the frown come over his face.

"What's this?" he asked, bending lower.

Emma realized her sleeve was still pushed up and

quickly reached for the edge to start to tug it down. He caught her hand.

"When did that happen?" he murmured, bending lower still as if to examine it.

Emma felt her face heating. "A long time ago. You need have no concern. I was just explaining to Alice what could happen if she played with your chemicals."

"I doubt that happened while you were playing," he said. Like Alice, he traced the mark with his finger, the touch gentle, sweet, raising an ache inside her.

He drew back and straightened. "Your shoulder is still damp," he said as if explaining a natural law. "It appears you haven't changed clothes."

She hadn't wanted to let Alice out of her sight. "I was busy," she said with a smile to her charge and a deep breath to recover her composure.

He stepped back to give her room to rise from the bed. "Go. Change. I'll stay with Alice."

"But your guests, Mrs. Dunworthy," Emma protested, rising.

"Are far less important," he replied. "Go."

Emma went. The rain had not soaked through her gown, so she only had to manage the outer layer instead of her petticoats and chemise. Indeed, the brown wool of the fresh gown had never felt more comfortable. Still, her arm tingled where he had touched her, as if he accepted this scarred part of her just as she was learning to accept his way of dealing with emotions. Her fingers were still trembling, but she managed the fastenings on the front herself and hurried back to Alice's room.

The sight of Nick sitting beside his daughter pulled her up short. The light from the fire etched the planes of his face, highlighted the wonder in his look as he gazed at the dozing Alice. Her heart melted. Why had she ever doubted she could love this man?

Emma tiptoed to his side.

"To think I might have lost her," he murmured.

Emma bent and put an arm around his shoulder. "But you didn't. You kept her safe."

"We kept her safe." He pressed her hand to his shoulder as if to hold her beside him. "You have consistently worked for my daughter's behalf, my behalf, Emma, and how have we repaid you? With accusations and recriminations. You deserve better."

He dropped his hand, and Emma straightened. "I could argue there is nothing better than being with Alice."

He smiled as if he agreed, then rose and drew her out into the nursery, away from the slumbering child. "I'd like to see if I might change your mind about that and provide you with something more. If I send Ivy up to watch her, would you join me in the withdrawing room?"

The withdrawing room? With her gloating foster father and the disdainful Mrs. Dunworthy? She'd had entirely too much of them for one day.

"I'm not good company this evening," Emma tried. "Perhaps after your guests leave."

He peered closer. "I will honor your wishes, of course, but know that Sir Humphry has returned to the inn and the Frederickses have already gone. They found a sudden desire to be back in London."

In London? Only one thing could make her foster father dash off so close to nightfall.

"Oh, Nick!" She clung to his hand. "I'm so sorry! He's gone to claim your design for his own."

"Perhaps," Nick replied, straightening. "But I can

deal with that matter another time. Join me this evening, Emma. There's much I must discuss with you."

His hand covered hers again, and she imagined she could feel the urgency, the fervent hope that she would agree. His day had been as difficult as hers, and she could only hope that Sir Humphry's report would stop her foster father's plans. Why shouldn't she grant Nick this small favor?

"Very well," Emma agreed, and he bowed and left.

Ivy arrived a short time later, walking into the nursery in such a decidedly odd manner that Emma jumped from her seat in the rocking chair, her knitting tumbling to the floor.

"What's happened?" she cried, rushing forward. "Oh, Ivy, please tell me Mr. Fredericks didn't strike you over an imagined slight to his wife!"

"Oh, no, Miss Pyrmont," the maid said, straightening now and pressing a hand to where her apron bloomed over her belly. "They were ever so nice to me, probably because they realized what I might see." She put her other hand behind her back and began tugging at her apron strings.

"What you'd see?" Emma asked with a frown.

"Yes, miss. This." She pulled off the apron to reveal a brown leather binder she'd strapped against her middle. "Mrs. Fredericks had Sir Nicholas's notes."

Emma stared at the binder as Ivy held it out to her. "*Mrs.* Fredericks?"

"Yes, miss, though surely it was for her husband. I was getting her dinner dress ready in the dressing room when she came in with this. Mr. Fredericks arrived right after. As soon as she told him she had it he decided to leave for London, and I got the task of packing. She slipped it into her trunk right in front of me, like I had no idea what it was. I didn't know what to do, so as soon as she left the room to bid Sir Nicholas goodbye, I went for Mrs. Jennings, and she advised me to lighten the Frederickses' luggage."

"So you brought the binder to me," Emma concluded.

"Well, you were accused of stealing it," Ivy said, mouth turned down at the injustice. "Seems only right you should be the one to hand it back. And this time, Mrs. Jennings and I will both stand behind you. I only wish I knew how Mrs. Fredericks got it to begin with. It's not like she was hanging about the Grange when it was taken."

She hadn't been, but someone else had. To Emma, there was only one person who knew the value of Nick's work, had had easy access to the laboratory and was so friendly with Mrs. Fredericks as to be willing to give the woman the notes. But she had no evidence. Would Nick believe her if she told him her suspicions?

She accepted the binder from Ivy. "I'll see it returned to its proper place, Ivy. Thank you, and thank Mrs. Jennings."

Holding the binder close, Emma went to meet Nick.

He was in the withdrawing room, standing by the window as if watching the twilight steal over the peaks, hands clasped behind his back. Mrs. Dunworthy was seated on the sofa, book open in the lap of her lustring gown. By the way her head was bowed, she seemed to be studiously avoiding him. Emma didn't do more than glance her way before moving to Nick's side.

"Ivy saw this among Mrs. Fredericks's things and thought it should be returned to its rightful owner."

Out of the corners of her eyes, Emma saw Mrs. Dunworthy raise her head. Nick accepted the leather binder from Emma with a frown, opened it and thumbed through a few pages as if to confirm it was his own work.

"It seems to be all here," he marveled. "So Fredericks did steal it. It seems you were right, Emma. He wished to claim my work for his own. But why? Surely he had his own ideas on the matter."

"Fewer than you might think," Emma said. "And I'm not sure he acted alone." She paused. If her suspicions were wrong, she would malign an innocent person. But if she was right, surely Nick deserved to know. But perhaps she should let him draw his own conclusions.

"How do you suppose he was able to lay hold of them?" she asked. "He was in London until recently, well after they disappeared."

"Charles thought your foster brother might have been in the woods," he returned, but she knew by the tapping of one finger against his banyan that he was already analyzing other scenarios. "I think he was wrong. How could Jones have subsisted until now? No, Fredericks must have had another accomplice closer to hand."

"Someone he could trust, someone you would trust enough to allow access to your work," Emma agreed, watching him. It was almost as if she could see his thoughts, sorting through possibilities, rejecting theories. She knew the moment he had a hypothesis. His face tightened, and he turned to eye his sister-in-law.

"Charlotte, what do you know of this?"

She had dropped her head again and now turned the page of her book as if she had been only half listening to his and Emma's conversation. The firelight glowed against her sleek hair. "About what, Nicholas?"

He strode to face her and held out the binder as if to show her the evidence. "About the theft of my notes, the prototype. You had access to the laboratory and a good friendship, it seems, with Mrs. Fredericks. But why you would want to hand Mr. Fredericks my work is beyond me. You knew how he'd accused me."

She raised her head once more, then carefully closed her book. "Yes, I knew. I thought it a shame the Royal Society didn't take more drastic action than asking you to leave. You should have been called before the Prince, your knighthood revoked. You deserved ruination for what you did to Ann."

He paled, and Emma had to hold herself still to keep from going to him. "Charlotte," he murmured, "you know I would have done anything to save her."

Charlotte rose to face him, regal, majestic. "Anything? Rather say nothing. You left her alone, you never even noticed she might be ill until it was too late. Your negligence killed my sister!"

Emma could stand it no longer. She moved to Nick's side, put a hand on his arm in support.

"No," she told Charlotte. "Consumption killed your sister. She was a grown woman, capable of contacting a physician. Certainly she must have been capable of getting her husband's attention if she wished it. Perhaps she didn't recognize the signs, perhaps she was afraid to learn the truth of her condition. But no one kept her from seeking help."

"Be silent," Mrs. Dunworthy hissed. "You know nothing about my sister."

"And I begin to think I knew her little, as well," Nick said with a shake of his head. "Certainly I didn't know you, Charlotte. I can understand why you would blame me, for until recently I've certainly been blaming myself. But I can't understand why you would do something that might affect Alice, as well. Or hadn't you considered her future when you tried to destroy mine?"

Charlotte raised her chin. "I would have protected Alice. I love her, which is more than I can say for you. You barely noticed her existence until this—" she waved dismissively at Emma "—this servant brought her to your attention."

"You encouraged me," Emma protested. "I thought you wanted to do the right thing and bring them together."

Her eyes narrowed. "I wanted him to suffer, to feel the loss of a loved one as I had, but that would mean he'd actually have to care. And you? You were supposed to be blamed for all this. Why else would I hire you?"

Emma stared at her. "And you say you care about Alice!"

"Indeed?" Nick frowned as if Charlotte's answer did not add up in his carefully constructed equation either. "You claim to love Alice, but my destruction would only have harmed her. You have no income of your own. Your station comes from being my chatelaine. If I am ruined, how would you fare?"

Charlotte leaned toward him, as if to impart a secret. "I've saved quite a bit from the household fund, scrimping on servants' wages here, on food there. You didn't care. You didn't even notice. That income would have allowed me to fare with great fortitude, knowing I'd avenged my sister and rid the world of one more man who cannot be bothered to see to the needs of his family."

One more man. Left destitute by her husband, dependent on another she could not trust, Mrs. Dunworthy had turned her bitterness on Nick. *I know too much about the dangers of bitterness, Lord. There, but for Your Grace, go I.*

"I will always see to the needs of my family," Nick

said. "Even yours." His frown eased, as if he'd made a decision. "I own a house outside London, too small for Alice and my laboratory. It is yours to use while you live."

She drew herself up, clenching her fists beside her gray skirts. "You're throwing me out?"

He raised his brows as if surprised she'd think otherwise. "Certainly. How would I trust you around Alice or Emma? Because I believe Alice is fond of you, I will ensure she visits, always chaperoned. I owe you a living for Ann's sake. If you have specific needs, write to my solicitor. I'll see they're met, within reason."

"How could Ann abide the sight of you?" she cried, mouth twisted. "You have no concept of family."

"That is quite enough," Emma said. "Your grasp on the subject is far feebler."

"And this from a nameless orphan," Mrs. Dunworthy sneered.

"She has a name," Nick corrected her. "And she has a better appreciation of family than any of us." He nodded to the footman, who stepped forward. "Charles, escort Mrs. Dunworthy upstairs and help her pack her things. I'm sure the inn will be glad to accommodate her tonight before she starts on her journey to London."

The light in the footman's eyes told Emma he took more than his usual delight in his duty. One last time, Charlotte lifted her skirts and swept from the room.

"We'll need to hire another maid," Emma said. "Without her around to continually sweep the floors with her skirts."

Nick chuckled. "And a footman for the nursery."

Emma smiled. "Thank you for insisting on that. And thank you for believing me. I think your precautions with Mrs. Dunworthy are very wise. Now, if you'll excuse me, I should return to the nursery to check on Alice."

In answer, he took her hand in his. "Wait a moment. I must thank you, for everything."

"You have," Emma said, but she couldn't make herself look away. The angles and planes of his face seemed to be softening, as if emotions were rising to replace the logic.

"Not sufficiently," he countered. "You have made yourself an indispensable part of this family. I'd like to settle that situation permanently."

Emma's heart quickened. Was this finally what she'd hoped for? "I'm listening."

"I realize I still lack a few of the finer points to being a husband," he said. "But I can offer you financial stability, some social connections. You have taught me the importance of making time for Alice and those I care about."

That was it? Money, Society, time? He still didn't understand. Despite herself, Emma sighed.

"Your offer is kind," she said, "but I was hoping for more."

She felt the movement of his finger under hers, tapping at her palm. He was dissecting what he'd said, searching for flaws in his logic, determining the need for additional evidence. How could she explain it wasn't logic that mattered most when proposing marriage?

Suddenly, his finger stopped tapping.

"Forgive me," he said. "This isn't my area of specialty. I neglected to explain two important points. I love you, Emma, and I'll do my best to make sure you never question that. You see, I am convinced that being near you is essential to my happiness. I thought I observed certain evidence that you might feel the same."

He was watching her, waiting for the least sign. Emma thought he might even have been holding his breath, he stood so still. Every part of him yearned for her to answer him yes. Every part of her agreed.

"You always were an astute observer, sir," she said with a smile. "Perhaps you can interpret my answer from this." She leaned forward and pursed her lips.

Nick felt Emma's hand trembling in his, saw her moving closer. He had little experience with love, but he knew her answer. He met her halfway, gathered her closer, kissed her with all the emotions that seemed to be dancing inside him. For once, he was satisfied that they were as reliable as a year's worth of careful observation.

He was in love with Emma, and she loved him in return. She had started a campaign to win his heart for Alice. Though they'd had an unusual courtship, he knew his heart belonged to Emma.

That wasn't a hypothesis, it was an inviolable law. And the rest of their lives would only prove it further.

Epilogue

From the doorway to the withdrawing room, Mrs. Jennings wiped a tear away from her eye. She knew she should be superintending the dinner arrangements, but she hadn't been able to resist checking on Sir Nicholas and Emma. And the scene in the withdrawing room went a long way toward assuring her that the future would be bright.

Dorcus approached from the dining room, and the cook put a finger to her lips to signal the maid to silence. Dorcus joined her and peered inside. Both her blond brows shot up.

The cook drew her back from the door. "Cover the roast. We'll give them a few moments before letting them know dinner is ready."

Dorcus nodded. "So she did it," she whispered. "She'll be lady of this house after all."

Mrs. Jennings smiled. "Oh, yes. She's perfect for the master and him for her. She'll keep him from disappearing into his studies, and he'll give her the family she's missed."

Dorcus shook her head. "If you say so. I'm just glad

we'll be shed of Mrs. Dunworthy. I could tell you stories."

"Be respectful, now," Mrs. Jennings warned. "And go on about your duties. I'll see to the master and Miss Pyrmont."

Dorcus bobbed a curtsey and hurried off. Mrs. Jennings took one more look at the embracing couple and sighed in delight. Yes, the future of the Rotherford family looked to be in good hands.

Thank You, Father!

Perhaps Sir Nicholas would reinstate her as housekeeper, she mused as she waited, or even hire a valet again. Heaven knows Mr. Quimby, the valet for the Earl of Danning, whose fishing lodge lay down the valley, must be considering a new position, and who could blame him? None of the servants at the lodge felt comfortable with the future of their positions, not with their master showing no signs of marrying and his cousin, the heir presumptive, gloating in the background.

Perhaps she should speak to Mr. Quimby on their next Sunday off together. Surely they could determine a likely candidate for a wife to put forward.

Her smile deepened. If Emma could wage a campaign to court Sir Nicholas, what was to say Mr. Quimby couldn't wage a campaign to find the earl a wife? All these gentlemen needed was a little prayer and help from the master matchmakers.

* * * * *

Dear Reader,

Thank you so much for choosing the first book in my Master Matchmakers series. I spent many years working with scientists as a technical writer. Their studies fascinate me, as does the marvelous way their minds work. Perhaps that's why I wanted to write about Nick and Emma's courtship.

Several scientists worked hard in the early nineteenth century to develop a safety lamp for the coal miners. Within a few short years, two natural philosophers and a machinist put forth designs that worked. But it was the design by Sir Humphry Davy, the natural philosopher who stood by Nick during his trials with the Royal Society, that was ultimately chosen for mass production. I envisioned Nick's lamp to be an early form of the propane lantern still in use today.

You can learn more tidbits about life in nineteenth-century England on my website at www.reginascott.com.

Blessings!

Regina Scott

Questions for Discussion

1. Emma seeks to find the perfect husband and family. What does family mean to you?

2. Emma loves Alice as if she were her own daughter. What ties build such relationships?

3. Nick struggles to believe that he is capable of loving because of a cold upbringing. How do we learn to love?

4. Nick is willing to forego sleep, food and time with loved ones to develop the safety lamp because of the deaths of miners at his property. What would justify putting your work first?

5. Mrs. Jennings, the cook, is willing to risk her position to see her master happy. Has anyone who served you, for example, a teacher or pastor, ever gone beyond their position to help you? How did you thank them?

6. Mrs. Dunworthy let her disappointing marriage and the death of her sister poison her spirit. How can we keep tragedies from making us bitter?

7. Mr. Fredericks is a horrible example of a foster father, willing to use even orphans to further his career. Describe someone you know who has either adopted or fostered children and how the family was blessed as a result.

8. The natural philosophers of the Regency period made observations of natural phenomena to advance knowledge. How can we use observations today to learn more about our world?

9. Seeing Emma and Alice's trusting faith, Nick begins to question his own. What events in your life helped build your faith?

10. The servants at the four estates in Dovecote Dale are determined to see their masters marry. Where have you seen someone play matchmaker? How did it turn out?

11. Nick has Emma and Mrs. Jennings to share his thoughts. Who in your life serves that role? How do you take that role with others?

12. Sometimes those around us think they see where we need to improve. When is it right to intercede in others' lives?

13. Nick accuses Emma of manipulating him. What's the difference between encouragement and manipulation?

14. The book had several themes. Name one that appealed to you.

15. How have you seen that kind of theme played out in your own life?

REQUEST YOUR FREE BOOKS!

2 FREE INSPIRATIONAL NOVELS
PLUS 2
FREE
MYSTERY GIFTS

Love Inspired
HISTORICAL
INSPIRATIONAL HISTORICAL ROMANCE

YES! Please send me 2 FREE Love Inspired® Historical novels and my 2 FREE mystery gifts (gifts are worth about $10). After receiving them, if I don't wish to receive any more books, I can return the shipping statement marked "cancel." If I don't cancel, I will receive 4 brand-new novels every month and be billed just $4.74 per book in the U.S. or $5.24 per book in Canada. That's a saving of at least 21% off the cover price. It's quite a bargain! Shipping and handling is just 50¢ per book in the U.S. and 75¢ per book in Canada.* I understand that accepting the 2 free books and gifts places me under no obligation to buy anything. I can always return a shipment and cancel at any time. Even if I never buy another book, the two free books and gifts are mine to keep forever.

102/302 IDN F5CN

Name	(PLEASE PRINT)
Address	Apt. #
City	State/Prov.	Zip/Postal Code

Signature (if under 18, a parent or guardian must sign)

Mail to the **Harlequin® Reader Service:**
IN U.S.A.: P.O. Box 1867, Buffalo, NY 14240-1867
IN CANADA: P.O. Box 609, Fort Erie, Ontario L2A 5X3

Want to try two free books from another series?
Call 1-800-873-8635 or visit www.ReaderService.com.

* Terms and prices subject to change without notice. Prices do not include applicable taxes. Sales tax applicable in N.Y. Canadian residents will be charged applicable taxes. Offer not valid in Quebec. This offer is limited to one order per household. Not valid for current subscribers to Love Inspired Historical books. All orders subject to credit approval. Credit or debit balances in a customer's account(s) may be offset by any other outstanding balance owed by or to the customer. Please allow 4 to 6 weeks for delivery. Offer available while quantities last.

Your Privacy—The Harlequin® Reader Service is committed to protecting your privacy. Our Privacy Policy is available online at www.ReaderService.com or upon request from the Harlequin Reader Service.

We make a portion of our mailing list available to reputable third parties that offer products we believe may interest you. If you prefer that we not exchange your name with third parties, or if you wish to clarify or modify your communication preferences, please visit us at www.ReaderService.com/consumerschoice or write to us at Harlequin Reader Service Preference Service, P.O. Box 9062, Buffalo, NY 14269. Include your complete name and address.

LIHI3R

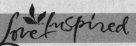
Gracie Wilson stood in the center of a Sunday school classroom at the Bygones Community Church. Her friend Janie Lawson adjusted Gracie's veil and again wiped at tears.

"You look beautiful."

"Do I?" Gracie glanced in the full-length mirror that hung on the door of the supply cabinet and suppressed a shudder. The dress was hideous and she hadn't picked it.

"You look beautiful. And you look miserable. It's your wedding day—you should be smiling."

Gracie smiled but she knew it was a poor attempt at best.

"Gracie, what's wrong?"

"Nothing. I'm good." She leaned her cheek against Janie's hand on her shoulder. "Other than the fact that you've moved one hundred miles away and I never get to see you."

What else could she say? Everyone in Bygones, Kansas, thought she'd landed the catch of the century. Trent Morgan was handsome, charming and came from money. She should be thrilled to be marrying him. Six months ago she had been thrilled. But then she'd started to notice little signs. She should have put the wedding on hold the moment she noticed those signs. And when she knew for certain, she should have put a stop to the entire thing. But she hadn't.

"Do you care if I have a few minutes alone?"

"Of course not." Janie gave her another hug. "But not too long. Your dad is outside and when I came in to check on you the seats were filling up out there."

"I just need a minute to catch my breath."

Janie smiled back at her and then the door to the classroom closed. And for the first time in days, Gracie was alone. She looked around the room with the bright yellow walls and posters from Sunday school curriculum. She stopped at the poster of David and Goliath. Her favorite. She'd love to have that kind of faith, the kind that knocked down giants.

"You almost ready, Gracie?" her dad called through the door.

"Almost."

She opened the window, just to let in fresh air. She leaned out, breathing the hint of autumn, enjoying the breeze on her face. She looked across the grassy lawn and saw…

FREEDOM.

To see if Gracie finds her happily-ever-after, pick up
THE BOSS'S BRIDE
wherever Love Inspired books are sold.

LIEXP0813